Silver Mo

HAV
GREAT NOVELS
OF
EROTIC DOMINATION

If you like one you will probably like the rest

A NEW TITLE EVERY MONTH

All titles in print are now available from:
www.onlinebookshop.com

Silver Moon Readers Service
The Shadowline Building
6 Wembley Street
Gainsborough
DN21 2AJ
United Kingdom

Electronic editions of all Silver Moon titles can be found at:
www.adultbookshops.com

If you like one of our books you will probably like them all!

If you want to be on our confidential mailing list for our free 20 page booklet of extracts from past and forthcoming monthly titles write to:-

Silver Moon Reader Services
The Shadowline Building
6 Wembley Street
Gainsborough
DN21 2AJ
United Kingdom
or
info@babash.com

or leave details on our 24hr UK answerphone
08700 10 90 60
International access code then +44 08700 10 90 60

New authors welcome
Please send submissions to
Silver Moon Books Ltd.
PO Box 5663
Nottingham
NG3 6PJ
or
editor@babash.com

Slaveworld Embassy first published 2003 Silver Moon Books
ISBN 1-903687-23-3

SLAVEWORLD EMBASSY

BY

STEPHEN DOUGLAS

Also by Stephen Douglas
Slaveworld
Royal Slave
Slave School

Preface;
All the novels in the Slaveworld series form self-contained stories and can be read and enjoyed in isolation. However, if you're one of Stephen Douglas's many fans and have read Slave School, the events described in Slaveworld Embassy begin some two weeks before the conclusion of that novel. Now read on……!

CHAPTER ONE

When a young biochemist, just out of university, is offered an extremely well paid job, budget no object, that must be carried out in conditions of absolute secrecy in a hidden private laboratory, she'd have to be a fool if the thought 'organised crime' didn't occur. Hayley liked to think she was no fool. Corporations have their secrets, but very few legitimate businesses have state of the art laboratories hidden in the cellars of secluded old country mansions.

Mr Crown, her employer, claimed to be an American. It was possible. His accent didn't sound in the slightest stateside to Hayley, but to be fair, you didn't have to be born in a country to legally hold its passport. Secretive, wealthy, permanently accompanied by his two silent hoods and a blonde floozy, her first guess had actually been Russian Mafia. He'd once casually let slip that his wealth mostly came from Silicon Valley, but Hayley wasn't sure whether or not to believe him. The man didn't know the first thing about computers.

The offer though, was very attractive. The prospect of doing real and challenging work, in her own perfect lab — especially when the future held only a dull low paid job in a giant multinational, testing haircare products — was very tempting. She'd still looked hard at the deal, and the two very complex compounds the mysterious Mr Crown wanted her to synthesise. Neither was illegal, but possibly only because nothing like them existed in the world yet. One, the easier, seemed to be some sort of growth hormone, the other a stimulant of some kind. But as far as she could tell, not a very powerful one. It seemed unlikely to be the next Ecstasy. Mr Crown had the exact formulae, but no idea how to manufacture the complex compounds.

Which raised the interesting possibility that the formulae had been stolen! But Hayley was intrigued, and the money was just too good to turn down. The task had taken her the better part of six months. And when her employer had said he wanted to see the results of her work immediately, he really did mean immediately! She'd heard the private jet go over. Only Mr Crown ever landed a Gulfstream at the little local airfield.

Hayley pulled herself out of bed and smothered a yawn. So much for her first lie-in in six months. She sighed as unfamiliar sounds and voices echoed around the big old house, she was used to having the rambling wood-panelled stately pile to herself. Taking long walks in its secluded grounds, her work and solitude disturbed only by the woman who came in to cook and clean for her two hours each day, she'd come to think of the place as her own. Home. Just pulling on her robe, wearing only a long T-shirt, Hayley yelped in shock and outrage as without ceremony the door to her bedroom was opened.

"The master wants to see you in the study, with your work."

It was one of Mr Crown's two henchmen. Bodyguards, chauffeurs, cooks, butlers and personal assistants, the two silent nameless men seemed all those, and more. Not just servants, they were clearly trusted confidants.

"Don't you ever knock?" Hayley demanded.

The man thought about it for a moment.

"No," he said simply, and turned to go, leaving Hayley spluttering helplessly. Some people! But there was nothing to be done. She dressed, collected two samples from the lab and obediently reported to the study. Besides, she was more than a little curious to know what she'd been making.

"Excellent. Excellent!" Mr Crown said holding the two vials of liquid up to the light. "Do have a seat."

The stimulant could be injected, or allowed to dissolve into the bloodstream in solid form, if surgically implanted. Mr Crown had been quite content with a liquid form to begin with, and he was paying. Hayley watched with fascination as he prepared two syringes, carefully measuring a small amount of each of the drugs.

"Are you going to try it now? With no tests!" she blurted.

"Oh I'm sure your work is excellent," her employer said

mildly.

Hayley was quite sure she'd got it right too, but she certainly wouldn't inject an unknown substance into her own body on someone else's say-so. Mr Crown carefully tapped the two syringes and squirted out a little of each drug to remove air bubbles. Rather him than her! One of the interchangeable goons served tea, the other propping up the doorway.

"Are you going to tell me what I've been making, now?" she asked.

"Well this one," he held up a vial, "makes a woman's breasts grow larger."

Hayley felt herself grin; first surprise — she'd never imagined that that was what she'd been working on — and then a dawning realisation as to how rich the drug could make whoever owned it. For those who wanted breast enlargement, a cheap, simple injection would be far more popular than expensive, uncomfortable, cosmetic surgery.

"And this one, is a very powerful sexual stimulant."

Hayley nodded politely. She'd believe that one when she saw it. Spanish Fly? But if it was real; well, you only had to look at how popular a legitimate drug like Viagra was!

"Thinking of renegotiating your salary and working conditions?" Mr Crown asked with a faint smile.

Hayley grinned nervously, a little flustered at having her thoughts read so easily, but she felt no real personal danger, even alone in a secluded house with just the mysterious Mr Crown and his two hoods. He still needed her. Only she knew how to make the stuff!

"Actually, so was I," Mr Crown told her softly.

Hayley suddenly realised he had prepared syringes from both vials. She was the only woman in the room, and while a man might occasionally need a little pick-me-up in the sexual department, the second vial...! Hands on both shoulders forced her back down into her chair as she tried to get up, the second goon forcing her arm down onto the armrest and quickly, expertly, using a roll of black masking tape, he secured her.

Hayley kicked and screamed, but there was no one to hear her at the secluded old house and the two men were not only strong, but seemed to be quite expert. Frighteningly expert! Within moments she was totally helpless, secured to the wooden-framed chair, tape around her wrists, arms, ankles, legs, waist and neck. Trembling, trying not to cry, she forced herself to stop screeching and speak calmly.

"Lots of people know I'm here," she said quickly.

Mr Crown laughed. "Your life is not in danger, if that's what you were thinking. And given the nature of your work, I very much doubt you told more than one or two people where you were. As for those one or two, if they call, you will be allowed to tell them all is well."

He nodded to one of his men, who put his fingers tight under her jaw and forced her mouth open. The large red ball they strapped into her mouth didn't stop her screaming, just reduced the volume a little. Mr Crown sat back in his chair, watching with a faint smile, as first one needle and then the other was pushed into her upper arm. She tried to talk reasonably, to promise anything, but the obstruction filling her mouth turned her words into whimpers and unintelligible pleas. Tears welling in her eyes, saliva welling in her mouth, she forced herself to meet Mr Crown's eyes.

"You'll be ready to fuck within half an hour or so," he told her conversationally," and it will be the best sex of your life. By tomorrow I'll be able to whip you to orgasm; humiliation, pain and shame will arouse you and by the end of the week you'll be desperate to please me, all thoughts of escape gone, if it means you get to be allowed to come just once more. Within two weeks, your tits will be large, firm and heavy, just the way I like them, and between serving me and my men, you will make more of this aphrodisiac for me. So that I can make more willing slaves."

Hayley shrieked in horror, shaking her head.

"Fetch Summer!" he ordered one of his men over her shoulder.

"You're wondering why?" he asked her calmly.

"Mmmmm!" Hayley wailed.

"My name is Prince Samuel," her tormentor told her. "I am an exile in this world, stranded here by enemies. I come from a parallel universe, an Earth with a history different from yours; and I wish to go home."

What? He was mad!

"I was abandoned here with just two loyal guardsmen, a single slave, and fortunately, some technological trinkets to sell. The technology is ahead of your world's. It's taken me a while — too long — but I'm a rich man in your world now, and now I can gather the people and equipment who can make me a Gate, so that I can return to my own reality," he continued, as if talking to a bound, gagged, woman was normal. "To preserve secrecy, and to ensure their loyalty, my research team will have to be slaves, and your work has given me the means to control those slaves. You will call me Master; my men, Sir. If your conduct, both in the laboratory, and when being used for sex, is not satisfactory, you will be severely punished. Understood?"

Hayley shook her head again. No, no, no! This couldn't be happening to her. Mr Crown smiled, and clearly not caring if she believed him or not, went on to describe a world of slaves. Where nobles ruled and peasants served them. Where when the working class stepped out of line, they only went to jail for violent crimes. The litterlouts, the tax evaders, those who raised their voices to their betters or forgot to bow their heads, were sentenced to sexual slavery. They could be bought and sold throughout their sentence, their value going down as a slave got older and approached the release date set by the courts. And if you were too old to enjoy, then your children served your sentence once they turned eighteen.

And then the goon sent to fetch Summer returned leading Mr Crown's young mistress, naked, with a collar and chain! Hayley had never even imagined seeing a genuine slave in her life, but sometimes you just know you're in the presence of the real thing. She had seen Mr Cr... Prince Samuel's, girlfriend on a couple of occasions before, usually wearing something sprayed on, hanging onto his arm and every word, showing a lot of leg and cleavage, and had dismissed her as a bimbo without two brain cells to rub together.

Led into the room by her lead, the cute little blonde was naked, perched on her toes in high stiletto heels, a chain hobble making her take small, neat, steps. Huge heavy tits quivered and swung with every step, a metal bar set through each nipple. The naked girl had a slender waist, a perfect hourglass, emphasising the generous flare of her hips, and her arms were strapped behind her, elbows touching. Hayley offered a silent apology for every dismissive 'piece of fluff' thought she'd ever had.

Prince Samuel stroked a buttock, planting a light kiss on a large breast. He reached between the girl's legs and stroked his fingers into her. The blonde gasped, her knees buckling a moment, and then forced herself back into position. Standing passively motionless, head up, legs slightly spread.

"This little toy is from my reality," the Prince said conversationally. "I'd only just bought her at a pet shop, a present for my fiancée, just before I was stranded here in this benighted world of yours."

His gaze settled on something in the distance only he could see.

"Isobell, my betrothed, likes torturing girls with big tits even more than I do," he said with a fond smile.

Then his eyes were back on Hayley, hard and cold. He stepped over and pulled her head back by her hair so that she was looking up at him upside down over the back of the chair.

"I want you to study and try to learn from Summer. She's quite an accomplished sex toy. A nice fuck, takes good whip. Sometimes I don't have to punish her for two or three whole days."

He dismissed his men.

"You two can have Summer tonight. I'll be breaking in the new slave."

"Yes, Sire," they echoed happily.

Trembling, Hayley whimpered in fearful terror as her

captor bent the pretty little blonde forward over the desk, facing her. Summer was incredibly placid.

Mr Crown tied a length of string to each nipple to hold the girl down, bent forward over the desk, tying the ends off to the desk's legs. Amazement and horror warred in Hayley's mind as the Prince unlocked the hobble and pulled Summer's legs wide; tying her ankles to the desk legs on his side. Hayley had of course heard of bondage, but the image that came to mind was a woman spreadeagled on her back on a bed. Not tying a girl down with string knotted tight around her nipples!

Summer's over-large breasts were pulled out into tortured cones, lying part-flattened on the desk, nipples and the areolae around them stretched out far beyond what Hayley imagined physically possible. Not that she could have ever imagined such a thing; not in a million years!

The man who called himself Prince Samuel tied a length of rope tightly around the girl's waist and then looped a length through the blonde's mouth, once round her head, and back to the waist. Summer's head was now held up firmly, spine arched, perfect teeth resting on the rope through her mouth and forced to look directly into Hayley's eyes. With sick fascinated horror, Hayley realised she was going to see the girl ravaged right in front of her.

And Mr Crown still wasn't finished. Two lengths of thin cord were tied — actually tied! — around the base of each over-large breast, the thin cord digging into heavy flesh as the man pulled slip-knots tight. Summer groaned softly as each cord was pulled tight, cutting deep into the blonde's flesh, her breasts now bulging, squeezed out as well as dragged towards the desk's edge by tortured nipples. The cords were looped over her shoulders like bra straps. Hayley suddenly realised the girl hadn't made one squeak of protest. Hadn't tried to twist away or even flinched, as she was tied down in a manner deliberately calculated to shame, humiliate and hurt.

She was used to it.

The Prince stood over his victim, one hand lightly stroking her backside, the other plucking the taut stings tied to her nipples. He met Hayley's eyes.

"Now, if you got the formula right, that aphrodisiac should be starting to kick in about now," he teased. "Nipples getting hard are they? A bit hot and bothered? Perhaps wondering what it would be like to exchange places with Summer?"

Hayley groaned in soft denial, horribly aware of the heat in her groin, totally at a loss to understand why watching the top-heavy blonde being so cruelly bound could be turning her on. She wasn't a sadist. It had to be the drug! And she would be forced to make more, she realised.

The Prince turned his attention back to his perfectly docile, long ago broken-in

sex toy. Summer's arms were unstrapped, and a leather cuff buckled around each wrist. Her arms pushed up behind her back and crossed, the Prince tied the lengths of cord lying over her shoulders to the cuffs. Hayley couldn't believe what she was seeing. She wanted to look away but she just couldn't. He'd actually tied

the collared girl's wristcuffs to her boobs!

Prince Samuel, Hayley's self-proclaimed master, pulled a strap from a desk drawer, and lightly stroked the broad leather band back and forth across the blonde's buttocks. His victim moaned in soft, helpless, animal lust.

"You'll learn to submit too," he told Hayley. "And you'll learn to please."

"No!" she cried out in gag-muffled revulsion, twisting her head away.

Leather landed on flesh with a vicious crack, the blonde's squeak dragging Hayley's eyes back to the bizarre spectacle being acted out in front of her. Tied to a chair, she was only a metre away from a naked girl bent over the desk, wristcuffs tied to breasts, tied down with her nipples! Prince Samuel swung the strap across Summer's buttocks again.

The helpless sex slave responded with a distressed cry, eyes wide, teeth biting deep into the rope tied through her mouth that held her head up. The girl's tormentor swung the strap again, the crack shockingly loud, a ripple running across her haunches, Summer squealing this time. The

Prince slowly undressed, swinging his strap across the blonde's reddened, twitching, buttocks between removing items of clothing. The first tear ran down the gasping, trembling, slavegirl's face as he stepped out of his trousers.

The Prince was putting real bite into his strokes, the naked blonde getting quite shrill now, Hayley couldn't help but notice. Real pain, no play-acting! And again and again leather bit into Summer's buttocks. The flogged girl was deliberately pushing herself forward onto the desk, Hayley suddenly realised; she still had enough presence of mind not to yank back on her tied down nipples and further torture herself.

But she couldn't help twisting and squirming, squeaking and sobbing as she was thrashed, and every time her bound arms jerked, she'd yanked the nooses a little tighter around her own big breasts. As Hayley watched breathless, the heavy mounds had ballooned out into perfect spheres, skin stretched shiny taut, crushed nipples purple now. Only when tears and saliva ran freely down the bound melons, twitching buttocks scarlet, did Prince Samuel toss aside his strap and drive an erect cock deep into the bent-forward girl.

Summer's head was driven up with a cry of ecstasy, teeth tight on her rope bit, as she was impaled to the hilt.

"Don't think this is just about sadism," Prince Samuel told Hayley conversationally, hands light on his gasping, bent-forward victim's hips, leisurely pumping his cock in and out of the helpless blonde.

Summer's eyes were glazed, a little groan of pleasure forced out of her each time the Prince thrust into her. She whimpered in pain when her abused tits were squeezed, but the casual maltreatment only seemed to make her hotter.

"As you will discover, when you are granted the privilege of serving me, power and submission, are in their own ways, very powerful aphrodisiacs."

He patted a buttock, still pumping his shaft hard and deep into the helpless sex slave bent forward over the desk. Hayley watched, mesmerised!

"And combined with the little drug cocktail you

whipped up for me," he squeezed the blonde's abused breasts again, making her wail in mingled pain and pleasure, "this will be you soon," he promised Hayley with a cruel smile.

Gagged, tied to a chair, Hayley felt the first tear run down her cheek. Her nipples were aching hard now, breasts lust swollen, and there was a raging heat between her legs. The aphrodisiac she herself had manufactured was turning her into a bitch on heat! Surely she could resist! Could you actually train someone to enjoy being kept naked and bound, to enjoy degrading servile sex, to enjoy pain even? To enjoy being owned? Hayley realised with horror that she was wondering what it felt like to be flogged, to have rope digging into her flesh, to be utterly helpless — just like Summer — and it was making her hotter!

The cock-impaled tit-tortured blonde cried out in ecstasy as she was forced to orgasm. Hayley, watching with growing arousal, realised that she half-believed now. Half-believed in alternative realities, and the Gates that could be made to allow travel between them! Half-believed that possibly, Mr Crown really was a Prince in his own slave-owning world.

He would lure in or kidnap more young university graduates and students like Hayley, to make his Gate to a parallel universe; the physicists, mathematicians, and technicians he needed. And the drug Hayley was forced to manufacture would make them hard-working, willing, slaves.

Toiling in the Prince's secret lab by day, by night the research team would become sex toys, playthings for the Prince and his men to abuse, humiliate, tease, torment and enjoy. She was more than bright enough to realise that if Prince Samuel's parallel universe was real, and his research slaves were successful, he would want to leave no witnesses behind him, so that possible retribution could not follow. Especially, he would not leave behind a team who knew how to make a dimensional Gate. Trying to ignore her growing arousal, Hayley tried to picture the Prince's Slaveworld in her mind. Tried to imagine what it would be like to be taken to a world where she could be legally owned for the pleasure of others. Surely no woman raised in freedom could endure what she'd just seen Summer put through.

Not once, not occasionally, but daily!

Chapter Two

On another world, the world Prince Samuel called home, exhausted, breathing raggedly, naked and bound, a former British police officer was being forced to advertise her own sale. Legally property here, a sex slave, she knew in a few days the capital's finest auction house was going to sell her to the highest bidder at a public auction!

Once the fantasy would have excited Susan, the reality should have terrified her, but a week or so's unrelenting, desperately humiliating training in which she had been casually punished and forced to orgasm without her consent again and again, had left her almost mindlessly obedient. No doubt exactly as her captors wanted, her thoughts became a confused whirl when she tried to think for herself. Good girls were praised, petted and given treats; bad girls were punished. It was so much easier to surrender and be just the docile, attractive, sex object the auction house wanted her to be, the sexual plaything they were going to sell, rather than wrestle with guilt and shame when she was forced to enjoy what was done to her.

Susan loved bondage, being controlled during sex, and had long known she was sexually submissive, but she'd never imagined just quite how subservient she could become with a little expert training. She had suspected — known! — that she belonged here on the Slaveworld right from the start, but her quite palpable need to please, to obey, scared her a little. If total devotion could be trained into her, and she became everything whoever bought her wanted her to be, would anything remain of her own individuality?

Since having been put up for auction Susan had spent almost the entire week in this one cell, with one wall made of glass and looking out onto a busy city street, so that pedestrians and street traffic could look in on the auction house's displayed merchandise. Permanently naked and bound; she had slept, eaten, used the toilet, been groomed, teased, sexually tormented and exercised, in full view of any passer-by. And almost every waking moment the auction house staff had had her walking on a treadmill in a posture collar, stiletto heels and manacles, with her arms bound behind her back. Fitted with a teasing dildo and a fat plug strapped deep inside her ass, Susan knew she was being prepared for the moment when she would walk down the catwalk. They were training her to be graceful, sexy, docile and hot, when she was paraded in front of the buyers; teaching her to walk with her head held up proudly, hips swaying, breasts jiggling and with the cute little ass-wiggle that would fetch the best price.

In the glass walled cage — some pedestrians not even bothering to look because sex slaves were such a common sight — an electronic spirit level swinging from each nipple ring quickly ensured Susan put the required tit-jiggling bounce and short-stepped sway, one foot in front of the other, in her stride. The wire-trailing shock dildo/butt plug strapped into her automatically delivered a bolt of agony deep inside her body if her big breasts didn't sway and quiver enticingly with every step. Naked apart from stiletto heels, for hour after hour, pussy and ass stuffed, red wires trailing from her anus, the shocks had kept her going! Susan thought it had been going on for about a week, but it was easy for slaves to lose track of days and even weeks.

Certainly she had toiled on the treadmill for many days, the butt plug also shocking her if she didn't keep up, as well as training her to walk with a sexy sway and display her boobs properly. Sweat gleaming on her flanks, juices running down her inner thighs, her saliva dripping from around her ball gag, in a haze of lust Susan had watched pedestrians and city traffic pass by, the occasional aristocrat pausing to look over her bound displayed nudity; young Lordlings, more eager and less restrained, pressing their noses longingly up against the glass. Her pedigree, reserve price and auction date scrolled across an LCD display, and Susan knew her sale had also been advertised in magazines — fashion, motoring, gardening and the like, as well as trade — and of course on the Slaveworld's 3D TV home shopping channel.

Occasionally the nobles who paused to look over Susan's displayed torment had a pretty sexual toy on a collar and lead, or they parked their pony girl pulled carriages by the kerb. Even as she looked into the eyes of people who were quite openly and obviously wondering what Susan would be like to take, torture and humiliate — to own — she found herself envying their slaves. They had been chosen!

Susan was for sale because she'd been rejected. She still didn't know what she'd done wrong, why Frances had put her up for auction. It wasn't the money. When Susan had defected from British Intelligence, she'd made a deal that had set her fellow agent up with a title, riches and a small country estate. The other half of the bargain, unspoken but understood, was that Susan would then be Frances's slave, free to enjoy the Slaveworld naked in a collar, but protected from its excesses. Why had Frances sold her? Why? As her sale approached, she'd grown more and more determined her next owner would find her pleasing.

It was almost dusk and nearly the end of this day's ordeal on the treadmill, when, quite shattered but still in a haze of lust Susan noticed a young Lady had parked a pair of pony girls on the busy street outside her cell's window-wall. Young, probably no more than eighteen, her eyes lingered on Susan's heavy breasts a moment and then trailed down her sweat-gleaming body. Susan was well aware that the base of her dildo projected down between her thighs, the crotch strap threaded through it, so that potential buyers could see how large a shaft penetrated her. She thought she'd endured every possible humiliation, but such a frank appraisal from a girl clearly younger than she was caught her by surprise.

Just for a second, Susan had made the mistake of looking at the girl with a cop's eyes, wondering what mischief she was up to, if she was old enough to legally drink — or here, drive those pony girls — and then she remembered where she was. Naked, on display with her arms strapped down her back, her ball gag making her drool down her own body and teasing herself with a fat dildo with every step. Dripping wet, Susan felt a flush touch her cheeks; and then a bolt of agony seared her deep inside her body, inside her back passage. The butt plug had shocked her.

Tears stinging her eyes, Susan forced herself to take shorter, faster steps on the softly whining treadmill, one foot in front of the other, deliberately within the limit of the manacle chain locked between her ankles. Good sex toys displayed themselves properly. She put a deliberate bounce in her stride, hips swinging, making her big breasts jiggle, bounce and sway as they were supposed to. The mercury switches hanging from her nipple rings only activated the shock dildo pushed hard up her ass when her boobs didn't bob enough.

Thinking like a sex object again, Susan found she could meet the girl's eyes easily now, a little shame was so exciting. The young Lady's lingering gaze travelled back up, and finally reached Susan's face. The girl was just window shopping, she told herself. Surely too young to afford an expensive plaything like Susan. The young Lady's eyes went back to her breasts, and Susan found herself hoping the girl was admiring the trails of saliva that ran down the heavy globes, not the ample size and weight of her boobs themselves. Here on the Slaveworld, as she'd discovered to her cost, many big tit lovers were also very much into tit torture.

Susan dismissed the thought from her mind. "Just window shopping," she told herself again. "She can't afford me!"

To her horror, she saw the pretty young girl fish the Slaveworld's combined ID and credit card from a belt pocket, and insert it into a slot beside the cell's wall-window. Almost immediately the treadmill started to speed up, and Susan was forced into a trot, yelping behind her ball gag as the butt plug repeatedly shocked her for not keeping up. She had to stay inside an invisible box of light beams to avoid triggering the ass-stretching shock dildo.

Once she was back in the centre of the treadmill, the

shocks stopped. The treadmill was only running a little faster, but in manacles, able to take only small steps, Susan had no choice but to trot to keep up. In stiletto heels she had to run on her toes like a sprinter. Her inner thighs sliding easily across each other, coated in her own juices, her breasts bounced and she gasped around her ball gag, as she felt the fat dildo that penetrated her stirring anew. Walking, she just teased herself to distraction, arousal without relief; but trotting, her internal dimensions shifted more! It felt like the shaft was flexing and pumping inside her.

Susan could feel sweat running down her body, between her buttocks, little pleading whimpers slipping past the large bright-red ball buckled into her mouth, and still the girl didn't withdraw her credit card. The pressure of her crotch strap tight across her clitoris was maddening, but lubricated by juices and sweat it was not quite enough to make her come yet. And still the dildo pumped and flexed inside her, rubbing up against the butt plug, the two invaders inside Susan's body separated by only a thin membrane of flesh.

Lungs burning, thighs and calves aching, Susan was desperately focused on the young girl who was tormenting her. The aristocrat had a faint smile on her face, watching with evident pleasure, the way Susan's breasts moved.

She couldn't be! She was! Susan suddenly realised that she was being made to run in a dildo, ball gag and hobble just so that a spoilt young aristocrat could watch the swing and bounce of her big breasts! Humiliated pleasure cascaded through her, consuming her, exploding into an orgasm of stars and hot flashes. Orgasm after orgasm, ecstasy piled on ecstasy, but somehow each orgasm was still separate, pleasure earthing in nipples and groin. Pain, her anal tormentor repeatedly shocking her, triggered and intensified the tail end of her multiple orgasm.

And then there was just pain, shock after shock, from the cruel butt plug. Panting on her knees beside the treadmill where she had fallen, arms strapped down her back, Susan dragged herself to her feet and forced herself to step back onto the machine. Back in position, the anal shocks finally stopped. Her audience had grown while she ran, a couple of young Lordlings, a nice looking couple and an older Lady.

Then, to Susan's horror, the pretty young aristocrat inserted her credit card in the receptacle again and the treadmill began to whine faster. Breasts bouncing, thighs pumping and her dripping dildo stirring inside her again, forcing her back to unconsenting arousal once more, Susan begged for mercy in gasps around her ball gag, but knew she wouldn't be heard past the thick glass. Somehow she suspected the sweet looking young Lady on the street outside wouldn't have been swayed to mercy even if she could hear her. Susan was just a sex slave! And here, where she had chosen to be, sex slaves, quite legally, existed only to be enjoyed.

Still in the English Kingdom's capital, Londinium, only half a mile away from the former police officer in her display window, another countryman of Susan's was finding it easier to adjust to Slaveworld life. But then it was much easier for a master than for a slave.

Holding a serving tray, Jacob stood obediently at the foot of the British Ambassador's bed, waiting for his current master to finish having sex with Jacob's own young wife. Jacob was naked, wrists cuffed to the tray, a gag filling his mouth. His cock — swollen to bursting — was bound and padlocked in an Arab-strap tight around the base of the shaft and his balls twitched and flexed helplessly each time Amanda squeaked and gasped.

His bride of only three months threw back her hooded head, the restraint Jacob himself had padlocked her into — tight, shiny black form-fitting latex — and cried out in ecstasy around the built-in cock gag that filled her mouth. She was sitting astride the Ambassador, arms strapped behind her back wrist to elbow. Thin, very tight straps, digging deep into soft heavy flesh, were buckled around the base of each large breast, flesh ballooned out into taut shiny sensitive balls of flesh. The lightest lick or squeeze made her groan, her nibbled nipples clearly quite unbearable. A breathlessly tight cincher belt nipped her waist cruelly, and from it fine chains ran down between whip striped buttocks, and then up in front, on either side of her pussy, holding in place a fat ass-stretching butt plug.

Their exacting training had taught Jacob and Amanda that a stuffed ass was just one of the many things that made a female sex slave a more responsive, willing, screw. The humiliations, forced pleasure, punishments, almost permanent nudity, control and restraints that they had been daily subjected to, also made them more of a pleasure to own they had learnt. As with fitting the tit straps, Jacob himself had been the one to force the heavy pear-shaped plug into Amanda's ass. It was frequently his duty to prepare his young bride for someone else to shaft, and he'd watched her enjoyed often enough now to know that the tit straps and butt plug really did improve her performance.

The British Ambassador was a small, wiry, man, easily twice the age of his twenty-year-old ride, with a surprisingly large cock. His normal expression was one of faint worry, but now there was only a cruel grin on his face. He controlled Amanda with a vicious little clamp on a length of cord, spring-loaded metal jaws with sharp little teeth, biting into her clitoris. With pained little high-pitched yelps, Amanda's hips bucked in time with his tugs on the tormented nub, thrusting herself hard and deep onto her user's cock, heavy strap-bound breasts swaying.

A painful tit squeeze refocused Amanda from her forced orgasm, and like the obedient, well trained, very willing sexual toy she now was, she was soon again docilely obeying the tugs of her user's cord. Snorting through her hood's nostril holes, there was a gleam of sweat on Amanda's flanks now, her ribs showing and stomach swelling around the waist-cincher with every gag-obstructed breath. The big-breasted sex object was quite clearly exerting herself to the maximum to please.

Jacob just couldn't take his eyes off her. Even if he hadn't been instructed to watch his wife's shafting, he couldn't have looked away at any price. He wanted to fuck her so much! Or save her from her ordeal! To be free to bind, torture and abuse her himself. Or rescue her? He was just so confused. But one thing that he was sure of now, was that there was little left of the shy young virgin he remembered from his wedding night, both of them so nervous. Amanda was a truly magnificent sexual animal now, tamed by her bonds, trained to the point of excellence and clearly a superb ride. He hadn't even been able to get a good look at her on their honeymoon night, Amanda quickly slipping between the sheets, and of course you couldn't expect a free woman, who had worn a head to toe robe and veil since adolescence, to flaunt herself like a slave. Now with heavily enlarged breasts, a neat wasp waist — and the cosmetic surgeon had also added a little to her hip bones to make her appear more spankable — skin flawless velvet and her acne cleared up, Amanda had proudly performed sex in public and been led down city streets on collar and lead, naked, knowing she was gorgeous.

Her shiny golden hair — another cosmetic change — pulled back into a ponytail out of a hole in the back of the hood, flicked this way and that, as with desperate cries Amanda tossed her latex-coated head back and forth, her user reaching up to suck straining hard nipples. Jacob's wife had not been permitted a tan, her pale peaches and cream skin marking easily, previous punishments showing up very clearly on the stretched taut skin of her bound breasts. There were whip marks, vivid red lines, on her belly and buttocks as well as the strap-bound globes. Jacob had put them there himself while Amanda shrieked and squirmed, chained standing in a spread X mounted on a dildo pole. The Ambassador's idea of foreplay.

His parents had warned him not to marry young; to wait until he was thirty or thirty five as they had, but he'd been so in love. Jacob wasn't stupid, he knew the world he lived in, and he knew when you said, "For better, for worse. For richer, for poorer. In sickness and in servitude," it was legally binding, not just a promise to whichever Gods you believed in. The Lords and Ladies set great store in the sanctity of marriage

Jacob knew that legally, married slaves could not be separated. When one was sentenced to sexual servitude, the other had to share the sentence. But Amanda, his childhood sweetheart, had always been such a quiet, respectful girl. Law abiding and sensible.

They'd only had a week together before the arrest, the nightmare of the trial, and Amanda's actions still baffled Jacob. Working evenings part time on the hatcheck counter at the opera house, she'd been caught on security camera molesting the patrons' checked-in, bound, sex slaves! He just didn't understand it. She had never showed the slightest interest in the sexual habits of their betters during their two-year engagement. They'd never even kissed. Sometimes ex-slaves, it was rumoured, or those helplessly turned on by the sights and sounds you just couldn't avoid on the streets of the big city, got up to some kinky stuff, but she'd never even seemed to be interested in sex all that much.

Very shy, he'd only eventually been able to persuade Amanda to have sex again after that first time, with a rolled up cloth in her mouth. But surely that had only been because they were living in the family home. His parents in the next room, separated by just a thin wall. The night before her arrest she'd suggested he tie her wrists to the tops of her thighs, so that she didn't scratch his back or bang on the headboard and disturb his parents. But it had seemed reasonable at the time.

In court Amanda had denied the charge, which had infuriated the judge who had doubled their sentence to fourteen years! Once auctioned and obedience trained, they had teased and tormented each other, put on sex shows and been enjoyed together in many beds, but were always gagged when alone. Amanda clearly thrived on humiliation and discipline, and Jacob had never, might never while collared, have the chance to put the question he so desperately needed to ask. Was she so unhappy with the prospect of a humble life, no prospect of wealth, so disappointed with their sex life, that she had deliberately chosen slavery?

Or had she secretly lusted after a collar, serial number and pedigree all along? The only way in the world she could ever turn heads on the city streets, be the centre of attention, be admired, and lusted after.

The only way a peasant or working class girl would ever be attractive to a noble, was naked, bound and owned.

They belonged to the King's Household now, under the control of the Chamberlain, but had yet to be enjoyed by a member of the Royal Family. They had only served visiting foreign dignitaries in the guest suites so far. Now they were on temporary loan, a housewarming gift to the new British Ambassador; until the man bought his own slaves.

Jacob felt self-pitying tears well in his eyes, as orgasm approaching, the Ambassador began slapping his voluptuous young ride's tits. Amanda squeaked in pained lust at each blow, hips bucking frantically now as her agonisingly clamped clitoris was yanked faster and harder. Her juices coated the cock that impaled her, saliva dribbling down her neck under her hood.

The hood made his wife almost anonymous. She could be any slave. And watching the big-titted sex object being fucked, ass stuffed to bursting point and with her arms bound behind her, squeaking with every slap and thrust aroused Jacob like nothing ever had in his life. Tossing her latex-coated head from side to side, sweat gleaming on her body, she was just fantastic. Just like the many helplessly bound pets, poodles and pony girls Jacob had seen Lords and Ladies use and abuse in the park when he was a groundskeeper there. Trying not to look too obviously, and working with a permanent erection.

But the face he'd pulled this tight hood down over belonged to Amanda, his sweet and innocent childhood sweetheart! Deeply ashamed of his own arousal, his barely controlled lust, of taking pleasure in his own wife's abuse, Jacob watched the Ambassador squeezing his young bride's strap-bound breasts with helpless longing.

It just wasn't fair! The man was apparently exclusively heterosexual, Jacob just here to whip tease Amanda during foreplay, and then lick the Ambassador's come out of his wife and off her body after he'd finished, so that the man could enjoy Jacob's complete and utter humiliation. Her fluttering hands bound behind her, Amanda cried in pained ecstasy again, nipples brutally squeezed and twisted.

The bitch! She put a collar around his neck, then she got all the sex. The lucky lucky bitch! Jacob hadn't been allowed to come for over a week, hadn't been allowed to have sex with his own wife for a full month though he saw her screwed every day. He so desperately needed to come, longed for a master or mistress who would enjoy him and leave Amanda, frustrated and desperate, holding the serving tray. The only consolation here was how often he was allowed to whip her.

The British Ambassador came with a soft grunt and flopped limp, Amanda ordered to sit still on his softening cock. Jacob stepped forward and offered the chilled drink he'd been holding, very aware of his wife's huge slave-tits heaving as she panted, the heat that radiated off her body, the musk of her — sweat and juices — bound tits a nice shade of pink now. It briefly occurred to him he didn't actually know where Britain was, but he supposed it wasn't too important.

The Ambassador's first language seemed to be English, though he spoke with an accent, and the British Isles was the old Roman name for both the English and Scottish Kingdoms combined, wasn't it? Possibly one of the old American colonies? He knew there was an independent Principality called New York. And the Northern fiefdoms, where European descended serfs supplied the Indian Nations with industry, modern medicine and sex slaves so that they could maintain a nomadic way of life in comfort, were referred to collectively as New England. Perhaps from somewhere around there, Jacob mused.

The British Ambassador ran his hands over his panting ride's naked body, the top-heavy sex toy still sitting astride him.

"I think I'll ass fuck her next," the man mused, his hooded plaything groaning softly as her big breasts were handled. "Is she a good butt fuck Jacob?"

Shamed, mortified, aroused anew, Jacob obediently nodded. He had not yet been allowed to have anal sex with Amanda himself, but he'd seen her with a cock or strap-on dildo deep between her buttocks often enough to know what his pretty young bride liked. He found himself suddenly very conscious of the chains from Amanda's waist-cinching belt, running down between her buttocks and down either side of her pussy, digging deep into her belly and holding in place the fat plug Jacob himself had forced into her back passage. He so desperately wanted to fuck her, and just knew he wasn't going to be allowed to while under the British Ambassador's control. Seeing a humiliated tear run down Jacob's cheek, the Ambassador smiled.

Oh Gods, would this never end?

CHAPTER THREE

In the Royal Palace in the centre of Londinium, in the Queen's bedchamber, Their Most Royal Majesties, The King and Queen of England, were making love. The sex toy they shared was of course of the highest quality, another formerly British girl, well aware of what an honour it was to be the meat in this particular slave sandwich.

The King and Queen maintained entirely separate chambers in different parts of the palace, amorous visits like this taking place by prior arrangement. The two had long ago decided that one of the key ingredients to a long and happy marriage was to give each other some space. It seemed to work. After four decades of marriage, they still loved each other and shared slaves with each other as often as many a young married couple. Today the Queen was host, and it was her slave they shared.

A cock pumping deep into her sex, licking her own juices off the strap-on dildo the hard flesh rod had just replaced, Precious groaned softly in pained lust as her milk-heavy breasts were squeezed by two pairs of hands. Victoria's favourite pet was secured in the centre of the bed on her knees, body bent forward, wrists buckled together behind her back. From above, a winch chain pulled the girl's arms up above and behind her and kept her body in position, the padlocks hanging from her clamped nipples brushing back and forward across the satin sheets as her big breasts swayed back and forth. A strap with anklecuffs on it, running across the bed and secured underneath it, kept her firmly in place, legs spread wide, bent forward, and perfectly secured to be enjoyed doggie style.

King Philip had started off kneeling in front of the girl, his penis in her mouth, his Queen taking her pet from behind with the strap-on. Leaning over the slavegirl they used, they had kissed slowly and passionately around the winch chain that dragged the young sex toy's wrists up above her. Victoria had come quickly and easily, Precious, as always, a delightful ride; then they'd switched. Now letting the lush plaything lick clean the dildo just pulled from her own body, Victoria watched fondly as her husband worked his shaft deeper into her property from behind, doggie style, as she had done.

Leaning forward to kiss her husband again, carelessly ramming the dildo she wore deeper into the slave's mouth, Victoria idly squeezed the bound toy's big breasts harder. Precious whimpered in pain as the hugely swollen globes were squeezed together. Philip's hands touched hers a moment, then he released the painfully distended melons, letting his hands slip onto the top-heavy brunette's hips, to pull her back harder and deeper onto his cock. Udders abused, but pussy filled to the hilt, the young dairy slave gasped in pained delight with each thrust.

The King had an easy grip, the generous flare of Precious's hips a convenient handhold for anyone using her doggie style. The British slave had a broad eighteen-inch iridium steel band permanently nipping her waist. Bonded into place, when sold or finally released from her sentence, it would eventually have to be cut off her. She'd worn the shiny decorative restraint, and a matching collar, for a full six months now, ever since Queen Victoria became her fourth owner. To begin with the palace grooms had had to use a high pressure jet of water from a small flat nozzle pushed under the belt to wash her and were only able to feed a fine silk cloth under the polished belt to dry her with after. Now Precious had acclimatised, it wasn't too difficult to squeeze a soaped finger under the metal belt and a towel could be forced under afterwards, if she breathed out.

King Philip's preferred choice of sex slave was a delicate natural blonde, usually a slavegirl but occasionally a boy toy; and naturally slender, not voluptuous with a trained-down wasp waist like Precious. Lushly spankable with huge tits, Precious was also far too tall to be his ideal slave, a fraction under five feet eleven. And while admittedly beautifully proportioned for her height and weight, she was clearly a powerful girl. If she wasn't so docile she could have been a champion mud wrestler, and in harness and bridle she could — with a little whip — manage to pull a hunter's pony trap alone through a day's hunt. Female hunting hacks usually came in pairs or teams of four.

Philip preferred a delicate slave, where Victoria absolutely delighted in having such a powerful, vital, animal tied down under her during sex; riding the magnificent, brown-haired beauty to exhausted, tormented, surrender. And she just loved the way the big girl so placidly allowed her driver's whip and reins to totally control her when pulling a pony trap. Precious had always taken good whip. The lovely brunette was twenty two years old now, and had been a slave since she was nineteen. The King, in his second century himself, usually also preferred a more mature slave than Precious, ideally thirty or so years old. But over the months, Precious always being the slave Victoria wanted to share with her husband when it was her choice, he'd grown comfortable with the powerfully built dairy slave and had even given her a few rides and punishments alone. Prodded, while he wouldn't actually trade her for one of his own more delicate girls, Philip would now reluctantly admit that the tall hazel-eyed brunette was a pretty good ride; and he certainly wouldn't have any other slave's milk in his tea.

Mouth full of dildo, hanging face down under her winch chain, ankles secured wide, gasping softly as she was shafted doggie style, beautiful wide eyes looked up into Victoria's in contented devotion when the Queen leaned back from her husband's kiss. As Victoria pulled back, her strap-on dildo slipped out of the lovely girl's mouth. She reached over for a discarded ball gag, and then held out the restraint in her palm. Just like a pony being fed sugar lumps, Precious strained forward without hesitation. There was a momentary pressure against Queen Victoria's hand and then the large red ball was behind the docile slave toy's teeth. Her body still rocking back and forth under the winch chain as she was ridden, the King's fingers digging deep into the flesh of her hips now, his juice-coated cock sliding easily in and out of her, the top-heavy plaything still had enough presence of mind to hold her head as still as she could while her mistress secured the ball gag with straps buckled tight behind her neck and under her chin.

No fuss! Victoria's lovely pet knew that except when performing oral sex, being fed or having her teeth brushed, there would almost always be a gag, tongue clamp or a bit tightly buckled into her mouth. She expected it. As with constant nudity, restraints and frequent humiliations and punishments, for one of Queen Victoria's slavegirls, a permanent gag was a perfectly normal part of being owned for sex.

Little ripples ran across the gagged brunette's hips as the King pumped his shaft deeper and harder into her, his pelvis slamming up against the bent-forward girl with every stroke now, her milk-swollen breasts swaying back and forth faster. The kneeling sex slave's hands, pulled up above and behind her by the winch chain, were clenched into tight fists, teeth biting deep into the big red ball that filled her mouth now. Left hand twisted into the girl's hair, holding Precious's head up and arching her spine, King Philip produced a thin multi-stranded whip, and began lashing his ride's haunches, forehand and backhand, faster and faster!

Squeaking in hopelessly mingled pain and pleasure, vivid fans of red lines marking her buttocks and curling down over her ivory hips, her user's lash licking down firm thighs, the well-trained sex toy thrust herself back onto her rider's penis in time with his whip strokes.

Looking into the whipped girl's face with interest, Victoria found herself aroused anew, but decided a second round could wait until she had her pet alone. She licked her lips. She'd seen the lovely sex slave whipped many a time, but it was never boring. Precious always took pain so well; born to be owned. King Philip thrust into and lashed his young mount faster, Precious squeaking with each whip thrust. Vivid red lines splayed down her thighs, the gasping pet's once creamy haunches soon glowed an angry scarlet, a sheen of sweat on her flanks now. The placid plaything had been tanned a light gold when Victoria first took possession of her, but the Queen preferred a paler slave, and had kept her out of the sun. Ivory skin marked more easily.

From in front, wide innocent tear-bright eyes and copper highlights in her dark hair contrasted equally nicely with the large red ball buckled tightly into the girl's mouth. At only twenty two and youth treated, she still had decades of hard use in her yet, Victoria knew. The bent-forward plaything, forced to gasp with pleasure every time King Philip thrust into her, wailed in distress as Victoria scooped up her breasts, and deliberately squeezed the swollen melons hard together.

Creating a dairy slave was easy enough. A small artificial vat-grown gland was surgically implanted in the slavegirl's body. Releasing the correct chemicals and hormones, fooling the body into thinking it was pregnant, in just two weeks you had a girl who needed milking. Her appearance was humiliatingly improved, she provided her owners with tasty produce and to many, made a very exotic sex toy. When overdue a milking, helped along with tight nipple clamps, a dairy slave's udders could become quite hugely — and painfully — swollen.

Most dairy slaves were milked twice a day, sometimes three, but Victoria only allowed Precious to be milked properly on special occasions — parties and the like — and before putting her to bed. During the day, a little and often, just enough to prevent damage, she liked to keep her pet permanently tormented with cruelly swollen udders. And as well as the discomfort, allowing the young brunette's already big tits to become painfully distended, skin shiny taut as if breast roped, much improved the tall slavegirl's already spectacular figure. As placidly as she had been trained to accept her permanently cinched waist, gag, constant restraints and total nudity, Precious had learned to live with enormously swollen breasts and a tight metal clamp almost constantly screwed down on the base of each nipple, a heavy padlock swinging from each clamp. Victoria had the only key.

Letting those same weighty steel padlocks hanging from the sex slave's clamped nipples slip between her fingers,

Victoria sank her fingers deeper into the milk-heavy mounds, squeezing in time with her husband's thrusts. Tits swollen to bursting, Precious cried out in anguished delight, the heavy globes so sensitive, even the lightest squeeze hurt her more than King Philip's whip now. Her husband was almost ready to come, Victoria saw. The rhythmic thwack, thwack, thwack of his lash across the brunette's haunches was faster, the helpless girl's ass a burning scarlet. Head still held up with a handful of hair, gasping around her ball gag, the plaything's eyes were glazed now, unseeing!

And still the superbly docile slave thrust herself back onto King Philip's cock in time with his merciless whip strokes. Bent forward on her knees, ankles secured wide, swaying under the winch chain that dragged her arms up above and behind her, mouth stretched wide by a huge red ball, milk-swollen breasts mercilessly squeezed, Precious suddenly went rigid, and then shrieked in ecstasy behind her gag. Experiencing a familiar thrill of triumph, Victoria smiled, Philip sighing softly as he pumped his come into the bound slave he'd so cruelly enjoyed.

Gasping, trembling, rib cage visibly swelling with every shuddering breath, a little tit squeeze quickly focused the now drooling sex slave's eyes on Victoria's. Total surrender was always fascinating to watch, something the Queen thought she would never tire of. Helpless in her bonds, a fusion of pain, pleasure and humiliation working their familiar magic, forced to come without her consent, the big-breasted pet had been totally subjugated once again. Best of all, Victoria could see the knowledge in her eyes! As she was enjoyed, ridden, used — overwhelmed! — the lovely sex slave knew she had surrendered her will, her humanity, and become exactly what her pedigree said she was. A sexual toy.

Victoria patted her property on the head, and slid off the bed, pulling on a robe. Two of her husband's slender blondes served afternoon tea on the sunwashed balcony, Precious in her bonds, semen dripping slowly out of her sex, forgotten for the moment. Victoria saw no point in untying the girl if she was going to use her again later.

"So you're going to declare Alfred your heir?" she asked heavily.

Philip sighed. "My love, Samuel is my son too. I haven't given up on him but I have to be a King first, and a father second. The Kingdom needs an heir. Both nobles and peasants need to know who their next king will be. I'm not getting any younger."

"You're not decrepit yet. I think if you asked Precious, she'd say she'd just been pretty well fucked."

King Philip chuckled and reached out to squeeze her hand, clearly grateful for her attempt to lighten the mood. Victoria looked bleakly at her garden below, where a naked slave strapped to a pole with a crosspiece, was serving as a scarecrow. Lining the path that bordered the garden and a broad expanse of lawn, a dozen or so naked sex slaves were secured spreadeagled, upside down, to wooden frames angled to face the sun. The girls were being tanned under their chins, the underside of their breasts and on their inner thighs. All modern cellblocks of course had sun lamps, but any Master-at-Arms worth his salt preferred the old way. An artificial tan never quite compared to the real thing, and besides, the odd slave staked out in the grounds here and there, made an attractive garden ornament.

"Why not just ask the British if they have him, now that they've sent us an Ambassador and we've established diplomatic relations?"

"We've been over this," he said wearily. "Control over the Prince of Wales gives them too much leverage over us. If I declare Alfred my heir, then Samuel becomes just another Prince, of value only to the family, you and I, not the Kingdom. They would have no reason to hold him against his will."

"But...!"

"No!" King Philip said firmly. "It's gone on too long. Too may people know Samuel is missing. Rumour is feeding on rumour — he's abdicated, he's been assassinated, he's insane. I've left it as long as possible."

Samuel, her son, had been missing for over six months now. The Royal Security Police investigation had found no trace of him, his driver or a slavegirl he'd bought at a pet shop just before disappearing. The Prince's limousine had been found abandoned by the docks. The best lead, the only lead, was that the one-way Gate to Britain had been activated without authorisation on the day of his disappearance, the two RSP guards at the facility also now missing. If Samuel had chosen to journey through the Gate for some reason, or been forced through it and stranded, he was definitely somewhere in the world of the known alternative Britain. Only Lady Franklin, née Philips-Webber, the one-way Gate's inventor, had the expertise to align one with another possible reality. But within that one parallel universe, he could be anywhere on the planet.

RSP agents seeking him had found no trace, but it was hard to explore a whole country, let alone a world, when that world's Intelligence Services were hunting for you, and still keep a low profile. The most hopeful scenario was that Prince Samuel was keeping a low profile himself, had somehow blended in, awaiting rescue. Possibly British Intelligence had him. The worst case, for a stranger alone on an alien world; was anything you could think of. You only had to look at what happened to pretty young Britons brought here! Her favourite sex toy, Precious, had once been an innocent, sexually inexperienced, British student.

No more searchers could be sent to the alternative reality. The newly signed treaty specifically forbade unauthorised visitors, intelligence agents sneaking around and getting up to mischief. And the British would notice. Once you knew what to scan for, a Gate activation could be detected up to 300 miles away. They surely had the whole country covered by now, as did the Kingdom.

"Can't you just wait a little longer?" she pressed.

King Philip shook his head. "Do you think I want to disinherit my own son? I've hung on as long as I could. Even the Privy Council are pushing me now."

Their second son, Gregor, amidst a whirlwind of rumour that he had somehow done away with his brother to take the Crown himself, had publicly renounced his claim to the throne. Irrefutably clearing his name by taking himself out of the line of succession. In part a noble gesture yes, but with more than a hint of pragmatism, as Gregor had never wanted the responsibility of the Crown in the first place, much preferring the luxurious slave-owning life of ease of a Royal Prince.

Next in line was Prince Alfred, son of King Philip's brother. Samuel's cousin, was an intelligent, thoughtful young man, who Victoria in no way suspected of conspiring against her son, and who would probably make a good King, she reluctantly conceded. But once he was named the Kingdom's heir, it could not be changed. If — when! — Samuel returned, it would be to find he had been cheated out of his birthright.

"I want to meet the new Ambassador. I'll throw him a reception or something. If he knows anything about Samuel he might let something slip in a relaxed setting."

"Unlikely if he's a professional, but worth a try. You won't mention Samuel yourself!" her husband half warned, half asked.

"No," she finally agreed heavily.

King Philip nodded.

"Is there nothing else we can do?" she said sadly.

Her husband had a suddenly thoughtful look on his face.

"What?" she asked.

"There is one thing we haven't tried," he mused. "Desperation!"

"Desperation?" Victoria echoed.

The King nodded into the bedroom where Precious still knelt naked in her bonds in the centre of the Queen's bed, head hanging.

"It doesn't break the treaty to send Precious to Britain. We would just be sending her home."

"Precious! What could she do?"

"If you could slip her past British Intelligence, she knows Samuel and how he thinks — he owned her — so she could surely spot him, even if he's disguised himself. And she knows her way around. If you think about it, she can blend in better, would know how to spot a foreigner, better than any of our own agents. And if you tell her not to come back without him, I think we can agree that that would be more than motivation enough?"

"Desperation," Victoria repeated with a slow grin.

Precious loved her unconditionally. The devoted pet, threatened with a return to her old life, never to kneel at Victoria's feet again, or to feel her lash, really would be quite desperate to find Samuel. Once before she'd quite voluntarily chosen to put a collar around her own neck rather than return to her own world. Motivation an RSP trooper on eighty Crowns a week, constantly looking over his shoulder, fearing capture, could never equal her. And they didn't even have to break the treaty, something she was secretly quite willing to do even if Philip wasn't, if it got her her son back.

"She'd be desperate to succeed, right enough, but she's no detective," Victoria said thoughtfully.

"So get her one," Philip said carelessly. "Or are you worried you might not get her back?"

Victoria said nothing.

"Sorry, I apologise," he said after a moment.

Of course Victoria would put her son before a mere sexual plaything. If there was even a chance of getting Samuel back, it was worth any risk to the top-heavy brunette. Slaves, even superb ones, could be replaced. Sons could not!

The King agreed to hold off declaring Alfred his heir just a little longer, to give her a chance to explore this new idea's possibilities. They arranged to share one of Philip's blondes the evening after next, a thirty two year old girl on what would then be the last day of her service before being set free. The King then pecked her on the cheek and took his leave, pausing in the bedroom to give Precious a satisfied pat on the behind.

Thoughtful now, Victoria selected a whip, letting her eyes roam over naked, bound flesh. As always, hers to use, abuse and enjoy as she wished, until now existing for no other reason than to give Victoria pleasure. But now, perhaps, the tall brunette had another use?

Head hanging, still on her knees, legs secured spread

wide, upper body hanging from bound arms pulled up high behind her back, the naked plaything was breathing slowly and deeply, hugely swollen breasts swaying gently back and forth. Her ball gag making her drool, a strand of saliva trailed to the white satin sheets. The top-heavy brunette's head came up slowly with a long soft groan of pleasure behind the mouth-filling ball gag as Victoria stroked the whip back and forth between her pouting pussy lips.

She had intended to give the gorgeous sex toy a good whipping anyway; an excellent way to work off a little frustration, anger and worry. Now very thoughtful, for the first time in months truly a little hopeful, her property was still going to be firmly whipped. But now, purely for pleasure!

When the long thin lash was completely coated in her husband's come and her property's juices, Victoria laid her chosen weapon lightly across firm, beautifully curved haunches. The bound girl's ass was still attractively reddened from her lashing as she was ridden doggie style, but as Victoria had discovered long ago, an extra dose of pain only made the placid slavegirl hotter and more compliant. Precious shrieked as a vicious stroke left a raised welt across both her reddened buttocks.

Music to any ears.

She gave the girl another, and then another, the hazel-eyed plaything's milk-swollen breasts squashed into the sheets one moment, then swinging free, as she twisted and squirmed under her winch chain. Just from the sound of her yelps, Victoria could tell the lovely sex toy was biting hard into the huge red ball that still stretched her mouth wide open. Another stroke, then another, braided leather licking across twitching flesh with a viper crack, and Precious cried out louder. The big-breasted sex slave with the permanently nipped wasp waist and Victoria's brand burnt into her flesh high on her right buttock, had the most pretty squeal.

Victoria paused to admire her handiwork, stroking velvet flesh lined with raised welts. Gasping around her ball gag, Precious's body swayed back and forth as she panted, ankles still secured wide to the bed strap holding her firmly in place under the winch chain. The buttock under Victoria's grip twitched as she let her palm glide across whip-burnt flesh, the panting plaything's skin burning hot against the cool of her palm. Involuntary muscle contractions made the tortured hemisphere flex and quiver under her hand, but although her property's breath was ragged, Precious wasn't sobbing just yet. Juices glinted between plump chastity-ringed sex lips.

Possibly thinking she was being punished for poor sexual performance, the experienced slavegirl took twelve whip strokes with comparative ease, but number thirteen clearly caught her completely by surprise. Just across the upper thighs, a blaze of pain right across her pussy made the top-heavy beauty squeal, lunging forward to the limit of the winch chain pulling her arms up behind her with a maddened cry, legs straightening and belly almost touching the satin sheets under her before her bonds pulled her back into a kneeling position.

Quickly, giving her victim no time to think, catching the moment, Victoria subjected her property's quivering haunches to lash after lash, welts soon criss-crossing Precious's presented backside. The helpless brunette wailed in ecstatic, tortured, helpless, exultant, agony as she was whipped to orgasm, shudders racking her body.

Queen Victoria let her tongue trail slowly up the fluid-glistening whip. Tears ran down her pet's cheeks, and these were also sampled. Delicious! Fully aroused again, she tossed aside her robe, settling herself on the bed in front of her gasping, trembling, pet and removed the girl's ball gag again. The luscious twenty two year old had been whipped to orgasm uncounted times, but the experience still seemed to leave her dazed and confused, eyes lust glazed. Normally the lovely brunette wouldn't need telling, but it wasn't until Victoria pushed the dazed girl's head between her thighs that Precious came out of whatever trance she was in, and began obediently performing cunnilingus as she had so many times before.

Idly handling milk-swollen tits a moment, Precious gasping pain onto her pussy — the poor little tart really did need milking, her udders were quite hugely and painfully swollen — Victoria flopped back onto the bed. Looking down her own body, she met the former British student's eyes a moment, the brunette sex toy's nose mashed into her pubic hair, tongue deep inside her. The Queen sighed as her property's expertly trained tongue worked its familiar magic. That reminded her!

"Precious. Show me your tongue," she ordered.

Clearly puzzled, the freshly whipped slave of course still responded immediately.

"No, the underside."

The hazel-eyed girl reared up to the limit of her bonds, tongue right out and almost touching her nose, nipple clamp padlocks swinging as her swollen udders bounced together. Viewed from this angle her permanent metal belt almost seemed to cut the lovely plaything in half, digging deep into silky flesh, belly squeezed into a taut swell. Oh yes, there it was. The collared girl's original name was tattooed on the underside of her tongue. She'd been called Jenny once, but Victoria had forgotten. She rarely saw the tattoo herself as the girl was always mouth controlled with some sort of restraint, or performing oral sex, in her presence. At a snap of her fingers, the docile slave's head dived back between Victoria's thighs, tongue obediently burrowing deep into her sex.

"I have a little job for you, Precious," Victoria said softly.

Again she saw surprise in her pet's eyes, but the bound girl knew better than to stop tonguing her without permission. Apart from being praised with "Good girl," and the like when given a pat or stroke, Victoria only ever normally spoke to her property to command her.

"I'm going to send you back to your homeworld to perform a little task for me. I will not take you back, you will not be allowed to come back; unless you succeed."

The brunette's lovely eyes widened in horror. Fresh tears welled in her eyes as she waited for the joke's punch line, and then realised her mistress was deadly serious. Queen Victoria laughed, letting her head drop back onto the bed, looking up, and leaving the horrified sex toy kneeling between her thighs to get on with gently pleasuring her.

Philip was right. Precious was exactly where she wanted to be. Wanted no other life! Forced to pretend to be Jenny again, back in her own reality, the top-heavy chattel would search for Samuel with nothing short of naked desperation. She would spend every waking second trying to find him! It only remained to make sure she had a fighting chance. Access to the resources and information she would need.

She was well aware Philip hadn't actually meant she should get a detective to accompany Precious to Britain, just give the girl access to a professional's advice. But the more Victoria thought about it, the better the idea seemed. Some of the British agents the RSP had captured over the last few months, although probably not trustworthy, surely had the skills she needed. And again, there would be no treaty violation.

She decided to let Samuel's fiancée, Lady Isobell, in on her budding plan. The girl was bright and had been to Britain herself when she'd worked on the original Gate project. She might have some input of value to offer, and it was safe enough; keeping it in the family would not add to the rumour mill.

Victoria felt secrecy was important. Assuming Samuel had been deliberately stranded in the alternative reality, those responsible might try to sabotage a rescue effort. Besides, Isobell had been moping around like a lost weekend ever since Samuel had disappeared. The prospect of a little action might buck her up.

Trembling, breath ragged, naked and gagged, Susan waited in line to be sold. She still couldn't quite believe this was real, that this could really be happening to her, and wasn't just one of her darker fantasies.

The hammer cracked down on Lot Fourteen, with a cry of, "Sold! To the gentleman in the second row," and with a pounding heart she watched Lot Fifteen led forward. She was a lush-bodied, doe-eyed blonde with full firm breasts, a neatly nipped waist and long legs. Led with a collar and chain, the lovely girl had sparkling pendants clamped to her nipples, her wrists were pulled up high behind her back and secured to the back of her collar with a short length of chain. High stiletto heels with a built-in manacle chain forced the naked girl to take short neat steps, hips swaying, as she was led down the catwalk, bidders calling their offers.

"Thirty three! Do I hear thirty four?"

Cruelly, the girls waiting for their turn could see the lower part of the catwalk and the auctioneer, who was intimately handling the helpless slaves, who were no more than livestock, displayed naked and tagged, while he cajoled and encouraged rich, powerful, ruthless people to bid for them. Susan, watching as the auctioneer stroked Lot Fifteen's behind as she was paraded past him, was desperately aroused despite a hollow pit of fear in her stomach.

She groaned in soft, helpless, forced pleasure, as fingers sank deep into the firm heavy weight of her own breasts, the over-large globes lifted and squeezed together. As her tormentor shifted his grip, stroking thumbs over erect, rigid, aching nipples she whimpered; the lust-swollen mounds, lubricated by her saliva, sliding easily together. Her ball gag was making her drool again!

The young man gleefully teasing her, looking little more than a boy in the auction house's pageboy uniform, grinned. Unable to resist, like a dog with a squeaky toy, he forced her to moan for him again, and then again, a longer drawn out wail, roughly squeezing and kneading her breasts; until an older supervisor's barked command brought him to heel. The teenager tied a tag to her left nipple, Susan gasping at the sharp pain when he yanked the knot tight, thin white string biting cruelly into the swollen nub. Saliva trickled slowly down her breasts. The boy happily hefted the heavy melons, as if weighing fruit on a market stall, surreptitiously looking around for his supervisor, and fingers sinking deep into her boobs again, with a cruel twist forced one last long helpless wail out of Susan, pain and pleasure inexorably mingled.

She was getting used to it. The humiliating new dimensions her breasts had been grown to — just a simple injection — delighted most men and many women, and a naked, bound, gagged girl, who could not say no or pull away, could be handled with impunity anywhere. Here, where slavery was legal and commonplace, an aphrodisiac-treated sex slave was expected to enjoy and appreciate strangers inspecting her. Clearly taken with her, deciding she needed a little bit of extra humiliation, the teenager held up the tag now tied to her nipple so that Susan could see what was printed on it. She was Lot Seventeen! The boy slowly stroked her belly, patted and squeezed a buttock, and moved on.

Her wrists were handcuffed behind her back, a huge bright-red ball was tightly squeezed into her mouth, straps tight across her cheeks and under her chin, and she wore nothing but for four-inch-stiletto-heeled sandals. She was secured to a hitching rail by a lead clipped to the shiny metal ring set through her clitoris. Breasts heaving, nipples so hard it hurt, and desperately aware of the slightest sway, swing or tremor through the lead clipped to her pierced clitoris — driving her to distraction, juices running down an inner thigh, even though she'd tried so hard to breathe lightly and stand as still as possible — Susan suspected that even without restraints, she would have still been quite powerless to resist. A well-trained girl was always placid and obediently docile, when she was groped by a stranger.

Unlike Susan, not all of the naked slave toys waiting to be sold into a life of degrading, sadistic, humiliating, sexual service without the possibility of escape, were fully broken in. Clearly panicking, Lot Sixteen needed a few touches with a cattle prod to get her going, and a choke chain to control her on the catwalk. Clearly she was a new slave with no previous owners. Unlike the voluptuous, top-heavy Lot Fifteen, and Susan herself, her figure and face, while attractive, were unremarkable. And as Susan knew only too well, here, in this strange land, there were many who thought a sex object should look like one. And here, Slaveworld owners had the means to make the physical enhancements they wanted!

The bidding on Lot Sixteen was still quite lively. There was room for all sorts of owners, and some masters or mistresses liked the challenge of breaking in, sexually and obedience training, unbroken or wild slaves themselves. A pair of Arapaho Indian girls sold earlier, exotic imports from North America, had been completely untrained and kicking, twisting and screaming behind gags, had had to be auctioned hanging naked from their wrists, slid along a railing above the catwalk like sides of beef in a slaughterhouse. Susan by comparison, hopelessly eager to be auctioned, helplessly excited by the idea of being owned; while still bound, could be much more lightly restrained to show how docile she was.

Owned! She shivered; caution, humiliation and lust warring inside her. Her nipple with the Lot tag tied to it throbbed in time with her heartbeat. Quite legally owned. A pretty plaything, to be used for the sexual gratification of others. Publicly owned!

Outside the auction house was a city where naked, harnessed and bridled pony slaves pulled carriages down city streets alongside limousines and trams. Where courts of law would sentence shoplifters to five years sexual service, naked in a collar. Where pet shops sold whips, chains, and humans. Where nude sex slaves were led along bustling pavements on collars and leads. And where no one would comment if a Lord or Lady chose to have sex with a bound slavegirl in a public park, as long as they didn't obstruct passers-by.

It was not a world Susan had been born into. But six months ago, in a discovery that would forever change her life, she had found that there were parallel universes, alternative realities, and that Gates could be built to travel between them. A spy for British Intelligence, seconded from the police, Susan had stepped through a dimensional Gate, and found herself in the Slaveworld. Entranced, seduced, tempted, though never imagining quite this outcome, she had defected.

Imagine a world, just slightly different from your own.

The continents in the same place, the same moon in the sky, the same fish swimming in the sea and the same birds in the sky. Just a slightly different history. A reality in which the First World War was never fought because a single assassination failed. A world in which a South American Columbus discovered Europe. Or a reality where you don't, and never did, exist, because your however-many-times-great grandfather was killed in the British defeat at Waterloo.

In this reality, the Roman legions and their Lords had never really withdrawn from Britain, had just been gradually assimilated as the power of Rome waned. There had been no Dark Age, just slow measured scientific progress which had left a technologically advanced world, and an entrenched society of nobles, soldiers, serfs and slaves. Where every man and woman, from King and Queen in their palace, to the lowest peasant in the fields, considered the existence of sex slaves quite natural, normal, the way things had always been; and always would be.

"Lot Seventeen!"

Completely naked, perched on her toes in stiletto heels, a ball gag filling her mouth and with her wrists handcuffed behind her back, Susan followed the insistent, teasing, pull of her humiliating clit lead towards the catwalk. She felt herself flush hot; her thoughts a confused whirl of thrilling shame, fear and overwhelming lust. Led by the same boy who had tied the Lot number tag to her nipple, every tug on the ring set through her clitoris was a delightful, deliciously cruel, torment; quite impossible to ignore or disobey! As she was pulled towards the bright lights, head held up proudly, taking small, neat steps, one foot put in front of the other, Susan was very aware of the fuck-me sway in her stride and the way her big heavy slave breasts quivered, jiggled and swung with every step; but it required no conscious effort.

The previous week spent in the auction house's display cell, visible to anyone on the street outside, had trained her to display herself as a purely sexual object quite to perfection. Although gone for the moment, the manacles and posture collar that had been locked around her ankles and neck while she toiled on the treadmill, meant she now took small neat steps with a sexy sway and boob-jiggling bounce, head held up, quite naturally. It would probably be several more days before she could bring herself to truly believe that a bolt of agonising pain wouldn't sear her anus if her over-large breasts didn't sway and bob enticingly with every step.

Oh God! Susan's heart skipped a beat. There were at least two hundred people on the auction house floor, all of them looking up at her naked body. A second T-shaped catwalk projected out from the first into the sea of buyers. There were four rows of plush seats for the elegantly dressed aristocrats, and standing jostling behind them, the more soberly dressed slave dealers and company buyers. Her training came to her rescue, and the memory of restraints, the hours on the treadmill, the countless shocks and repeated orgasms she'd been forced to while on public display, ensured Susan didn't falter.

"Lot Seventeen is a twenty three year old brunette, youth treated, all standard implants," the auctioneer announced.

'All standard implants' meant a surgically implanted contraceptive and a very powerful aphrodisiac slowly, permanently, dissolving into her bloodstream. The aristocrats liked to keep their slavegirls permanently hot and wet, continually ready to be used. Like a bitch on heat, Susan was always eager to be enjoyed. She couldn't help herself. A barked command, a stroked buttock or a squeezed breast, and her nipples would obediently rise, her breasts swell with lust and juices would flow. Her arousal was almost instant, total, and completely beyond her control.

Wafer thin coin-shaped sensors under the skin, attached to the skull at her temples, monitored her brainwaves, any orgasm recorded on the owner's personal computer. Some owners liked to know how many times they'd made their property come, how effective this or that chastity belt was, and of course, a slave toy was not allowed to give herself pleasure; to masturbate. Owners sometimes allowed, and frequently forced, slaves to come, but their sex toys were otherwise expected to endure raging sexual frustration for as long as necessary. Knowing that only through docile obedience would they be permitted the pleasure they craved.

Susan's final implant was a pea-sized locator tag implanted in the left breast. At the touch of a button, her owner could use orbital satellites to track her position anywhere on the face of the planet, to within five metres. It was a useful device. Sex slaves, knowing that escape was absolutely impossible, didn't need to concern themselves with the possibility. And so never had to feel guilty about placidly submitting; to being forced to enjoy the humiliating sexual indignities they were put to.

Susan was also now very limber. She could perform a full splits, touch her elbows together behind her back, sleep comfortably hog-tied and wear a ball gag all day without jaw ache. Every muscle, ligament and joint in her body had been stretched, flexed and twisted at the same clinic that had performed her other 'improvements'; it was a standard treatment not even worth mentioning. Her skin was flawless velvet, moles and freckles surgically removed, every last hair follicle except pubic hair and eyebrows permanently stunned.

The youth treatment the auctioneer mentioned was one of the technologies that had specifically attracted British Intelligence to this world. Here, they had a rejuvenation treatment that added at least twenty years to the average lifespan, dramatically slowing ageing. The aristocrats were all much older than they actually looked. Mostly reserved for nobles, the treatment was occasionally given to a favoured slave, so that he or she could be enjoyed for longer. Treated herself, Susan would look only a few years older, twenty six or twenty seven, by the time she was fifty. The treatment substantially added to the length of her service compared to the average slavegirl, usually released around the thirty-year-old mark, which of course raised Susan's auction value. With a shiver of fear, Susan was well aware she could be into her sixties by the time she appeared thirty years old. Still serving!

"She is five foot two tall exactly, and there is a reserve price of fifty K on this slave," the auctioneer continued.

An excited buzz swept the hall at the announcement of Susan's reserve price, even though most buyers would have already seen her pedigree in the auction house programme or in an advertisement. She caught the whisper, "One of the New Ones!"

From knowledge of the Slaveworld gained as a spy, Susan knew why the auctioneer had pointed out her height. At five foot two inches tall, Susan was eligible to compete as a show pony. Dressage slaves competed in pairs in public competition, from local shows to the international Olympics, in a combination of beauty contest and training and obedience display. The dildo-stuffed dressage pony girls were always top-heavy, competition rules requiring a bust measurement twice the tightened girth size, but they also had to be cute little things.

As a serving police officer, Susan had been just under five foot three inches, but here the Slaveworld's surgeons had taken two vertebrae out of her spine to reduce her height, and then stretched her legs a little, bringing her exactly to a lush, curvy, dressage-eligible five foot two. That was if her new owner even wanted to compete her in the arena of course. She shivered. There were after all many many other uses for a legally owned slavegirl.

In addition to the rejuvenation treatment that would keep her young for longer, another factor raised Susan's value. For many months, a rumour of a new improved aphrodisiac had swept the Kingdom. Slavegirls so hot and wet, so willing to please they barely needed any training and could be screwed unconscious by an old man. 'The New Ones', were mostly owned by Royalty so far, but a few were now starting to come onto the market.

Susan actually knew there was no new aphrodisiac, but the rumour, like most, had a grain of truth to it. Once treated, a frigid slavegirl who didn't like sex, could be whipped to orgasm, trained to like whatever sexual use she was put to. A hot girl became a bitch on heat, constantly craving sex. And when a genuine submissive was treated, you had a hopelessly devoted girl who worshipped the ground her owner walked on. Sexually, Susan had always secretly been very submissive.

The drug had been around a long time now — the aristocrats used a milder non-additive version themselves — and each new generation was slowly building up an immunity. If a slavegirl's mother or father had served a few years for littering or failing to show a noble the proper respect, then the girl was slightly less susceptible to the treatment. If both parents had been treated, she would be still less susceptible. If a grandmother or grandfather, had served ten years for unpaid tax maybe, then the drug's effect was further diluted. And of course, that was not forgetting great grandmother's seven years of service as a champion mud wrestler. Almost all working-class families had a few former slaves in the family tree somewhere. It was hard to avoid.

So there was no new treatment, but it was true there were some hotter than usual sex slaves about. British girls! It was a trade that British Intelligence and their agents were supposedly trying to stop, though Susan hadn't seen much evidence of it herself on her own spy missions. 'The New Ones', as she very well knew, were in actual fact, girls kidnapped from home. Girls with no resistance at all to the very powerful drug, brought here to serve the depraved sexual appetites of Slaveworld's English Royalty and the Kingdom's rich and powerful.

Other slaves could be trained to enjoy their sexual use, but British girls could take more of everything; more pain, more sex, more humiliation, and still want more! Susan herself had effectively been given a dose probably twice to three times as powerful as the other sex slaves on sale. Her every waking moment, when not being enjoyed, was characterised by desperate frustration and a burning need to be just that little more pleasing, obedient, sexy. The more delightful she was to own, the more she would be enjoyed. She was still genuinely upset that she'd been sold once, and couldn't imagine why her fellow defector Frances, hadn't wanted to keep her to use, abuse and enjoy!

The men and women who would bid on her knew nothing about dimensional Gates or alternative worlds, but if they had, it wouldn't have mattered to them. The aristocrats were born and raised to own, the peasants, born to serve. To them it didn't really matter which world Susan had been born on, just that she hadn't been born a noble. And here today, if the new aphrodisiac wasn't available to the general public yet, then that made the few New Ones who came up for auction all the more valuable in their eyes.

Probably her past would not even be questioned. Her new owner would just rename her, and enjoy her.

"Lot Seventeen has pierced nipples, navel, clitoris, and five pairs of chastity rings. The bar code is on the ass," the auctioneer continued matter-of-factly.

At the end of the T-shaped catwalk — surrounded by seated aristocrats looking up at her naked body — following the insistent tug of her clit ring, Susan was wheeled around by the young man holding her lead. Her hands cuffed behind her clenched into tight fists, Susan bit hard into her ball gag, whimpering, as in a clearly practised move the boy gave the lead a swaying tug back and forth, making Susan swing her hips from side to side. Giving all the buyers a good rear view.

The bar code with a serial number printed underneath was on her right buttock, all slaves were similarly marked somewhere on their bodies to facilitate their purchase and sale. If you won a slavegirl at the card table or betting on a racing pony, you didn't want to have to mess about with complicated forms and pedigrees — just a sweep across the bar code with a scanner or personal computer, and ownership was transferred. The tattoo was a liquid metal. It didn't fade like ink, and would remain on her body, perfectly sharp, forever. Her juices smearing her inner thighs, Susan was led back up the catwalk.

"As you can see, the tits on this item have been quite heavily enlarged," the auctioneer said calmly.

The pageboy leading Susan paused to allow the man to

heft a breast, the heavy globe filling his palm, flesh spilling between splayed fingers. Naked, helplessly bound, being intimately handled in front of well over a hundred fully dressed people, Susan groaned in soft pleasure. The man's fingers sank into her flesh just from the weight he held.

Here, if an owner desired a top-heavy slavegirl, with big, firm, heavy tits to slap, whip, rope and shock; then they could have one! The bigger the dose the slave was injected with, the larger her breasts grew. There were slender slavegirls about — they were fashionable in some circles — and it was every aristocrat's birthright to own the physical type that pleased them most, but most girls were improved only a little; about a third, like Susan, quite substantially. It was perhaps unsurprising that the first male explorers to the Slaveworld from Britain had christened the place Titworld.

"Admittedly a little unfashionable, but just think of the fun you could have with them!"

The auctioneer held Susan's breast up by a nipple ring a moment, the whole weight of the full globe hanging cruelly stretched from the ring set through her flesh, before letting it drop and waving on the boy holding her lead. Her clitoris tugged again, Susan whimpered, and helplessly followed her lead.

"She has a twenty one inch waist, easily belted or girthed down to a pretty eighteen inches with natural thirty six inch hips," the man who had just so casually handled her continued.

Her hourglass figure was the work of the same cosmetic surgeon who had widened her eyes and dyed her irises a dark violet. The spotlights aimed at the catwalk were very bright, dazzling her — no doubt so that the buyers got a good view of what they were bidding on — but she could make out the people in the front row easily enough. Lords and Ladies, elegant in their finery. Men and women, old and young. And any of them might buy her.

An old woman wearing pearls and a tiara, looking shrunken, wrinkled, her hands trembling, clearly at least a hundred years old, and maybe more with rejuvenation treatments, let her eyes trail over Susan's naked body. Her gaze was steady and clear. Please not her! On the other side of the catwalk a monstrously fat man gave the quiver and sway of her big, ring-tipped breasts an approving nod, and made a note on his programme.

Some of the nobles were the owners of her fantasies though. Handsome, ruthless-looking, dashing men and beautiful, cruel women. A stunning young couple in the second row caught her eye, but she looked in vain for any sign of interest from them. Maybe they were waiting for the slaveboys' auction after. Obediently holding up her head, her ball gag making her drool on her breasts, stray comments and snatches of conversation drifted up to her out of the buzz of voices.

"Look at the size of those tits!"

"....so I'd bid up to sixty two, no more."

"....but I'd want to use her as a carriage pony as well. Do you think she's got the stamina?"

"I certainly wouldn't mind giving it a ride. Lovely ass on her, hasn't she?"

"We can't afford her! Not if you want that blonde as well."

"....with those tits? Trust me. Any eighteen year old boy will love her. She's the perfect birthday present."

"Looks a bit sulky to me."

"That's the one. Please buy her for me Daddy!"

Sitting next to her resigned-looking father, the young Lady was in the front row, wearing a pretty soft-red summer dress. She was very attractive, her sweet, clear, voice carrying easily to Susan over the shuffling, rustles, coughs and murmurs of two hundred people. She also looked about eighteen, the legal limit to own a sex slave in the Slaveworld English Kingdom.

Susan almost stumbled, immediately recognising the young aristocrat as the same Lady who had made her trot on the treadmill until she dropped in the glass-walled display cage. The auctioneer gave Susan a stinging slap on the behind as she was led past again, her handcuffs cutting into her wrists behind her back as she jerked.

"As you can see, firm and toned haunches, perfectly

spankable. Who will open the bidding on this magnificent young animal?"

A man raised a hand.

"Thank you. Fifty. Do I hear fifty five?"

The old woman flicked open her fan. A bid. The auctioneer took more bids, stroking Susan's bare flesh now. The father of the girl in the red dress, seeing something expensive about to happen, was reluctantly prodded into raising a hand when the auctioneer pointed out how stiff and swollen Susan's nipples were, rolling the fat nubs between his fingers. She gasped, almost coming, when another tug on her clit ring pulled her down the catwalk again.

"Sixty two? Sixty two for this superb slave? My Lords and Ladies. Look at the swing of those hips, the way those huge heavy tits quiver with every step."

Susan felt herself flush scarlet again.

"Can't you just imagine her chained to your bed? Fighting in an oil pit? Or in harness and bridle, a nice fat dildo in her, pulling your pony trap down the Strand?"

The auctioneer thrust a careless hand between her legs, pushing his fingers inside her body, Susan's hips bucking as she thrust herself onto his hand. Teeth clenched tight into her ball gag, she wailed softly as she came, panting helplessly around the obstruction now, breasts heaving, hundreds of eyes on her body as the auctioneer stroked her wetness up her belly, matting her pubic hair. Dazed, shattered, the pageboy firmly squeezing and kneading her big breasts from behind now, the bidding became a flurry. Susan looked helplessly back and forth, meeting the eyes of the people who wanted to own her.

"My Lords and Ladies. I draw your attention to page two of your programme," the auctioneer called. "This slave has been whipped to orgasm on a dildo pole only four seconds off an Olympic qualifying time! Imagine what you could do with her with a little professional training. I can't let her go for just seventy eight thousand crowns. Do I hear eighty?"

Susan had been evaluated when she'd first arrived at the

auction house, but hadn't realised she'd done so well. Whipping slavegirls to orgasm while mounted on a dildo pole, fastest to three, was a popular sport all over the Slaveworld. Like dressage and mud wrestling, the sport was played at all levels, from friendly amateur bouts at village shows, to international competitions.

Susan couldn't really imagine herself winning a national Polewhip championship, but the very thought of being impaled on a dildo and whipped in front of a live audience, and on TV all over the world, left her dripping wet and hotter than ever. And she'd once thought being publicly sold at auction, naked and bound, would be the realisation of her fantasies. She was a very, very long way away from masturbating while wearing her own police-issue handcuffs now, the first steps on the path that had led her here, about to be quite legally bought at a public auction.

"Daddy! You promised!"

"Oh all right!"

The beautiful young aristocrat raised her hand.

"Sold! To the young Lady in the red dress."

Nipples being rubbed across each other, lust-swollen breasts squeezed hard together by the auction house boy, her clit lead still looped around his wrist swaying back and forth across the fronts of her thighs, an erection poking her between the buttocks, Susan gasped in mingled shock and pleasure as the hammer cracked down. She was led off the catwalk, perfunctorily hooded and hog-tied, and left to lie on her stomach on the floor.

In her own fantasies there had been no gap between being on the auction block, and finding herself tied spreadeagled on her handsome, dashing new master's bed. Here, reality proved a little different. Her tightly-tagged nipple throbbing painfully now, Susan eventually realised that of course her pretty new owner couldn't be expected to collect her property straight away. The beautiful young Lady might wish to bid on other Lots. Susan shivered, taking comfort from warm soft velvet skin pressed against hers, other hog-tied slavegirls piled up around her. She'd known a woman might buy her, but hadn't expected to find herself owned by someone so young!

CHAPTER FOUR

Lady Abigail paced impatiently back and forth across one of the auction house's collection suites, waiting for her chosen sexual plaything to be delivered to her. Her father sat on one of the plush comfortable settees, his amusement at her impatience to get her hands on the girl clear, and temporarily taking his mind off muttering about how much the top-heavy little brunette had cost.

"You could have had her delivered you know," he said mildly.

"Daddy!" Abigail protested. "I want to play with her now!"

Her father nodded with reluctant understanding. After all, he had been young, sex mad and impatient himself once. And as he well knew, even if the auction house's shipping department made the morning post, the pet crate containing Abigail's lovely new sex toy would not have reached the family estate until that afternoon. Some playthings you just wanted to harness, mount and ride straight away.

"And then I can buy her some nice restraints after, and show her to my friends this afternoon," she added with happy, cruel, anticipation.

Some pets didn't like being orgy fodder, preferring to be used exclusively for the pleasure of the owner they had been trained to love and adore, but Abigail was sure her new purchase would like being shared. Knowing the truth behind 'The New Ones' Abigail was pretty sure Lot Seventeen could be trained to enjoy almost anything she chose to do with her.

She scrolled through the sex toy's pedigree on her personal computer, the small, light and expensive belt-worn device. Age, measurements, height, weight, education, skills, history, surgical improvements and previous owners were all listed. Any information a potential buyer might wish to know, was public record, with pictures. If they had access to a holo-projector, any noble could even call up a life-sized image of Abigail's new pet, naked, in various restraints, indistinguishable from the real flesh and blood girl unless you tried to touch.

The before and after pictures of the girl's face showed a light touch, lips just a little fuller, cheeks hollowed and eyelids stretched out into an exotic almond shape, giving the top-heavy slave an appealing look of wide-eyed innocence. Her irises, once an uninteresting washed out grey/blue, were now dyed a beautiful dark violet. Quite lovely. Too many slave toys were given flawless magazine-cover faces; perfect, but devoid of personality.

Fortunately for Daddy's bank balance, a cosmetic surgeon had already trimmed down the sex toy's waist, because while Abigail liked a lush, curvy, plaything, she just absolutely refused to bed a girl who couldn't be corseted down to a nice eighteen inch wasp waist. "Lovely," she sighed. And those big heavy tits were going to be an absolute delight to rope, torture and shock. Unfashionably huge, which didn't concern her unduly; though now Abigail thought about it, big tits did seem to be back into fashion this season.

Partly, Her Majesty Queen Victoria II had set a trend in Royal circles with her current deliciously top-heavy pet, Precious, and also, the New Ones were all big girls. People assumed it was some side effect of the new aphrodisiac treatment, but Abigail was privy to the truth. It was just so much more humiliating for the kidnapped British girls to find themselves so substantially 'improved', and humiliation and shame made them hotter, wetter, better and more docile slaves. Local girls, although they might sob a bit at the time, were used to the idea of breast enlarging injections. Just as a brunette slavegirl might suddenly find herself blonde, or be put on a diet or force fed, so she knew an owner might consider a larger bust.

In Abigail's opinion, slavegirls released once they'd served their sentence usually came out ahead of the game. So, a peasant girl might find herself up a few bra sizes when she was set free; but she also got perfect teeth, flawless skin and a pretty face that she didn't have to pay for — and would never be able to afford — into the bargain. And big-titted ex-slaves were allowed to jump to the head of the hospital waiting list if they developed back trouble in later life. You couldn't say fairer than that.

She scrolled on through Lot Seventeen's pedigree.

Lady Abigail had already decided she would have a ring set through the tip of the girl's tongue; useful when combined with a tongue clamp, for clipping a lead to if you didn't want the stimulation of a clit lead. Abigail never clipped a lead to a slavegirl's collar unless she was thoroughly bored with her. The brunette was almost three years older than Abigail herself. Twenty three years old at the moment, her twenty fourth birthday in a little over a month. She would try to think up a new name for the big-titted plaything to answer to before then, so she could be fitted with a nametag for her birthday. Pets, unlike interchangeable household slaves, were always re-named. It helped them feel more owned and loved.

Finally a pageboy led Lot Seventeen into the suite, along with one of the auction house's representatives, and Abigail could shut off her 'comp' and study the real thing. Her chosen purchase was still naked, drooling around the huge ball gag tightly strapped into her mouth, with her wrists still handcuffed behind her back. And she was still being led with the same clit chain with which she'd been displayed and sold on the catwalk, the brunette's eyes looked a little glazed. Being led about with a lead clipped to the ring set through her clitoris all day was undoubtedly tormenting the pretty little sex object to utter distraction. Her four inch stiletto heels, everyday wear for slavegirls, tip-tapped prettily on the marble floor, firm, weighty tits jiggling and quivering; but the bound slave was still focused enough to come to attention, head up and ankles together at a snap of the salesman's fingers.

"I do apologise for keeping you waiting, My Lord, My Lady. We've had a very busy day."

Abigail waved away his excuses with a careless gesture, her eyes drinking in the full glorious curves, lingering on erect nipples, a neatly trimmed vertical tuft of pubic hair above a plump pussy and a row of five chastity rings set through each sex lip. The pussy rings were pretty, but might have to go, she thought. They would protect the slave when Abigail whipped her between the legs!

The gagged girl was breathing hard, almost snorting through her nose with every breath, nostrils flaring and eyes wide, her gaze nervously darting back and forth between Abigail and her father before settling properly on her new owner. As the salesman bustled about her with a hand-scanner, scanning retinas, the ID chip implanted in her body and the bar code tattooed on her right buttock, with every cheerful little beep from the machine, the pussy-led sex object's breath became faster, harder; more ragged! Helplessly caught by Abigail's rapt gaze, she was almost panting around the large red ball filling her mouth by the time the salesman gave her a last approving pat on the behind.

The handcuffed, clit-led, brunette was also trembling just a little, which added a delicious little quiver to her spectacular tits. Saliva ran in rivulets down the big gasp-heaving globes, her stomach swelling and flattening with every fearful, excited, breath. Still naked and bound, as she'd been paraded down the catwalk, auctioned to the highest bidder like so much livestock, now the gorgeous creature faced the final indignity of being sold. The appraisal of her legal owner!

Abigail grinned slyly as her father thoughtfully squeezed and kneaded a buttock. The pretty sex toy was quite clearly a beautifully spankable little beast.

Finally the irritatingly slow salesman set up the credit transfer. Lady Abigail waited impatiently while her father paid for the bound and gagged girl with an electronic bank transfer, and then she finally got to run her own belt-comp across the bar code on the doe-eyed sex toy's ass. The machine gave a little chirp of its own, and the pageboy handed over the lead clipped to the trembling slavegirl's pierced clitoris.

Her slavegirl! Bought and paid for. Abigail's to enjoy as

she wished. When she wished, how she wished, as often as she wished. Abigail now owned every last hair on her head. She even owned the saliva trickling down the panting sex object's heaving tits and the juices glinting between her plump sex lips. The salesman dismissed the pageboy and bowed a final time.

"May I wish you every pleasure in using her, My Lady. However, if she is in any way unsatisfactory, the auction house will of course buy her back, minus the house's commission, if she is returned in good condition within two weeks. Please keep your receipt."

"Yes, yes," Abigail waved him away.

Typical flunky! They always wanted praise and attention, just for doing their jobs. The ball gag's straps across her purchase's cheeks and tight under her chin really did suit the girl, Abigail thought. So pretty, and you could just drown in those wide dark eyes. Abigail couldn't wait to see them well with tears. Return her? Not a chance.

"Thank you, I'm sure she'll give years of pleasure," her father, less distracted, assured the salesman for her, snagging the bill of sale.

Lady Abigail pulled the top-heavy sex toy forward a pace with her lead, the naked, handcuffed, plaything gasping helplessly as she was tugged closer with the ring set through her clitoris. Breath ragged, there was an attractive hint of fear in the slave's wide dark eyes; and bright shining excitement! Totally mesmerised by Abigail now, she didn't flinch, barely seemed to notice, when Abigail's father thoughtfully hefted a full, firm, ring-tipped breast.

"Big tits. She'll need a lot of whip mind," he warned.

"I know," Abigail breathed, still looking into beautiful almond-shaped eyes helplessly, fearfully, fixed on her own.

There were three people in the room, but only two players. And the sex object, perched on her toes in stiletto heels and with her wrists locked behind her, held in place with a pussy lead, was intelligent enough to realise it too. Daddy was just an extra in this drama. He hefted the breast he held a couple of times, and then with a rueful nod turned back to the sofa to pick up his hat and cane.

Actually, Abigail suspected the top-heavy plaything would need very little breaking in as opposed to her sexual and obedience training, which was going to be a long and exacting process. Possibly years! The suggestion that large-breasted slavegirls needed a lot of whip, was just a phrase common to her parents' generation. The old wives tale was quite pervasive, dating back to the days before big tits were just an injection away, perhaps even back to Roman times, when a lush voluptuous slave toy would be more likely to earn her supper in her owner's bed while skinny and not so pretty property worked in the fields. Pampered pets, pure sexual playthings, not working animals, of course soon got ideas above their station, and had had to be taught that they were not lovers.

Many of the older slave-training manuals still recommended harsher punishments for top-heavy toys. And on some of the more conservative country estates, where the old ways were considered best, it was still unremarkable for a big breasted slavegirl to get twelve of the best, and earn herself a week permanently gagged, hooded and in a pin-lined tit harness, for an offence that would gain a slender girl only six cane strokes. Abigail decided the as yet unnamed brunette, was going to be disciplined the old way.

Her father finally realised he wasn't going to have her full attention for some time to come.

"Oh all right, I'll leave you alone to play," he said. "I'll tell your mother not to expect you for dinner tonight, shall I?"

Lady Abigail let her eyes trail slowly down Big Tits' displayed body once more, and then back up to her beautiful eyes again. Her property, trembling lightly as she panted, but with juices glinting on her pussy rings, looked like she had quite a bit of stamina.

"Yes, I think so."

"Okay, have fun," he said, and then added in a sly dig, "though if she's worth half of what she cost, I'm sure you will!"

"Daddy!" Abigail protested. "You did say I could have

'anything' for my birthday."

"Yes I did," he sighed. "Just try not to get bored with this one too quickly."

"I won't," she promised.

She had promised the same before she knew, but this time she was sure it really would be different. Ordinary slavegirls just didn't seem able to keep her interested, no matter how often she had them punished for their lack of docile, masochistic, sex appeal. After a few months, she just lost interest in them, and wanted a new one.

The problem, she'd eventually realised, was her eighteenth birthday treat. Abigail had lost her virginity enjoying a superb sex toy call Jenny, an exquisite, top-heavy girl, just nineteen years old at the time, with hazel eyes and a long dark mane of copper-highlighted hair. Although tall, a shade under five feet eleven inches tall and powerfully built, her birthday treat had been amazingly docile and very eager to please. The sex and torture had been amazing! Unfortunately, subsequent slaves just hadn't matched up.

To start with, Abigail had just tried to match the physical type, though in her preferred blonde. A docile, but tall and powerful girl, with large heavy tits — born to pull a pony trap — who took good whip, but something had always been missing.

At the time Jenny had belonged to Lady Franklin. Lord Franklin was Abigail's godfather, which was how she got to sample the girl. What Abigail didn't know then, was that her godfather's second wife was actually a traveller from another dimension, another reality, which the inhabitants called Britain. Her godfather had headed up the research team here, which had invented the dimensional Gate, and Lady Franklin had invented the other half of the Gate in Britain. To form a stable portal, two Gates had to link together.

Jenny, renamed Treasure had subsequently been passed on to Lord Franklin's daughter, Lady Isobell, and then had been briefly owned by the Prince of Wales. She answered to Precious now, Queen Victoria's brand burnt into her right buttock, and like Lady Franklin herself she was also originally from Britain. One of the first of the New Ones! Brought here by Lady Franklin.

Out of the bedroom, Abigail's passion was racing ponies and Lord and Lady Franklin just happened to own a champion. Abigail wanted to drive her. To begin with, after much pestering, she had been allowed to exercise and train pony girls alongside the grooms, her godfather while indulging her, clearly expecting her to eventually lose interest. But she hadn't, and finally they'd both given in and allowed her to take up the reins against professional drivers on a real racetrack. Driving Lady Franklin's Black Beauty, Abigail had won again and again.

The black girl wasn't the greatest fuck in the world, though she had a nice tongue on her, but from the moment Abigail clipped the proud racing pony's reins to her nipple rings and pulled and buckled her crotch strap and bit tight, until she whipped her naked, sweat-lathered, sobbing mount over the finish line; there was a rapport between them that other drivers just couldn't quite equal. Nobody could whip a faster lap time out of the black girl. Beauty had had many winners' rosettes pinned to her breasts, and Abigail had a cabinet filling up with gold cups. Beauty was also a former British student, another of Lady Franklin's original research team. The crowd loved her!

Regularly driving Lady Franklin's champion pony girl, breaking Beauty in with her own unique brand of sexual torture, Abigail had become friends with the Lady's stepdaughter, Isobell, until then just another family acquaintance. Gradually the whole Gate story and the Franklin's part in it had come out. It wasn't exactly a state secret, just a subject best not talked about. Abigail could go along with that. Because by then she'd finally realised what would satisfy her. A British slavegirl, all of her own! And now she had one. She held out a hand, palm up.

"Cunt!" Lady Abigail ordered.

The as yet unnamed British slave obediently stepped forward and pressed her crotch into Abigail's cupped hand. Her flesh was silky soft, a luxuriant caress, satin set with steel rings.

"Tits!" Abigail ordered.

The naked and gagged slavegirl with her hands locked behind her back immediately dropped to her knees and pushed the over-large globes into Abigail's waiting, held-out hands. Ringed nipples, aching hard, pressed eagerly against her palms; warm, heavy, velvet flesh spilling out of her grip. Gods, her tits were huge! The docile slave, looking up at Abigail from her knees, moaned in soft helpless pleasure as her lust swollen flesh was kneaded, squeezed and pulled, the firm, weighty mounds lubricated by saliva, slipping and sliding together.

"Cunt!" Lady Abigail barked again, finally forcing herself to let the placid plaything's heavily enlarged tits drop.

Her property sprang back to her feet and obediently pushed her pussy into a waiting palm. The pretty slave cried out, a wordless gasp of pleasure, as Abigail slowly let her middle finger stroke up through the bound girl's sex, between her ringed sex lips, probing deep. The ball-gagged brunette was dripping wet. Slowly, teasing, she lifted the finger to her own lips and equally slowly sucked the digit.

"Mmmm! You taste nice, pretty toy."

The docile slavegirl flushed, shame, fear and excitement warring behind her wide eyes. Another rivulet of saliva ran down a breast, the heavy globes rising and falling faster still as the bound toy panted. Her hips bucked, a little squeak forced from her, as Abigail again stroked her fingers back through her property's pussy. Then she pushed all four fingers into the girl and the sex toy wailed in helpless delight, throwing back her head, ramming her crotch forward onto the fingers penetrating her.

"Open your eyes pretty toy. Look at me," Abigail coaxed softly.

The teased slave's dazed eyes floated open, hips still bucking to Abigail's strokes, so hot and wet she couldn't help herself gasping with every little finger thrust. Lady Abigail scooped up the slave's lead, still hanging from her ring-set clitoris, and clipped the lead's chain to the chinstrap of the brunette's ball gag. She flipped the suede handle and spare chain out of the way over the girl's shoulder.

"Head up, until it hurts," Abigail commanded softly. "Give yourself a little pain, and then maybe I'll give you a little pleasure."

The forcibly aroused slavegirl obediently lifted her chin, painfully dragging up at her own clitoris, the pierced nub cruelly stretched. The chain lead lay taut between her big pant-quivering breasts, and dug lightly into the gentle swell of the tormented plaything's belly and Abigail was delighted to notice the first tears welling in her lovely dark eyes.

"Good girl," she whispered, stroking the gagged toy's baby-soft belly a moment before slipping her fingers back into the slavegirl's sex.

Twisting deep, all four fingers to the knuckle now, the handcuffed and gagged girl cried out helplessly. Again, she obediently squeaked and moaned as her owner's fingers stroked back and forth between her pussy lips, and then deep into her body once more, but there was a desperate, pleading note to her cries now, pain and pleasure mingled. Head up, teeth clenched hard into the large red ball strapped into her mouth, her clitoris was agonisingly stretched, the chain from chinstrap to pussy pulled cruelly taut up her body. Abigail was entranced.

Timing the slut to perfection, just as her cries were becoming breathless, Abigail let her fingers slip out of the quivering sex toy, up, rubbing back and forth, faster and faster, across the girl's stretched, chain-tormented clitoris. The unnamed brunette squealed in ecstasy.

Abigail pulled her property back into place with her nipple rings — the girl had staggered back a couple of paces — and unclipped the lead from her ball gag's chinstrap. She left the restraint still attached to the brunette's clitoris however, swinging between her legs, in case it was needed again. Panting harder, tits heaving, her rib cage showing with every gasping gag-obstructed breath, her new pet forced herself back to attention, head up and ankles neatly together.

"My name is Lady Abigail. You may call me Mistress," she told the drooling plaything she'd just forced to come. "I own you now."

There was nothing but eager acceptance in the slavegirl's eyes. Abigail walked slowly around her conquest, the obedient plaything standing motionless. As her father had done, she thoughtfully squeezed and hefted a buttock. Oh yes, very spankable! Firm and toned muscle underneath, but enough padding to give a nice ripple when a whip or paddle landed. According to her pedigree, updated by some meticulous sergeant, the cute little brunette had spent the last two months being worked as agricultural labour on a historical re-enactment farm. There, on the orders of her supposed owner — really another offworld spy — she had been force-fed daily to add a half stone to her weight. But as a working animal, given plenty of whip, she'd gained the weight in all the right places, mostly hips and tits!

As long as the girl was fit enough to pull a pony trap or pedal a tandem bicycle through the streets of Londinium, Abigail had no intention of allowing her to lose any weight. She loved a lush, voluptuous body tied down under her during sex. She walked back around her plaything, lightly trailing fingernails over a hip.

"I haven't decided what I'm going to call you yet, so you'll just have to answer to 'Hey you,' or 'Tits,' until I do, understood?"

The brunette nodded obediently, an attractive hint of a blush again touching her cheeks. Abigail reached out and slowly but firmly lifted a large breast up high by the nipple ring, pierced flesh and the areola around it nicely stretched, the breast itself pulled up into a cone; and delivered a palm-stinging slap to the full globe. Heavy flesh bounced under the blow, and swung back beside its twin with a delicious quiver, now marked with a vivid handprint. The naked slave gasped. Without pause, Abigail raised the other melon, and swung another hard slap, her palm's crack on unmarked, lightly-tanned flesh, very loud in the still room. Another red splotch marked the handcuffed sex toy's flesh.

Then again, and again! The pretty toy held herself obediently still as her big breasts were firmly and repeatedly slapped, just making little twists and twitches away from Abigail's blows, squeaking softly at each stinging crack. Abigail was ambidextrous when it came to slapping tits; as were the owners of many top-heavy slavegirls. You could spank a slave's behind all over one handed, but to get both tits equally scarlet meant slapping with both hands.

She carefully marked her property's heavy udders all over, a nice red blush at first, and then with slap after slap, a burning, stinging, scarlet. Her victim's squeaks became louder, a hint of a pleading whimper slipping past the mouth-filling red ball gag, but the handcuffed girl managed to keep her ankles neatly together, and her head up, properly raised, still meeting her tormentor's eyes. The first tear ran down the brunette's cheek, pooling on the ball gag's strap tight across her cheek. Her palms stinging now, Abigail delivered a last few blows, until both ring-tipped melons were a deep throbbing angry dark red.

The docile sex slave whimpered as her punished breasts were stroked, the heavy mounds trembling and quivering as she snuffled. Delighted, Abigail sank her fingers deep into reddened flesh, cruelly squeezing and kneading. Her property cried out in anguished pleasure as her stinging, bruised udders were roughly handled, groaning helplessly in forced lust as Abigail twisted her fingers painfully deep into burning hot flesh. Her moans became even louder as she let her tongue trail slowly, sensuously, over the big heavy mounds she held squeezed together.

On sensitive stinging skin, Abigail knew her tongue probably felt like a metal rasp! Exquisite torture. Finally she allowed punished flesh to drop, and again walked slowly around her gasping, trembling, naked property. The lovely girl's juices ran down an inner thigh, nipples standing out harder than ever, her beautiful doe eyes starting to look a bit glazed over again now, after a stimulating punishment right on top of being forced to come. Abigail let her palm stroke down the velvet curve of her property's belly, fingers brushing through soft down, and lightly cupping a dripping sex.

The drooling brunette thrust her crotch urgently against Abigail's palm, a soft plaintive pleading moan escaping her. Abigail flicked a nipple with her free hand.

"Do you think you deserve another orgasm yet?" she teased.

Clearly quite desperate for release, almost crazed with all-consuming lust, the tit-slapped slavegirl managed to obediently shake her head. Abigail laughed, a peal of uninhibited delight, and wiped the docile sex object's juices off her palm on a firm silken thigh.

"Good girl!" she praised.

She could feel her pet's eyes watching her warily as she examined and then selected a whip from the selection in a wall rack. Abigail gave the long thin lash an experimental swish, braided leather hissing through the air. The unnamed slave's huge tits quivered quite beautifully as she flinched. Abigail unlocked the girl's wrists, the key to the handcuffs hanging in the usual place, from a pierced earlobe like an earring.

"Now this is a test," she told the slave, the ball-gagged sex toy clearly obviously very surprised to find herself free of her restraints. "You exist only to please me now. Do you understand that?"

The naked slavegirl nodded, arms now obediently folded behind her back, wrist to elbow. Abigail stroked her spine with one hand and with the other toyed with pubic curls. The lovely slave arched her back with a soft sigh, eyes closed in pleasure.

"And you do want to please me, don't you?" she whispered in the gagged girl's ear.

The placid slave nodded emphatically.

"I'm going to whip you now," Lady Abigail told her property. "Spread your legs wide, bend forward and hold your ankles."

The brunette obeyed with gratifying speed, heavy slap-reddened tits swaying under her, her long dark hair trailing down her back and spilling over her shoulders. Her chastity-ringed pussy pouting nicely between her thighs from behind, the sex toy moaned in pleasure when her mistress stroked a finger along her pussy. Abigail lifted the girl's head by her hair, stroking the whip under her chin.

"I'm going to give you a chance to prove you deserve to be owned by me," Abigail promised with soft menace. "You see, the test is, the whipping doesn't stop until you pull away."

Abigail saw fear dawning in the slave's eyes as she realised what was expected of her. She stroked the lash back and forth across an obediently presented behind, her property's buttocks involuntarily twitching at the touch.

"Now I know how many whip strokes I expect you to be able to take, how many a good girl can take, and if you pull away before I'm finished, you'll be back on the auction block in a week. You don't want to be sold again, do you?"

The bent-forward girl made an emphatic if gag-muffled "No!" noise, visibly bracing herself into position. Preparing herself for the whip!

"Remember," Abigail teased. "You can stop me at any time. Just pull away!"

Savouring her power and the top-heavy slave slut's submission, she stroked the whip back and forth over the trembling buttocks. The only sound in the room was the girl's ragged breath, a strand of saliva trailing to the floor from under her ball gag. The brunette had a simply lovely ass, and would look quite delicious padlocked into a waspie corset or waist cincher, Abigail thought.

She swung the whip in hard in a wide, hissing, arc! Braided leather landed on light gold flesh with a vicious thwack.

Her naked property squealed in agony behind her mouth-filling ball gag, taking an involuntary step forward, head jerking up and tits swinging forward; and then forced herself back into position. Abigail gave her another savage, full-force cut, her victim's shriek totally uninhibited. The gasping slavegirl flinched with a little unconscious squeak as Abigail laid the lash across her quaking buttocks once more, but still held position. Bent forward from the waist, legs spread wide and holding her own ankles, her clit lead, still attached, trailed to the floor between her legs.

And knowing she could pull away at any time, no restraints on her, she was submitting herself to atrocious pain, for no other reason than to please Abigail. Naked, wearing only four-inch stiletto heels, her mouth stuffed with a huge gag, suddenly there was a sheen of sweat on the trembling sex toy's lovely flanks. Perfectly parallel lines marked her buttocks.

Leather bit into flesh with a vicious viper crack, and the bent-forward sex toy jerked forward another half pace with a desperate squeal. The girl took four more whip strokes quite well, but after the seventh stroke sobs were suddenly racking her body, a forlorn plea in her squeals. But she still held her own ankles tightly, bent forward from the waist, ready to take more. Obediently presenting her ass to Abigail's lash!

Giving her property a moment to recover, Abigail stroked the welts she'd put across the brunette's behind so far. She'd never owned a slavegirl with the bar code on the ass before. It was usually hidden on the underside of the breast with top-heavy girls, but she decided it could stay on this girl's buttock. Quite pretty.

The big-titted sex toy took five more lashes well enough, though she was getting quite shrill now. Abigail was impressed. She was putting real bite into her swing, making no pretence of teasing, delivering pain you just didn't expect a girl not chained between two whipping posts to be able to take. The next stroke drove the girl to her knees, clutching her whip-marked ass. Abigail pulled the girl back to her feet by her breasts, and then licked the tears off her cheeks, dipping her fingers into the sobbing girl's dripping sex to mix tears and juices.

The taste of subservience. Delicious!

Having sharp fingernails sunk painfully deep into her punished tits, and then fingers penetrating her pussy, seemed to steady the trembling plaything, and to Abigail's amazement, when released, she bent forward and held her ankles again. What a simply perfect toy! She obviously had no idea how much pain she was expected to endure. And despite her sobs, the brunette could still be made to moan in forced pleasure when Abigail stroked her whip back and forth between her dripping sex lips. She swung her lash again and again, revelling in high-pitched, pitiful, cries. Whip stripes criss-crossed her property's haunches now.

After maybe twenty five, thirty or so, whip strokes — Abigail had stopped counting at six, the least she'd expected the girl to take — she finally broke the docile sex toy. Her sobbing plaything dropped to the floor, writhing helplessly, clutching whip-burnt flesh. Abigail tossed the handcuffs on top of the girl's body, and settled herself on a settee.

Amazing endurance, even though the New Ones, British girls, were reputed to take good whip. The curvy sex object was going to be an absolute delight to own. Naked on the floor, the former British policewomen managed to drag herself to her knees, wiped her eyes, locked her own wrists behind her back without hesitation, and then crawled to her younger owner's feet. Teasing her, Abigail deliberately frowned, looking away, her expression firm. On her knees, Abigail's chosen pet made a soft pleading noise, begging for forgiveness, deliberately pushing her weighty tits into Abigail's hands. She finally consented to look down into imploring eyes, while idly kneading and squeezing the big heavy ring-tipped mounds again, making the whipped slavegirl groan in pleasure.

"Well, I expected you to be able to take a little more pain than that, but that was adequate," she allowed.

Relief palpably washed over the yet-to-be-named sex slave. Naked on her knees, her lust-forced moans as her slave breasts were roughly mauled were suddenly quite uninhibited, now she no longer had to fear being sold.

"But I'll expect better if I test you again, mind," Abigail warned, raking fingernails across the well-slapped, ring-tipped, melons.

Her new pet nodded eagerly, only whimpering a little as her tits were cruelly scratched. Inspecting the handcuffs,

Abigail found her property had squeezed the metal bands cruelly tight around her own wrists.

"Stand now!" she ordered.

Then she stood herself, reaching up to unbuckle the slavegirl's ball gag and pulling the large red ball out of her helpless property's mouth by a strap. The pretty plaything just melted against her as Abigail thrust her tongue down the slavegirl's throat, her hands roaming over naked flesh as she wished. Exploring the gorgeous body that was now legally hers. To do with as she wished.

The helplessly hot, wet and quite desperately aroused slave-slut gasped pleasure into Abigail's mouth as fingers were once more thrust into her pussy. Having her whip-scorched buttocks stroked only seemed to make her hotter, her body heat almost searing through Abigail's dress. She pulled back for air, her naked property leaning forward, pushing up against her, and then moaning in soft protest when Abigail held back. A sharp, painful, yank of her pubic hair reminded the as yet unnamed slavegirl that she was here to be enjoyed, not to enjoy herself. Sex slaves were kissed when and for as long as the owner wished, no longer. Her handcuffed and thoroughly groped property, subserviently, apologetically, lowered her eyes, and Abigail rewarded her with another kiss on the lips, a burning whip-hot buttock in one hand, a huge heavily-enlarged tit spilling out of the other.

"Good girl," she soothed. "And if you continue to please me, you'll be kept in permanent restraints, especially during sex and punishment, from now on. No tests for good girls!"

She sank her fingernails painfully deep into both big slave tits again, making her property wince.

"What do we say?"

"Thank you Mistress," the thoroughly broken-in brunette breathed obediently, Abigail stroking thumbs across her erect nipples now.

"And what is your reason for existing?"

"To give you pleasure, Mistress."

"And do you want to please me?" Abigail asked, giving swollen hard nipples a warning twist.

"Oh yes Mistress," her totally subjugated property breathed softly. "More than anything!"

Abigail nodded to herself in satisfaction, having heard all she needed to. The lovely slave had nothing else to say she wanted to hear, and could now be kept permanently gagged, forbidden to speak when not mouth controlled, for the remaining years and decades that Abigail owned her.

Easy! Just like the old slave-training manuals said. Make the girl come while looking into your eyes. Humiliate and tease her; the tit slapping . And then make her co-operate in her own punishment, though of course the big-breasted slave had done nothing to deserve one. Result, one instantly broken-in slavegirl. Training her to please in bed would take much longer. But Lady Abigail had all the time in the world!

She stroked the placid little brunette between the legs again, scooping the slave's juices onto her fingers, and then smearing the fluid across the ball gag before forcing it back into her property's mouth. As every owner knew, an occasional little taste of herself helped keep a slavegirl docile. As Abigail buckled the restraint back into place, tight behind the slave's neck and under her chin, she was struck by how truly delicious her property looked with the large red ball filling her mouth.

Idly twisting and pinching ringed nipples, Abigail tried to imagine herself standing naked and gagged in only four-inch stiletto heels with her wrists handcuffed behind her back. A stranger handling her intimately, free to dispense pain, pleasure and humiliation at whim. Bought and sold, existing only to please. She knew she just couldn't do it!

The thought only even occurred to her because she knew the helpless pet's secret history. Slaveworld girls were raised in a world where slavery was a fact of life; the way things had always been and always would be. As a child, if you were unlucky you got measles, with adolescence came acne and the puzzles of sex, and once eighteen, legally an adult, for non-aristocrats, if you fell foul of the law, you could be sentenced to sexual service. Most girls hoped it wouldn't happen to them, but it was really just one of those things. The luck of the draw.

This sex slave, who according to her pedigree had once answered to Susan, had never even seen a real slave until six months ago, and had been raised in a world without slavery. An aristocrat's upbringing almost, knowing it could never happen to her. How much more humiliating, exciting, terrifying, could it be for her to find herself owned, existing only, entirely, for another's sexual gratification? Lady Abigail squeezed her property's lovely big tits together again and closed her lips over aching nipples, the heavy globes spilling out of her grip as she tongued and nibbled the ringed nubs.

She looked up into her purchase's placid eyes, sinking teeth deeper into aching, lust-swollen nipples. The broken-in slave whimpered in hopelessly mingled pain and lust, but without a hint of protest. Abigail walked contentedly around her motionless property one last time. Daddy had nothing to worry about. This sex toy wasn't going to bore her for a good long time! She stroked the welts criss-crossing the brunette's ass — all her own work — her plaything squeaking when Abigail thrust a finger into her anus.

"I know who you are," she whispered in the naked, gagged, plaything's ear, resting her chin on the girl's velvet shoulder. "I know about Gates, where you come from, who you were!"

The clearly horrified brunette flushed, Abigail happily playing with her huge tits again.

"You're not just some semi-literate peasant girl caught stealing a dress," Lady Abigail continued remorselessly, the teased slave's face scarlet now, eyes wide, "so I expect you to take more far more pain, far more humiliation, and be much better in bed, than any other girl I've owned. Because you chose to be here!"

The otherworld sex slave lowered her eyes in submissive acquiescence. With the contented feeling of a job well done, Abigail scooped up the now deeply shamed slave-slut's pussy lead, and led her property out of the reception suite without a backward glance. The cute little sex object gasped as her ring-set clitoris was tugged again and obediently followed her lead. She was going to be an absolute joy to own, Lady Abigail decided.

Resplendent in his scarlet uniform, Captain Scott, the Royal equerry, stood at an attentive parade-rest in front of Victoria's desk. Queen Victoria was absorbed in milking Precious, her naked pet on the desk on all fours between them, but each time she'd looked up, the man's gaze was always attentively, respectfully, on hers, over the naked girl's back. He'd seen slavegirls milked before, after all. Wrist and anklecuffs chained to rings set into the desk's surface, held the slave toy she milked in place while a choke chain from above pulled her head up. The Queen's fingers and thumbs were tight around the base of one udder, squeezing in slowly with both palms, and Precious moaned in mingled pain and pleasure as a jet of milk was squeezed into the bowl under her. As usual during her milking, the tall, powerfully built, dairy slave had a tight hood of heavy burgundy silk, pulled taut across her face, laced tightly down the back of her head. Tightening her grip around the base of the swollen globe a little lower, Victoria squeezed again, and then again, working down with each squeeze.

Just as whipping her compliant property was an excellent way to work off a little frustration, Victoria had found milking her property by hand instead of having the staff hook the brunette up to a milking machine in the kitchens with the other dairy slaves, very soothing, the perfect way to relax. The hooded sex toy groaned loudly with each jet of milk squeezed into the bowl under her. Because Victoria had allowed her pet's breasts to become so enormously swollen, what should have been a relief for the girl, was actually a very uncomfortable experience.

And so much milk to be painfully squeezed, twisted and wrung out of her, such huge udders, meant the humiliation and discomfort of milking could be made to last almost as long as Victoria wished. She knew Precious would be very frisky, desperately sexually aroused, when her nipple clamps were finally fitted again and padlocked into place.

Hands still working, slowly, rhythmically, the brunette groaning and gasping with each squeeze, she looked up over her pet's back again.

"Make it clear to the Ambassador that this is just a casual affair, nothing formal," she said. "Just a little reception, for me to personally welcome him to our world."

"Yes, Your Majesty," Scott agreed. "If he declines?"

"Oh I'm sure he won't. That wouldn't be diplomatic."

"Yes, Your Majesty. My Lady?"

"Yes?"

"On that other matter you wanted me to look into. There is one suitable girl amongst the captured British agents, a former police officer."

Victoria gave him an encouraging nod.

"She might not actually be a security risk," Scott continued. "She wasn't properly an agent, she just posed as a slave to reinforce the real agent's cover. Quite successfully by all accounts. And she had the chance to escape but gave herself up to secure freedom for another British agent. Unfortunately, she was sold at auction just this morning."

Victoria hefted the udder she'd been milking, thoughtfully weighing the silky mound in her palm. Still heavy with milk, but her fingers now sank easily into the over-large globe, skin now longer shiny taut as it was when bound. Precious whimpered as the clamp was screwed tight back down over the base of her nipple, a little shiver running through her as the heavy padlock was snapped back into place.

The top of the desk rotated, allowing her to swing the brunette around and work on the other breast. Precious breathed deeper, faster, as Victoria's key clicked into the second padlock. Her bonds still held the hooded plaything neatly on all fours over her milking bowl. Victoria placed the padlock in the small of her pet's back, stroked a buttock, and then returned to her most enjoyable task.

"Sold to anyone who might be willing to sell on?" she finally asked Scott, meaning a commercial buyer who might like to make a quick profit, rather than a private buyer who would undoubtedly have bought the girl purely for the pleasure owning her would bring.

"No, Your Majesty, a private sale, but you do know the young Lady."

"Oh! Who?"

The equerry pointed his personal computer at her wall-screen, and the former British police officer's updated pedigree was displayed on a split screen alongside a series of pictures, showing the slave, naked and variously bound. Nice big tits and a pretty face. A born show pony if Victoria was any judge of slave flesh.

"Oh yes, I know Abby," Victoria said cheerfully when she saw the name of the new slavegirl's registered owner.

Perhaps because she was so disinterested in palace intrigue and the social backstabbing that made up Londinium high society, one of Victoria's best friends was now the former professor Philips-Webber, Lady Franklin. Abby, Lord Franklin's goddaughter, often drove Lady Franklin's champion racing pony and Victoria knew her quite well. Lady Abigail was also a friend of Franklin's daughter from his first marriage, Isobell. The same Lady Isobell who was her son, Samuel's, fiancée.

That kept it all nicely in the family — no loose talk. Best of all, Victoria had even lent Precious to Abby for a ride on occasion, and so the young aristocrat should be quite willing to return the favour. On the down side, Abby had been trying to get her hands on one of the rare and very expensive British slaves for months, to the utter distraction of her father, mother and god-parent, and it was extremely unlikely she'd want to sell the new sex toy any time soon. Or let it out of her sight for more than a night.

Victoria unscrewed the second nipple clamp, Precious whimpering as blood rushed back into crushed capillaries, her breast so swollen with milk a white bead immediately formed on her nipple, hung a moment, and then dripped into the bowl under her. Without her breast being squeezed at all, another bead of milk formed. The brunette whined as fingers and thumbs closed tightly around the base of her udder, moaning in mingled pain and pleasure again, as

Victoria's palms squeezed firmly in.

Delightful! She looked up and waved Scott away with a careless, thank you, finally catching the equerry's eyes on Precious's naked body.

Victoria would have to make the loan worth the Lady's while somehow. Now what could she offer Abby for the loan of a superb new pet the young aristocrat had barely had a chance to fully enjoy yet? When realistically, Victoria might have to borrow the top-heavy sex toy for up to a couple of months.

At the very least, the British police officer would have to be replaced with something similar. Docile, pretty, with big tits. And of course, it went without saying, she would have to be a satisfying screw!

CHAPTER FIVE

When Lady Abigail had stooped to scoop up the lead still hanging between Susan's legs, looped the chain's suede handle over her wrist, and without a backward glance led her property from the auction house's reception suite, with a helpless gasp of pleasure, Susan had docilely followed the tug of her owner's lead, still clipped to the ring set through her pierced clitoris; hips swinging and heavy boobs jiggling with every step, as she had been trained. Her stiletto heels tip-tapping on the marble floor, she found herself wishing she was hobbled. It was easier to display herself in the approved manner with a short length of chain between her ankles.

Her buttocks burning, throbbing and pulsing in time with her pounding heart, she could feel each welt the whip had left across her backside; lines of fire! Her nipples aching hard; slapped, squeezed and scratched breasts very sore — the abused globes deliciously lust-swollen — and drooling helplessly around her ball gag, Susan was shamefully aware her punishment had only made her hotter. She desperately needed to come again, but when, or if, she would next be permitted an orgasm again was now entirely up to Lady Abigail. She found herself very much wanting to please the young noble.

Kissing, their tongues entwined, Susan naked and her owner dressed, cotton cool on her bare skin, her own wrists locked behind her back while the aristocrat's hands had roamed all over her body, had been just heavenly. Everything she had hoped for from slavery. The ease with which the pretty girl in the red summer dress had made her come, the assurance with which she had punished Susan and made her humiliate herself, was a little disquieting though. The Lady had just been testing her. Far worse was surely to come.

More disquieting still, was the shameful realisation that she was quite willing and eager to endure more humiliation and pain to please the young aristocrat. If it meant she would be praised, petted and called a good girl again. Allowed to come! Even knowing she was not a person in her owner's eyes; just a toy to use, abuse and enjoy — at best a pet — shamefully excited her. She was legally owned, and even her beautiful owner's inexperienced-looking youth aroused her.

How old was she? The aristocrat looked a young eighteen to Susan's eyes, the legal minimum to own a slave, but surely she had to be older. Her casual and obvious experience in handling a sex slave surely meant she'd taken the youth treatment and had owned many slavegirls over years. Outside the reception suite a young man in the auction house's pageboy uniform came to attention and bowed to the aristocrat.

"Your purchase came with this My Lady. My master said to ask, do you want it?"

The boy held up a T-shaped metal device that Susan recognised. The short crossbar was straight, the long rod curved, with a padlock set through a small ring at the end. Saliva running down her breasts, Susan stood motionless, head up, shoulders back and ankles together, from the moment her young mistress paused. Lady Abigail looked back, her eyes on the rise and fall of Susan's big breasts a moment, before her gaze trailed down, between Susan's legs. Just her owner's eyes on her made her heart pound faster, lust coursing through her!

"Yes, put it on her," the sweet-voiced young aristocrat decided.

At a snap of her legal owner's fingers, Susan set her feet apart, still obediently looking directly ahead. Holding still, she couldn't help a little ball gag muffled whimper as the young man, now on one knee, pulled and tugged at her sex lips. A faint smile touched Lady Abigail's lips. The short top T-bar lay across Susan's belly, the longer curved rod threaded down through the five pairs of rings set through her sex lips. When the padlock was set through the ring at the base of the rod and snapped shut, the rod couldn't be removed. A humiliating but very comfortable chastity device.

Sex lips squeezed — locked! — together now, very aware of the weight of metal hanging from her pussy, Susan watched her mistress clip the chastity rod's key to a bracelet like a charm. At another snap of her young owner's fingers she obediently put her ankles together again, breasts rising and falling faster under the aristocrat's appraising gaze. Helplessly drooling around her ball gag, she felt herself blushing again.

"Oh aren't you sweet!" her young owner crowed with a delighted smile, flicking first one and then the other, erect nipple.

Susan groaned, arousal making the fat nubs quite unbearably sensitive. She had expected her lead to be clipped to her ringed nipples now that the chastity rod hid her clitoris, but the aristocrat clipped it to the padlock on the chastity rod's base. A pull on her lead now gave Susan's locked pussy a pleasant tug, but didn't torment, or stimulate, like being led about by her pierced clitoris. As she was led out into the sunlight, Susan realised with a guilty thrill that she preferred the clit lead.

She had been led down Londinium's streets like this before, naked, gagged and with her wrists locked behind her back, and had loved every second of it. As always on the capital's streets, there were naked sex slaves everywhere, slavegirls outnumbering slaveboys by about three to one. On the streets between limousines, whipped along at a smart trot, pony slaves pulled carriages and pony traps. And faster, weaving in and out of them, slaves provided the power for tandem bicycles. The nobles had their own lane; trams, carts and delivery vehicles jostling for space in the workers-only lane.

On the wide pavements, shared — though the serfs always stood aside for a noble — many a Lord or Lady had a sex slave on a lead, often favoured pets or poodles. Susan felt right at home. When a Lady dressed formally, for say a day at the races or when attending a ball, a poodle, usually a voluptuous girl with large heavy breasts and a wasp waist, was as much a part of her outfit as hat and gloves. While on the other hand, pets, of either sex, and coming in all shapes and sizes, were more usually their owners' sexual favourites. It was possible for a girl to be both a pet and a poodle, Susan knew — she hoped to be herself — but sometimes, when for example the Lady preferred boy toys or slender slavegirls, the top-heavy poodle could be a purely decorative purchase. Enjoyed only by houseguests, or rented out to a hotel to serve as room service, when not on display.

Sunlight on her bare skin, hundreds — perhaps thousands — of eyes on her naked body, Susan was in her own version of heaven. As well as aristocrats and their nude property, here and there on the busy streets there was a flash of scarlet in the throng, a household trooper in dress reds; a groom, slave trainer and enforcer for a noble house. Most of the large crowd, no working class housing estates near the city centre, but many employed by the businesses there, wore dull colours, the women veils. Here and there, strolling in pairs, were black uniformed Royal troopers: the Slaveworld's police.

There was very little crime for them to concern themselves with. The auction block was always waiting for those foolish enough to litter, cross the street against the lights or fail to step aside for an aristocrat. They could see the results of anti-social behaviour, the sentence of the courts being carried out, all around them. A street sweeper's eyes momentarily lingered on the sway of Susan's heavily enlarged breasts, the rings set through her nipples, her firmly locked pussy and then guiltily darted away. The crack of leather on flesh and the squeaks of hard-worked pony girls were audible over the traffic noise.

It was even better now. The last time she hadn't been treated with the Slaveworld's aphrodisiac, which had made her hopelessly addicted to sex. Now frustrated beyond endurance, feeling her juices oozing between locked-together sex lips, Susan suddenly realised it was more than that. Before, the bonds and her nudity had been real, but the slavery hadn't. She'd been pretending, knowing she was really an undercover police officer not a slave, a secret agent from another world. It had all been a show, a delicious game. A fantasy come to life, excitingly dangerous, but never real!

Now suddenly, Susan had no hidden secrets. What you saw was exactly what you got. And what people saw was property, a sex object who existed only for the pleasure of the beautiful young Lady who led her. Shame at being turned on by the thought, hotter and wetter than ever, finally realising now that her servitude was for life, without limits, Susan suddenly felt goosebumps. What had she got herself into? How could she ever have wanted this?

She groaned in helpless pleasure as she was tugged to one side of the pavement with a yank of her chastity lock. Her owner looped her teasing lead over a hitching hook, and strolled into a bakery. A hand slid over the curve of a whip-burnt buttock making her twitch, another young Lord hefting and squeezing her breasts as she stood helpless outside the shop. Susan moaned in lust as the firm mounds were kneaded and pulled, sweat suddenly slick under the cuffs that held her wrists behind her.

The young man was being very rude! Beyond a little pat or stroke, it was normal to ask the owner's permission before intimately handling a slave. Lubricated by saliva, positively slavering around the ball gag stretching her mouth wide open now, her big heavy slave breasts slipped easily across each other as they were squeezed and pulled. She could do nothing but stand there. In the middle of a crowded street her young tormentor finally held both full globes up high by each nipple, flesh cruelly stretched, clearly delighted with the weight of the ring-tipped melons.

Deliberately, he slowly squeezed and twisted the fat nubs until Susan cried out in pain, nipples brutally crushed as well as agonisingly stretched, the whole weight of her over-large breasts hanging from the tortured ring-set nubs. With a twitch of a smile, satisfaction more than pleasure, the unknown aristocrat released her, and just walked on.

Nipples throbbing, suddenly made aware of her vulnerability, how helpless she was standing naked on a busy street, hands locked behind her and her pussy chained to a pet hook, flustered, Susan looked around for her mistress to protect her from further assault. Lady Abigail was visible through the shop window, having of course moved straight to the head of the line, just paying for a pastry. The aristocrat didn't seem to be aware her property had been molested. Further aroused by the unknown man, Susan straining to the limit of her pussy chain, leant into Lady Abigail's embrace as the aristocrat stepped back out onto the street.

"Did you miss me?" the Lady asked with a delighted laugh, squeezing a breast in one hand, free hand stroking up Susan's behind.

Susan moaned in pleasure as she was publicly handled, the aristocrat giving her a fleeting slave-kiss, licking the lips Susan's ball gag parted.

"I saw you bothering that nice young man though. Bad girl!"

Susan whined in soft protest. A mistake! She was instantly pushed up against the shop window, nipple rings touching with a click, breasts flattened up against the windowpane, the glass chill on her belly. Held in place with a hand between the shoulder blades, more a guide than anything, Lady Abigail swung a strap — her own belt — across Susan's buttocks. Susan squeaked at each blow, leather biting into flesh with a crack, squirming against the shop window. The sting would have been quite pleasant if she hadn't just been so thoroughly whipped.

Inside the shop, apart from one Lord who paused to admire the way her big breasts squashed up against the glass, the working class staff and customers pretended not to notice that a naked, gagged, slavegirl was being disciplined on the street right outside. A shop assistant, looking firmly down, restocked the shelves in the window right in front of Susan.

She wailed as the last blow fell, a blaze of pain across both buttocks, ass on fire again. Snuffling, Susan was pushed around to face her owner, back against the bakery window now. Lady Abigail's fingernails sank into her sob-quivering breasts as she delicately licked the tears off

Susan's cheeks. The aristocrat then lightly kissed her forehead, across her shoulder and down. Susan thought her breasts were being bitten for a moment; before she realised with a delighted sigh that the aristocrat was sucking love-bites into the ring-tipped globes.

Her chastity rod was unlocked, pulled free of her pussy rings, sex lips slowly flowering open, Susan crying out in ecstasy as fingers stroked across her clitoris. Dazed, helpless, her handcuffs scraping across the window glass behind her with a jarring screech, Susan gasped and squeaked behind her gag as fingers rammed deep into her dripping sex. The glass was deliciously cool on her punished buttocks! Hips twitching, slumped helplessly against the shop window, her owner sucking in deep hard mouthfuls of flesh, scattering more love bites all across her breasts, Susan looking blankly over her owner's head found she had an audience.

A pair of black uniformed troopers, police - one man, one woman - were watching with mild interest. Had been for a while, maybe even as she had been punished, but it had taken Susan a while to focus. Just as Susan herself might once have paused for a moment while on patrol, a world away, watching two lovers in a passionate embrace. No disapproval from the pair, no crime being committed, just a Lady quite legally enjoying her property.

As fingers twisted deeper into her sex, biting hard into her ball gag now, another mouthful of flesh sucked into her owner's mouth, love bites all across both big breasts now, Susan wailed plaintively; a forlorn plea for mercy, begging to be allowed to come! The man's eyes were disinterested, just watching the show, the woman's bright, excited. Susan rather suspected the female trooper would very much like to get her in a cell alone. With a shrug, the man turned to go on, and his partner reluctantly followed.

Then her mistress's fingers were stroking back and forth across her clitoris again, faster and faster. White-hot pleasure, earthing in nipples and groin consumed her, and Susan was again incapable of rational thought. She recovered to find herself on her knees, panting. Head hanging, she slowly focused on red splotches all over her breasts. Susan's handcuffs had minutely scratched the bakery window, and Lady Abigail carelessly told the shopkeeper she would of course pay for the damage, assuring him her pet would be thoroughly punished for the scratches.

"There... there's, really no need my Lady. It's... it's hardly noticeable anyway," the man stammered, cap in had, tugging at his forelock.

Whether he meant the money or Susan's punishment, wasn't clear.

"Oh no," Lady Abigail assured him. "I insist!"

Susan was made to kneel on all fours, her owner using the small of her back as a stool, while she nibbled on her pastry, waiting for a glazier to come and provide an estimate. Humming happily to herself, it was clear the young Lady was having a splendid day. The glazier arrived quickly — you didn't keep an aristocrat waiting if you knew what was good for you — and pussy again locked, wrists secured behind her, Susan was soon being led on her way.

She had expected to be punished and made to humiliate herself when introduced to her new owner. A quick and easy way to let a new sex slave know where she stood. But what had just happened outside the bakery was far more personal; intimate. Lady Abigail clearly intended to enjoy her to the limit. She felt a shiver of delight run through her, a careless tug on her again locked pussy making her take a half-skip to keep up. Now she knew her innocent looking young mistress would enjoy or punish her without hesitation, for the slightest infraction, on a whim. Anywhere!

Susan was now totally focused on her young owner, as she should have been from the start, she realised - no time for sightseeing! On public display, shamefully proud of the love bites decorating her udders, the marks on her buttocks, Susan understood now that simply being naked, helpless and available was not enough. That was her own fantasy, not Lady Abigail's. A sex slave could never be obedient, devoted or pleasing enough.

The aristocrat's skirt swirling and flicking around her calves, the faint breeze that ruffled her short hair, made Susan's heart pound faster. Her eyes kept going back to the red leather belt, which had so effectively doubled as a strap, around the slender Lady's waist. The aristocrat led her into a nearby hotel, and casually ordered a room. After booking her in, the obsequious clerk politely asked how long she would need the room.

"Oh, just a couple of hours," Lady Abigail said carelessly, sliding a hand down Susan's behind, and then slowly kneading a buttock. "I'm just going to give my new toy here a quick ride."

Even though she'd been led into the lobby naked, gagged and bound, Susan still felt herself flush scarlet as the clerk's eyes flickered briefly over her displayed body. Everybody within earshot had just been told Susan was about to be forcibly used for sex! Without her consent. But it was just an everyday transaction to her owner and the hotel's employee.

"Room 12, My Lady. I hope you enjoy your stay."

"Oh I'm sure I will. If Big Tits here doesn't want the punishment of her life."

The clerk smiled politely, and turned to the next guest, an ancient looking Lord leading a hooded slaveboy. A blonde slavegirl in harness and bridle, pulling a huge steamer trunk on wheels, obediently followed.

In room 12, Susan was given a shower, arms pulled up over her head, wrists secured to a ring set in the shower cubicle ceiling, while two naked room service slaveboys worked soap into every inch of her body. Lady Abigail sat watching happily, offering occasional helpful hints, like: "Work a bit more soap into her ass," and "scrub her tits harder. Use the brush with the stiff bristles!"

Clean enough to eat off and further aroused — the two male slaves had been quite edible themselves — Susan was chained to the bed and the boy toys dismissed. She lay on her bound arms, elbows strapped together, her wristcuffs chained to the lower pair of rings set through her sex lips.

Straps from under the bed to her collar, to a tight belt and to anklecukffs, held her firmly in place in the centre of the bed, legs spread wide, while lying on her bound arms raised her hips invitingly. Lady Abigail standing over her touched a light finger to Susan's lips.

"Don't talk, not a word," the aristocrat gently warned her. "You've got nothing to say I want to hear."

Her tone was soft, but the threat in her voice was quite clear to Susan. Swallowing a lump in her throat, she kissed the finger the Lady held to her lips.

"Good puppy."

The aristocrat patted her belly, flesh squeezed into a taut swell by the cruelly tight belt. Susan whimpered in pleasure as fingers briefly slipped inside her sex, and was then allowed to lick and suck her own juices off them as a reward for her own docile obedience. Firmly strapped to the bed, she could only watch helplessly as her legal owner undressed.

The aristocrat's body was slender, toned, with kitten hips and long legs, her breasts small and firm with upturned nipples. Quite beautiful! In Britain she could have been a model, the sort of lithe ideal that Susan had tried to diet down to, but had known she would never really manage. Watching the graceful girl, Susan was reminded that since her introduction to real slavery, she had in fact been forced to put on weight; over half a stone. She had a smaller waist than the aristocrat now, but only because a cosmetic slave-surgeon had been instructed to give her an hourglass figure, her hips, not to mention breasts, much heavier. Spankable! Lushly screwable!

She felt herself shiver in fear as the aristocrat laid out toys on the bed beside her, settling herself on her knees above Susan, thighs to either side of Susan's head. The beautiful young Lady leant over her, planting a light kiss on each straining erect nipple, and then touching her lips to Susan's pussy. Susan gasped in shock as hot breath and then soft warm lips touched her spread sex. It was just a fleeting touch, a tongue darting between her pussy lips for just a second, the aristocrat tasting her, but Susan was too hot, too wet, too desperate! A wave of pleasure coursed through her body.

She recovered her senses to find the aristocrat looking into her face with inquisitive interest, upside down, thighs gripping Susan's head firmly now, idly toying with her nipples.

"You are a hot one, aren't you?" the aristocrat mused, Susan panting softly as her nipples were rolled between thumb and finger.

"But in future, try and wait until I've disciplined you before coming. When pain and pleasure are combined, you'll find your orgasm much more intense," the pretty Lady explained earnestly.

Punished then, fingers twisting painfully deep into her flesh, Susan wailed in helplessly mingled lust and pain as her big breasts were firmly twisted and squeezed. Gasping, she couldn't, didn't dare, look away from her tormentor's eyes.

"And I will punish you if you come without permission too often," her young owner warned seriously. "Understood?"

Susan nodded obediently. Looking up into the aristocrat's face upside down gave her a new perspective. The young Lady had a delicately slender neck, a perfect heart-shaped face, eyes set just a fraction too wide. She really was quite stunningly beautiful. A smile briefly tugged at her lips as Susan moaned in pain. Finally her grip on Susan's breasts loosened, and as she stroked down, hands gliding down Susan's stomach to the tight belt, thumbs digging into Susan's belly, fingers then trailing back up to trace Susan's rib cage her expression became absorbed - intent. Susan clearly fascinated and enchanted her, would provide many months — perhaps years — of delightful, cruel, experimentation and sadistic pleasure. Overlying lust, and the joy of her power, it was the same frighteningly absorbed expression you might find on the face of a scientist looking down a microscope at a particularly fascinating bug.

Susan had once arrested a six-foot drunk alone. Now,

strapped to a bed, naked, with her legs spread wide, beginning to fearfully suspect that the angelic looking but spoilt aristocrat who quite legally owned her was a merciless sadist, she felt herself trembling with fear. The intense young woman, hands light on Susan's love-bite-decorated breasts again, didn't miss the fearful tremor. Another smile touched her lips. Good bug, it said.

Susan was also as aroused as she'd ever been in her life, nipples aching hard, the over-large breasts her mistress handled, almost painfully lust-swollen. A raging heat in her groin, hot and so, so wet, she could feel her juices flowing out of her, pussy lips pulled open and down by the chains that linked pussy rings to wristcuffs.

Lady Abigail selected her first toy. The base of a thin candle was pushed onto a spike projecting out of a spring-loaded, three-jawed clamp, which was allowed to close over an erect nipple. Susan gasped in pain as sharp metal jaws bit into the swollen nub, the matching candle and clamp followed in moments. The candles swayed back and forth as Susan panted, breath ragged, her love-bite-covered breasts rising and falling faster. She whimpered. And as the candles swayed in circles, pendulumed back and forth, her nipples were tugged this way and that in the clamps' vicious grip, the sharp little metal teeth digging deeper.

"Nice?" Lady Abigail asked.

Head held between her naked owner's thighs, Susan nodded obediently. Besides the nipple torture, it was quite clear that as her breasts, partly flattened across her chest under their own weight, moved with every breath, gasp and pant, the candles would sway, waggle — burn unevenly. And scalding hot wax would drip down onto the full mounds!

The aristocrat then held a long thin pin with an incense base, like a joss stick, teasingly before her eyes. Susan squeaked as the long pin was pushed deep into a breast. There was a sharp pinprick, no worse than an injection, the thin pin as sharp as any syringe needle. A firmly slapped boob, or electrodes attached to the nipples hurt far worse... but, this was different.

Someone was pushing pins into her breasts!

When a dozen pins had skewered each candle-decorated globe, only the top incense-covered two inches projecting from each gasp-quivering breast, Lady Abigail clicked a lighter on.

The elongated incense bead on the end of each deeply embedded needle caught easily, burning down slowly with an orange glow. The lighter clicked again, the candles soon burning with a steady flame. As Lady Abigail pulled Susan's head back, raising herself and thrusting her crotch into Susan's face, the first scalding droplet of hot wax seared a trembling slave-breast, running down and cooling halfway over the skewered mound. Susan's gasp of pain was muffled by her owner's flesh, the aristocrat squirming her sex down onto Susan's mouth.

Susan tongued and licked, burying her tongue deep inside her user's pussy, managing little snatches of breath as her beautiful owner squirmed back and forth. Lady Abigail tasted heavenly. Her mistress sitting on her face — smothered, stifled — gasping for breath only made Susan pant harder, breasts heaving, which in turn dripped more scalding candle wax onto the huge pin-skewered mounds.

Susan had had candle wax dripped onto her body before. She was ready for the delicious, anguished moment after the first sting when just for a second the molten wax burned hotter before the pain faded away as the wax dried. Molten drops of agony dripped and ran freely down her abused boobs now, clamped nipples painfully yanked this way and that as the candles wobbled and swayed back and forth.

Susan's surprised shriek of distress was muffled by Lady Abigail's pussy. She jerked rigid in her bonds as a blaze of pain was laid across her belly and curled down an inner thigh, the aristocrat happily squirmed down harder onto her face. Another blow followed, deliberately just to the other side of her sex. She was being pussy whipped! The next whip stroke licked across her belly, the tip of the lash curling down and striking directly into her pussy. Susan squealed.

Hips bucking, her thighs and buttocks trembling and twitching, Susan desperately tongued, licked and kissed her torturer. Trying to make her come, to bring her pussy whipping to an end. She squeaked and yelped as braided leather bit into her pussy lips, across her belly, down inner thighs, and occasionally — when she became really shrill — the flexible tip curled down across her whip-burnt belly and bit directly between her sex lips.

Pussy whipped, and scalding candle wax spattered all over her breasts, now short of breath and surely quite red faced, Susan was slow to notice the new sensation. She thought it was just the wax to start with. But it hurt. Really hurt! She finally realised the long thin pins, embedded in her flesh, were getting hot. The burning incense, glowing hot, was conducting heat right down the length of metal pins. Hotter and hotter, the pain was excruciating. It felt like red-hot wires had been poked into her flesh.

Susan had half expected to have her breasts punished, had known it was a possibility when she was being auctioned. It was unlikely that anyone on this world would buy a slavegirl with breasts as large as hers, unless they enjoyed a little tit torture. But this was pain beyond endurance! Tears streaming down her face, Lady Abigail's juices all over her mouth, Susan thrashed and bucked against her restraints, her user's whip biting between her spread legs again and again. Lady Abigail's thighs gripped her head harder. Her begging and pleas muffled by flesh, realising she had to make the aristocrat come, her ordeal would not end until she did, Susan forced herself to stop begging and try to firmly flick her tongue back and forth over the Lady's clitoris.

She couldn't breathe. Her boobs hurt so much, the pins stuck into her breasts burning as if they really were red-hot wires. And then the whip striking between her spread thighs caught her own clitoris once too often. Thighs gripping her head firmly, body arching up off the bed, Susan shrieked ecstasy into her torturer's sex, coming again and again, shudders racking her body. Her tortured slave breasts and a few more whip strokes between the legs quickly refocused her, and Susan was again obediently, docilely, lapping at her owner's sex.

She'd never dreamed she could endure being used so hard, so cruelly, so totally! This was why she had wanted the gentle Frances to own her.

The aristocrat enjoying her was quite relaxed, Susan realised, hips moving slowly back and forth, riding her face easily. The young Lady had probably come, maybe more than once, but Susan had been in no position to notice. Her breasts balls of unbearable pain now, the whip biting between her legs harder and faster, Susan realised her ordeal had probably only just begun. Lady Abigail would continue to ride and lash her, not just for sexual release, but for the pleasure her power gave her, for as long as she wished. Or for as long as her gasping, strapped-down mount could remain conscious.

Sure she was being suffocated, mouth full of pussy, her collar digging into the back of her neck, fervently wishing she was one of the lucky quarter or so of sex slaves allowed small breasts, her agonising tit torture made Susan frantic to please. But in a dreamy haze, she also realised she had no thoughts of rebellion or resentment, not a one. She just desperately prayed her young owner would be satisfied soon. The whip biting into her dripping pussy forcing her relentlessly towards another orgasm — a whirlwind fusion of pain and pleasure; quite beyond her control — Susan again urgently lapped at her owner's sex. Trying to make her torturer come.

Susan was not even sure if making the angelic looking young noble climax would end her own torment, but thoroughly broken, a docile ride now, she had to try all the same. Another whip stroke licked across her belly, the lash's tip curling down to strike in between her sex lips. Susan squealed, her hips bucking and causing more scalding wax to drip onto and run down her agonisingly skewered slave breasts. Lady Abigail's thighs gripped her head harder. Tongue flicking faster, Susan raised her hips to meet the next blow.

She didn't doubt for a second the experienced slave

owner sitting on her face, admiring her wax-coated, pin-tortured breasts, her tightly-strapped-down body and flicking a lash between her chained wide legs; also realised her ride was broken. She was not just a sadist, but an accomplished one. And Susan was now her helpless plaything. Overwhelmed by pain, exhaustion, lust and multiple orgasms, half suffocated, the thought still thrilled her.

Lady Abigail continued to ride and lash her tortured, half-suffocated, big-breasted, legally owned, sexual plaything until Susan was insensible!

Set in a quiet suburb of the Slaveworld's English Capital, Londinium, too near a working class enclave to ever really be considered exclusive, the new British Embassy occupied one side of a grand but outwardly unremarkable former townhouse. The newly formed Ministry of Offworld Affairs occupied the other side. The large greystone building was a fairly typical hollow square, a Roman derived design, with access to the central courtyard through a single narrow archway only just large enough to accommodate a single limousine or a team of four pony slaves abreast. Commercial deliveries were always made to the rear of a noble house.

A single black uniformed Royal Security Police trooper checking passes, and the Royal crest newly mounted over the archway told any passer-by that the building was now a government department, but gave no clue as to which branch. Most embassies were ostentatious buildings, mini palaces, a symbol of their country's prestige, and clustered close to the city centre. Here there was only a discreet brass plaque beside the embassy entrance inside the courtyard, not visible from the street outside. Local dignitaries and diplomats from other embassies would not be invited to grand receptions here, Ambassadors would not exchange greetings; they wouldn't even know this embassy existed!

A very discreet embassy.

Facing each other across the courtyard, the new British Embassy and the new Ministry of Offworld Affairs were separated from each other on one side by the archway leading to the front street. At the base of the square, the side of the building facing the archway, the townhouse had been further subdivided into three. By mutual agreement and Treaty, neutral territory, the buffer zone contained a customs and immigration department, and a bright shimmering Gateway to another world! Looking like a slab of mercury hanging on its side, bordered by the copper generating field, Londinium and London were now just a step apart.

Two Gates linked together were very stable, supported each other. One here, one in Britain, each requiring no more power than it took to run a TV set, could be maintained indefinitely. An official, sanctioned, diplomatic contact point between parallel dimensions.

The necessity had become pressing! The English Kingdom and its alternative history counterpart, Britain, had been in contact for over three years now, though the governments of neither had realised it at the time. At first, linked by just the original two Gates; one half of the portal created by Lord Franklin here, and the other half in Britain by his now wife, the former professor Phillips-Webber. Two purely scientific projects, with no goals beyond pure research; until each world saw what the other alternative dimension represented and had to offer. The two scientists found they were soul mates, clearly made for each other, and there had been no question of going their separate ways. Their marriage had been only a matter of time. In an attempt to bury the knowledge that alternative realities existed, that travel between them was possible, and so that she would not be followed, Phillips-Webber had brought her research team, her students, with her. The five turned out to be superb sex slaves. An absolute delight to own.

Such a bounty was hard to ignore, especially as Lady Franklin went on to develop a one-way Gate. One way, punching through from one world to another, was very unstable, only lasted about 15 seconds and required a phenomenal amount of power. But it was possible if you had access to a fusion reactor for half an hour or so. Once through, your agent could then set up a receiver Gate, the agent then only needing a modest power source to return home, as it was now two Gates linking.

The Chamberlain and the head of the RSP, both occupying the highest post a commoner could aspire to, had hatched a plan to collect a few more of these excellent slaves and win themselves the further approval of their masters. To begin with, just a couple of slaves, for the King and Queen, maybe the Crown Prince, and of course members of the Privy council.

British sex slaves were an instant hit. Both men were now going to retire as Counts, not Barons!

It had been a modest plan, and Lady Franklin, née Philips-Webber, the inventor of the one-way gate — in return for the collection of a couple of former students she rather wanted to own — had devised a simple method to select quality merchandise. British students seemed to be universally short of funds. At universities and colleges around the country, Slaveworld agents posing as market researchers for an advertising company, offering a modest fee for their questionnaires, soon had thousands of psychological profiles to choose from. The secretly sexually submissive could be targeted, quietly kidnapped and from the point of view of an entire country, was anyone going to miss a girl here, a girl there? Unlike the well regulated Kingdom, where ninety eight per cent of peasants were born, lived and died in the same village or town district, in the chaotic and unregulated otherworld, young people went missing all the time. The police barely even investigated unless there was clear evidence of a crime.

But the quiet little operation had just snowballed. Everybody wanted the New Ones. Princess Alice had been the first to formally request a British slave. The next day, Prince Gregor had demanded one. British Intelligence was aware of the alternative world by this time, had their own one-way Gate, and their agents were strolling around the Kingdom, passing themselves off as Lords and Ladies, stealing technology. The need for diplomacy had become self evident and pressing. Even the possibility of conflict with a nuclear power that could create a portal into your world, anywhere, with no warning; was just too dangerous!

The Kingdom had successfully rolled up most of Britain's spy network, and British Intelligence in their turn had a few RSP agents in cells, but individuals weren't important as long as those in power, the decision makers, could talk to one another. Pawns had always been sacrificed for the greater good. The important thing was that there should be official understanding and accommodation between the two nations. A Treaty and an embassy.

Captain Scott, the King's equerry, found the British Ambassador on the roof of his new embassy, eating ice cream. Sunning himself in shirtsleeves, his gaze wandered over the roofs and treetops of Londinium. They built higher in the otherworld, so Scott had been told, and he had no reason to disbelieve, but he found it hard to imagine. It would be like living in a canyon, surrounded by concrete walls. A city that diminished its inhabitants.

"My Lord, may I intrude for a moment?"

"Of course, of course," the new Ambassador waved his spoon expansively. "Do have a seat Captain."

Her wrists pulled back over her head and secured to the back of her collar, the married slavegirl who had been provided for the Ambassador's comfort and amusement, knelt in front of his chair. Kneeling behind his young wife, the tip of a swollen strap-bound cock twitching and flexing between her buttocks, clearly quite desperate to ram his shaft into pussy or ass — but too well trained and too fearful of punishment to actually do it — the boy toy half of the pair held up his wife's large breasts, squeezed together. Her cleavage was her master's ice cream bowl. Both slaves were collared and gagged, the slavegirl snorting through her nose a little, teeth clenched tight into the large red ball that filled her mouth.

"May I offer you refreshments?" the Ambassador asked politely, scooping another spoonful of ice cream from between chilled, squeezed together tits.

The Captain couldn't help noticing how stiffly the married slave's nipples protruded, melted ice cream running down her stomach from between heavy slave breasts to matted golden pubic curls. The naked plaything groaned softly, as, helplessly following Captain Scott's gaze, her husband unconsciously sank his fingers deeper into his lovely young bride's big tits. The firm mounds were whip marked, as was the girl's ass, her husband's body unmarked. Both had their wedding rings set through their noses.

"Thank you no," Captain Scott declined. "I just have time to deliver you an invitation actually. Then I really must be getting back."

The new Ambassador raised an enquiring eyebrow.

"More a reception in your honour, hosted by Her Majesty, Queen Victoria II. A sort of non-official welcome, as you can't do the usual round of embassy parties. A week tomorrow? At the Ministry?"

Scott waved to the building across the courtyard.

"I'd be delighted," the British Ambassador assured him.

"Thank you Sir. I'll inform her Majesty and have the written invitations sent out this evening."

The Ambassador nodded, scooping the last of his ice cream from between full breasts. "Are you sure I can't offer you something? A little sexual relief perhaps?"

Captain Scott checked his finger ring. "Well..." he murmured, letting himself be persuaded.

He was of course tempted. As an officer he was legally allowed to indulge himself with offered sex slaves of either sex, and his new girl-friend, Lady Frances let him use her property as he wished. But he couldn't legally own a slave himself until he actually married up into the nobility. Experience had taught him never to turn down an offered sex slave. And although he was now finally getting as much sex as a Lord, something he'd aspired to all his life, things still might not work out with the Baroness.

"Well actually, I may have a moment," he allowed.

"Be my guest," the Ambassador offered, waving to the kneeling slave.

There was a plea, and raging eager lust in the bound slave's eyes, but Scott saw no reason she should be allowed the pleasure of being fucked as he didn't really have time to enjoy her properly himself. Just a quickie. A little light relief! He unbuckled his breeches, and thrust a stiffening cock between heavy tits. Ample flesh enveloped his shaft as the heavy mounds were squeezed tight around his shaft, the pretty sex slave groaning as her chilled tits were squeezed. Scott thrust harder and faster between pleasantly cool flesh, pulling the ball gagged slavegirl's head up by her hair so that she was looking up at him. Her husband, kneeling behind her, tears of frustration and shame in his eyes, obediently squeezed his young wife's breasts tighter around Scott's penis at his command.

Captain Scott was aware of the Ambassador's eyes on him, the delighted smile on the man's face as he watched his visitor indulging in a little relief. Enjoying what was an everyday spectacle in a way that wasn't quite right or wholesome.

"You'd better not be watching me as if I were a slave performing for your pleasure!" he threatened softly, silently, inside his head, as he pumped come between big heavy tits. Even the most jaded, arrogant, rude, Lord or Lady, would not shame an officer, a valued subordinate of proven loyalty, in that manner.

No, the offworlder was just different, he decided, and looked at slaves differently to the way Scott did. No insult was intended. He stayed to watch the voluptuous slavegirl's husband lick mingled semen and melted ice cream off his wife's body, the Ambassador clearly taking great pleasure in the boy toy's humiliation.

"Sometimes he cries when I make him lick my come out of her," the Ambassador confided happily.

The lovely sex toy, naked on her knees, with her arms pulled over her head and secured to the back of her collar, clearly enjoying having her flesh licked clean, was oblivious to her young husband's distress.

"And he hates watching her enjoying being fucked," the Ambassador said loudly, deliberately teasing. "But when I let him whip her, he really gets into it!"

Tears ran down the humiliated slaveboy's cheeks, but he

was just carelessly ordered to lick his own tears off his wife's velvet flesh as well. The Ambassador stroked his palm down the kneeling girl's belly, thrusting his fingers into her. Hips bucking, eyes closed, the delicious sex toy wailed in pleasure as her husband lapped up semen that had splashed up under her chin and over her collar.

As Captain Scott took his leave, he paused at the stairs, looking back one last time. The new British Ambassador now had the naked girl bent forward over a table, wrists still secured to the back of her collar over her head, and was thrusting into her sex from behind. Firmly spanked as she was shafted, buttocks soon nicely pink, the ball gagged sex toy squirmed and twisted as a swollen meat shaft was rammed deep and hard into her body, squeaking in pain and pleasure around the ball strapped into her mouth. Her slave-husband, kneeling on the other side of the table, held her down with painful handfuls of breast.

As ordered, he was looking directly into the eyes of his beautiful young bride as she was spanked and fucked!

Legs wobbly, quite shattered, hoping her mistress wouldn't allow anyone to handle her terribly sore breasts just for the moment, Susan, again gagged and with her wrists locked behind her, stood placidly on the end of her lead in a plush red velvet elevator. Led from the hotel room after possibly the most intense, and certainly the most painful, sexual experience of her life — made to come so many times — she realised she still wasn't fully satisfied, needed more! Addicted to sex by the surgically implanted aphrodisiac, she would always crave more. This was going to be her life, every day like this. Even as a self-pitying tear ran down a cheek, Susan realised the prospect delighted and aroused her anew.

Protest was unthinkable. It was clear to her that Lady Abigail's every wish and whim would have to be obeyed, her desires and lusts, no matter how depraved, satisfied. Regardless of what that meant Susan herself had to endure. Even including, though a pussy whipping and tit torture were far preferable, sexual frustration! Now that she had been broken in, it was self-evident to her.

Susan found herself a little surprised, not at just how easily she'd been broken, but at how placidly she accepted the fact. Surely not all slaves succumbed so quickly. Perhaps just British slaves? Another explanation for the popularity of the New Ones, and the high auction price Susan had commanded?

As the uniformed lift operator surreptitiously admired her naked body reflected in the brass doors, Lady Abigail was again happily humming a little abstract tune to herself. The young aristocrat at least, was sated for the moment. Leading her naked property out of the elevator into the hotel lobby, she tossed her keycard onto the reception desk. The noble Lady smelt of almonds, the scent of the shampoo and bodywash she'd used in the shower after enjoying Susan. However, sweat, tears and juices had dried on Susan's own naked body, dried candle wax flaking off her thoroughly abused breasts when the ring-tipped melons swung and jiggled as she swayed across the lobby in her stiletto heels. Having had the sex slave washed before use; it clearly wasn't too important to the pretty young Lady to have her washed afterwards.

"Thank you my Lady. Did you enjoy your stay?"

The noble's eyes flickered back to Susan, who, heart suddenly racing, fearfully bit harder into her ball gag. Handcuffs bit into her wrists behind her back as she unconsciously squared her shoulders. Her beautiful owner reached out to lift a breast, her fingers sinking into the firm globe, admiring the pin-pricks where the scalding hot needles had been, the purple love bites and the red candle wax scalds that now decorated the over-large melon. Clearly reaching a decision, rewarding Susan in a public place, guests, slaves and staff all around, she lightly touched her lips to the upper slope of the heavy mound.

"Yes I did actually. Needs a lot more work, but she's going to be a superb fuck when she's fully trained."

Susan felt a thrill of pride even as shame made her flush, the clerk's eyes on her naked body a moment. Quite openly studying her. She felt her nipples swell tighter, juices oozing between the squeezed together sex lips, which her pussy lock again imprisoned. The clerk didn't have to pretend to hide his interest. Because they dealt with room service slaves, if their employer was willing to put them through college, senior hotel staff could qualify and be licensed to groom and discipline slaves, just as the household troops did.

"And the room service?"

"Have the blond one punished," Lady Abigail decided. "He seemed much more interested in his fellow than in preparing my little toy here for my use."

"Of course My Lady."

The clerk presented the aristocrat with her bill, urged her to call again, and politely turned to the next guest. An old Lady with a petite young blonde on a lead was assured all rooms came with a full complement of whips, shock dildos and the beds doubled as racks.

Still humming happily, Susan's owner led her back out onto the thronged streets, swinging her lead idly from side to side. Two streets down, then a left, in sight of the river, Susan's introduction to slavery continued at a pet shop. Wanting to be obedient, to be pleasing, Susan nevertheless followed her lead very reluctantly into the clearly exclusive establishment. She didn't like pet shops. The last time she'd been in one, she'd walked out with a pierced clitoris she hadn't previously had, and her upper arm stinging from a breast enlarging injection, though that didn't show instantly. It had taken over two weeks for her breasts to grow to their present humiliating size and weight.

An Arab girl with lovely olive skin and dark eyes, an exotic import probably almost as expensive as a British girl, hung naked from her wrists, slowly spinning, in one shop window. A trio of identical triplets, sprawled naked in chains, asleep, were in the other window.

Inside, a hog-tied slavegirl, suspended in a harness, hung over the door, heavy bells hanging down from her clamped nipples. The bells chimed merrily when the top of the door brushed over them, and then again as it swung closed. Cages lined the walls, glass display cases here and there, each containing a naked sex slave. Racks and shelves held rows of whips and dildos, harnesses and bridles hanging from pegs. In the back rooms of the cluttered shop, pony traps and slave tandem bicycles stood side by side.

In the centre of the main display area, a naked woman stood helpless, a locked bridle gag holding a huge orange ball in her mouth. Her arms and legs were free, but she was held firmly in place by a choke chain from a winch above; and below, a chain in an upside-down V linked her ringed clitoris to ring bolts set in the floor in front of her and behind her.

The blonde, about thirty or thirty five years old, had the very large breasts typical of the older slave, almost a match for Susan's. Making the breasts grow just slightly larger every six months as the slave's sentence progressed, kept the bust pleasingly firm, no droop, but it all added up. In thick black marker pen, someone had written across her stomach, 'ON SALE — FINAL REDUCTION'. Lady Abigail led Susan closer, one girl in a display case shrinking back fearfully, but another squashing her naked body up against the glass, licking her lips, a clear plea to be chosen in her eyes. Across one of the standing blonde's buttocks in the same marker pen was written 'MUST GO', with 'C450', crossed out, and under it 'C400'.

The pet shop owner, attending a young couple handling slaveboys' cocks between the bars of cages, looked back, a smile lighting his face.

"My Lady. How delightful to see you again."

Lady Abigail nodded imperiously, obviously taking it for granted that the owner of any shop she chose to patronise, would of course be delighted, and indeed she expected nothing less from a commoner. Susan was reminded again that the beautiful young aristocrat really was quite dreadfully spoilt, but that only made it more exciting to be in her power. The man waved an assistant over to the young couple, probably his son, there was a clear family resemblance, and ordered the young man to open the cage of the boy toy they wanted a closer look at. Presumably the pair were not regular customers, or were of a lower social rank than Lady Abigail, there being several tiers of nobility under the English system.

"Why so cheap?" Lady Abigail asked, kneading one of the on-sale blonde's buttocks.

"She's only got three weeks left to serve on her sentence, My Lady. Nothing to do with quality."

The clit-chained woman, her price written on her body in marker pen, head pulled up by the choke chain cutting in under her jaw, stood placidly motionless. Looking directly ahead, her free arms were folded neatly behind her back, ankles together, as Lady Abigail hefted her breasts, tugged erect nipples and slipped a hand between her legs, briefly penetrating, to taste her juices. The young noble concluded with a stinging slap, leaving a perfect handprint on the blonde's unmarked buttock.

Big breasts rose and fell faster, the bridled woman's lips parting to reveal even white teeth clenched tightly into the large orange ball strapped into her mouth, but her eyes sparkled with excitement. Clearly in no way distressed at Lady Abigail's interest, or being intimately handled by a girl who was ten, maybe fifteen years her junior.

"Youth treated?"

"No My Lady. She's a natural. She'll be thirty three years old on the day of her release."

"Experienced?"

"Oh yes My Lady. She was sentenced to serve fifteen years on her eighteenth birthday to cover unpaid tax and rent on her family's farm."

Lady Abigail stood in front of the naked woman, squeezing and kneading heavy breasts harder as she looked into placid blue eyes. Three weeks away from her thirty third birthday, the experienced slave moaned in soft, uninhibited, pleasure.

"Has she been hunted?"

"Yes My Lady. Seventeen captures, four escapes!"

"I'll take it," Lady Abigail decided. "My mother's hosting a hunt in two weeks. We can always use a few more prey slaves."

A prey slave, running loose with just her arms bound

behind her, was hunted by nobles driving slave-pulled pony traps, using rifles firing tranquilliser darts. Susan felt sympathy and envy for the blonde in a confusing mixture. The idea of being hunted darkly fascinated her. The aristocrat sank her fingers deeper into the blonde's breasts, forcing a louder moan out of the helpless woman who was going to be hunted for sport just one week away from being set free. If captured, she faced brutal sexual use and sexual torture in cruel games.

"What's it called?"

"Her last two owners didn't bother to name her, just kept her as a house slave, one of the pack, but before that as a young man's pet, I believe she answered to Fancy," the shopkeeper replied.

Lady Abigail held up the blonde's breasts by the nipple now, swinging the heavy mounds back and forth, bouncing them together.

"Are you listening to me, Fancy?"

The blonde groaned obediently around her ball gag, hands clenched tight into her own forearms behind her now.

"We have a little rule on my estate. Any slavegirl with less than three months to serve, who evades a hunt, is too good a slave to let slip away. You escape, and Daddy will appeal to the court to increase your sentence. Youth treated, you'll be good for another ten years service, maybe more! Do you understand?"

Susan felt herself gasp silently in horror as the woman nodded, her choke chain cutting into her neck as she did. So cruel! Unbelievably cruel. Assuming she wasn't captured anyway, the mature sex toy now had to choose between running hard and fast, and win herself another ten years in a collar or let herself be captured, and submit to the ordeal of the hunt orgy, traditionally a sadistic occasion.

A moment ago the woman had been only three weeks away from freedom, now she was panting in lust as her nipples were twisted, the full weight of both heavy udders hanging from the tormented nubs, but her eyes were bright and Susan suddenly realised the blonde was going to run as hard and fast as she could. And would regret it for the rest of her life if some young noble driving a pony girl team managed to shoot her with a dart gun on the hunt in two weeks' time.

"Will you take her with you?"

"No." Lady Abigail yanked Susan closer with a tug of her pussy lead to indicate her. "I've just bought a new toy. Still breaking her in. Have blondie delivered. You know the address. Second class post will do."

"Very good, My Lady." the man gestured to Susan. "May I?"

Susan was as docile as the blonde while strange hands explored her body. Both drooling around ball gags, sexual property on display, the two exchanged a knowing glance. The pet shop owner pronounced Susan to be of excellent quality, worth every Crown Lady Abigail had paid for her.

"Anything you'd change?"

"I might stretch her nipples out a little, My Lady. Did she have large tits before her bust was improved?"

The aristocrat nodded.

"Ah, there you are. The naturally big-breasted merchandise tends to a smaller nipple. And perhaps I'd have her lose a little weight?"

"No!" the aristocrat said firmly. "I like her with curves."

"Well of course, it's your choice. She's your property," the pet shop owner soothed, then understanding dawned in a light bulb flash. "Oh. You want to outfit her?"

"A harness and bridle. Perhaps a new pony trap and a selection of restraints," the aristocrat agreed. "And some torments and toys."

"Of course. If you would bring her this way, My lady," the man said happily, clearly having a profitable day.

Reluctantly, but helplessly following the tug of the lead clipped to her pussy lock, Susan followed. Lady Abigail spent the next hour or so happily selecting and trying out a variety of restraints, torments and decorations on her new purchase.

Susan was eventually led naked from the pet shop, perched on her toes in five-inch-stiletto-heeled pumps, a built in manacle chain making her take small neat steps. It was a little uncomfortable being forced to walk entirely on her toes, but a small price to pay to now be publicly acknowledged as a pet. Specially chosen, the cream of the crop! And she looked great in five-inch heels — her legs went on forever.

The handcuffs had clearly allowed too much freedom for Lady Abigail's tastes, and now Susan's arms were strapped together down her back, elbows touching, chains linking her wristcuffs to the new rings in her pussy. The strap above her elbows pulled back her arms, squared her shoulders and thrust her breasts out into even greater prominence. A broad tight collar held her head firmly up, and a breathless waspie-corset in matching black leather was crushing her in two. Her owner said she looked utterly adorable, an eighteen inch wasp waist something Susan suspected she was going to have to get used to.

Lady Abigail's lead was now clipped to a new piercing, a ring set through the tip of Susan's tongue. Knowing how good she looked in a ball gag, Susan wasn't too sure about the new look, but her young owner seemed happy. A tongue clamp, through her mouth like a bit, screwed down tight above and below her tongue, pulled it out of her mouth, her mistress's lead now clipped to the ring set through the clamped muscle's tip.

Her pussy rings had been cut off, as Lady Abigail deciding the chastity rings provided to much protection during a pussy whipping, just the ring set through her clitoris remaining from the original. Her nipple and navel rings had been allowed to remain, a new pair of rings had been set through her inner labia to attach cuff-chains to now adorned her as well as the new tongue ring. Susan's tongue was just a little sore but would be fully healed by tomorrow, Slaveworld anti-inflammatory drugs and painkillers were very effective. As well as being a point to clip a lead to, the ring set through the tip of her tongue would make her better at oral sex, she'd been told.

As decorative torments, a heavy chain swung between her nipple rings, and from the base of her corset to her pierced clitoris, taut across her belly, a cruel chain dragged up at the ring-set nub, teasing Susan to distraction with every step.

Pulled along with a jerk on her pierced tongue, chains from pussy to wristcuffs brushing enticingly against her inner thighs as she walked, inner labia delicately tugged and clitoris painfully stretched with every hobble-restricted step — still expected to swing her hips and jiggle and sway her big breasts for the appreciation of anyone watching — Susan was so very wet! Desperately hot. She could hardly think.

Yet again being led from a pet shop, her upper arm stung after a large, painful, injection. The proprietor had assured Lady Abigail her property's roots would be growing through in the light honey-blonde colour she had selected by tomorrow. Only months ago she had been quite resentful when her British Intelligence controller, a Ms Carson, had decided to make her a cute, fluffy, blonde. Now she didn't mind at all.

Stricter restraints clearly made her more attractive, and Lady Abigail was asked twice if Susan was for sale, while many people were allowed to grope and pet her. Susan sincerely hoped she'd never ever get used to total strangers stroking and patting her bottom, squeezing and twisting her nipples, hefting her breasts or pushing hands between her legs on a public street. It was so nice to be wanted.

Eagerly wondering what Lady Abigail was going to do with her next, Susan was led to a large pleasure boat moored on the Tamesis. A dozen or so young nobles, Lady Abigail's friends, had hired the boat for a day's cruising. At first, delighted to find herself being admired and intimately inspected by the group, as they discussed how best to restrain her, Susan suddenly realised Lady Abigail was going to let all of these people have sex with her. All of them! Susan met the eyes of the young girl holding her lead with a clear plea for mercy in her eyes. Please no! The aristocrat met her gaze with a cruel, sparkling, delighted, smile.

"Her tits are huge. Did you want such a big girl, Abby?" one of her owner's friends asked.

"Oh yes!" Susan's owner replied happily. "They're more fun to torture, and I've always found top-heavy sluts a better ride!"

There was not the slightest mercy in the aristocrat's tone or eyes, just a cool satisfied pride as her property was admired. Two dozen hands on her body, humiliation and fear only made Susan helplessly hotter, wetter, more eager!

A late lunch finished and the table folded away, Susan found herself the sole entertainment at a small impromptu party. Even though she'd realised in dazed, lust-confused disbelief it was coming, the policewoman in her was still outraged to find herself orgy fodder, the only slave in a room with a dozen or so young nobles. They were just kids. As the little clothing the young nobles wore dropped to the floor, one beseeching look from her beautiful owner immediately put Susan on her best behaviour; determined to please! In front of her peers, the normally confident young aristocrat who held Susan's tongue lead was unconsciously biting her lip, a faint worry in her eyes. Lady Abigail was clearly anxious that Susan might disgrace her.

Eleven aristocrats later, cocks having been pushed deep into her pussy, mouth and ass, strap-on dildos having been rammed into her sex and back passage, her head having been pushed between Ladies' thighs and having been forced to orgasm again and again, Susan could taste nothing but come. Sour, salty, gelatinous, slime coated her tongue. She'd swallowed so much she felt queasy. Lady Abigail, happily watching her perform, was quite relaxed now, sprawled on a couch, with a broad smile, a wine glass in hand. Susan was a hit. Her friends were very clearly enjoying her new pet, enthusiastically complimenting her on her choice.

As was common for orgy fodder, Susan had her right wrist and right ankle cuffed together, and on the other side, left ankle and left wrist. It was a convenient restraint that allowed the slavegirl to be enjoyed on her back, lying face down, kneeling astride a noble or sitting up and performing oral sex but still kept the plaything physically helpless. She was enjoyed one on one, three into one, and everything in between.

Gasping around the heavy cock in her mouth, sat astride another Lord and deeply impaled on his shaft, Susan squeaked in pained distress as her breasts were squeezed. The Lady behind, thrusting into her ass with a strap-on dildo, was wearing pin-lined gloves! There were little red dots all over the already well-tortured, come-covered melons. Wrists handcuffed to ankles, wearing only her new collar and waspie-corset, clit chain still dragging painfully up at her pierced, throbbing, pulsing, clitoris; semen splashed into her mouth again. Grunting as the dildo was forced deeper between her buttocks, Susan forced herself to swallow.

"I'm finished. Who's next?" the handsome young Lord asked in the beautifully cultured tones of his class, carelessly pulling his cock out of Susan's mouth, semen and saliva dripping down her body.

Another Lordling stood, tossing aside his robe. It wasn't just the original twelve, they were coming back for seconds now! She was exhausted. Deeply impaled front and rear, a hard cock rubbing up against the rigid dildo inside her, dozens upon dozens of tiny little pins torturing her breasts as the heavy mounds were lifted to her lips, Susan obediently licked come off her pin-speckled breasts. The ring set through the tip of her tongue felt strange as it trailed across her own flesh but it did seem to make her better at pleasing women orally.

Another erect cock was held before her face. Conscious of her owner's eyes on her and the lazy, predatory gaze of the rich, privileged, nobles lounging all around her, who had freely enjoyed and abused her, and those waiting their next turn, Susan licked slowly up the heavy shaft from between the unknown aristocrat's balls, and closed her lips over the shaft's purple head. The aristocrat let his cock rest on her tongue while he closed a clamp over each nipple.

Susan squealed. Too tight! Her nipples were being crushed, little spring-loaded metal teeth bit agonisingly into the abused nubs. She knew without being told the clamps wouldn't come off until the young Lord came in her mouth.

If then!

Hot meat brushing the back of her throat, wrists handcuffed to ankles, out of the corner of her eye, Susan saw her beautiful young owner take a small digital camera from her purse. Collared, her corset spectacularly cutting her in two, emphasising the flare of her hips and the size and weight of her breasts — a perfect sex slave's body — cocks in mouth and sex, a solid strap-on shaft deep in her ass, Susan's gang bang was carefully photographed from all angles. Under her, the man she was astride thrust up harder and faster, his hands tight on her corset nipped waist. Ass painfully penetrated, Susan bucked on the cock that impaled her, tugging on her own chain-tortured clitoris with every thrust. A new cock deep into her mouth now, forced to come and come again, in chains, without her consent, Susan was in heaven, body drenched with pleasure.

Her owner, the only aristocrat dressed now, noticing Susan was tiring, helpfully suggested that her friends apply a little more pain to the sex toy they were sampling. "To perk her up!"

Susan cried out in pain as the attractive young Lady thrusting a strap-on dildo deep into her back-passage twisted and squeezed her over-large breasts harder still with her pin-lined gloves.

"Yes, yes, that's it," Lady Abigail called in excited approval, moving in to get close ups of the tortured melons, and then the rigid shafts that impaled her helpless, bucking, gasping, sweat-gleaming, chained, property.

Finally finished with, her users sated, Susan was dragged limp from the cabin and hung from her wrists from the boat's mast while the cabin cruiser made its way slowly up river to drop Lady Abigail off at her family's riverside townhouse. The sun was low on the river by the time she recovered enough to notice, and shone bright in her eyes, a warm caress on her bare skin. Evening! Laughter, music and the chink of glasses echoed up from the cabin below. Susan was naked but for the collar and corset she'd been enjoyed in, a trophy on display to all, semen slowly leaking from her hard-used, pleasure-drenched, exhausted, body. As she swayed slowly back and forth to the boat's movement, listening to the party below, Susan dared to hope that her first day of service was nearly over.

Lady Abigail woke with a sudden start in the night, a shaft of moonlight streaming across the bedroom floor from between open curtains, wondering for a moment what had woken her. For just a second she felt disorientation, something different or wrong, as if when waking in a strange bed. But no, she was in her own bed in the family's riverside townhouse; safe and snug. She snuggled back up to her pillow, nestling her head in the small of a slavegirl's back, the naked slave tied across the top of her bed face down. Sliding a hand under the girl and sinking her fingernails deep into a large breast, Abigail smiled in lazy contentment and deliberately closed her eyes again. Her pillow whimpered in soft pain.

No, there it was again. Pushing up on one elbow she listened. A soft desperate rhythmic gasping was accompanied by the regular thrusting click of metal on metal; but that wasn't it. The sound of a slavegirl fucking herself to exhaustion while Abigail slept was a familiar and soothing sound, one she'd dozed off to many a time. It actually helped her get to sleep, knowing her property was suffering, so cruelly forced to exert herself through the night, while Abigail slept.

It was like strapping a dildo inside a girl and padlocking it into place. Even if the girl wasn't in the room, you could take pleasure in the thought of her; stuffed, impaled, forced to tease and torment herself with every step, breath and movement.

There! A light breeze had sprung up, and it was rattling the curtain's cords against the wall every now and then. A hot night, and she hadn't bothered to draw the curtains or close the French windows. Abigail idly patted her pillow on the behind, an old pet she'd grown bored with, and slipped out of bed. Her robe was hanging from a hook held in the mouth of a girl strapped to one of her four-poster bed's posts, another big-breasted nineteen year old plaything awaiting the auction block when Abigail finally got around to remembering to sell her.

"Lights," Abigail ordered, a soft light automatically illuminated the room.

She slid her fingers between the blonde's legs, taking a little taste of her juices. Weights hanging from nipples and sex lips, metal clamps biting into her flesh, kept the blonde awake and wet throughout the night. She gave the coat hanger's firm breasts an approving squeeze. The coat hanger moaned ecstatically, an eager plea in her whine. Since Abigail had lost interest in her, she was being shafted no more than once or twice a month, her last whipping a full week ago - the last time she'd been allowed to come!

Abigail just found it so hard to part with her playthings, even when they no longer enthralled or excited her. Besides, as she'd told Daddy, a good hostess always needed a few big-titted blondes about the place for the comfort of guests. A third slave with her arms strapped behind her back stepped up with a serving tray strapped to her waist, the outer corners supported by chains from nipple rings, offering a glass of water. Taking a sip, Abigail barely noticed a fourth slave, kneeling at the foot of the bed, wristcuffs chained to nipple rings, sliding slippers onto her feet.

The heavy-breasted ex-pets found it easy to remain awake all night, ready to serve their owner instantly when she finally woke. Not only were they all desperate to regain her favour, but they all knew from personal experience just how severely Lady Abigail would punish a slavegirl who disappointed her. Only her alarm clock, a hog-tied girl on a table on the bed's other side, who would cry out loudly when her strapped-in anal shock dildo delivered a bolt of agony deep inside her body, was allowed to sleep.

Abigail walked out onto the balcony, the night air refreshingly cool. The new slave was mounted on a small but solid waist-high table, so that she would be visible to anyone on the street below through the thin bars of the balcony's railing. Abigail still couldn't resist the feeling of wanting to shout, 'Look what I've got!" just yet. The bedroom's light behind Abigail, the girl in her shadow, moonlight glinted in hard points of light off highly polished stainless steel chains, and gleamed off the sweat-sheened flanks of her naked prize.

Abigail walked slowly around the table, delighting in the beauty of her new purchase, admiring the British girl's lush curves and flawless skin, savouring a familiar thrill of power as she surveyed the brunette's utter helplessness, her delicious suffering and abject submission. The knowledge that the gorgeous creature she had yet to name was no longer a free person with her own wants, wishes, hopes and desires; simply a plaything to be used for Abigail's gratification. The softly gasping brunette was secured on all fours, still fitted with the decorative eighteen-inch corset with its built-in tormenting clit chain.

The sex slave was unaware of her presence. Abigail had fitted the top-heavy plaything with a tight shiny-black latex hood, the only opening at the mouth. A ring gag buckled behind her teeth held the bound, soon-to-be-blonde's mouth, wide open. Broad leather cuffs buckled around ankles, calves and wrists, padlocked to rings set in the table, kept the girl firmly in place. A final chain from the top of her hood to an ass hook buried deep in her anus, pulled the beautiful toy's head hard back, spine arched, thrusting big heavy tits forward between her arms.

An automated vibrating dildo mounted on a mechanical piston thrust slowly and deeply in and out of the gasping, moaning slavegirl, the dripping wet girl ramming herself hard back onto the shaft that penetrated her with each piston thrust forward. To keep her refreshed, held in place with a short chain clipped to her tongue ring, a large bottle suspended above the British girl's face slowly dripped semen into her wide open mouth. She'd swallowed about a pint so far, but the bottle suspended over her mouth still held plenty more. And to keep the sweat-sheened toy focused, to remind her that pleasure had to be earned, a small pot of stinging nettles was set in a recess in the table just in front of her. With an anguished wail, each time the former British police officer thrust herself back onto the rod mechanically reaming her, her big tits swayed into and through the broad green leaves.

The delicious, delightfully cruel part was the small rod in the brunette's right hand. Her thumb was firmly holding down the red button on the rod's end. The on/off switch for the vibrating dildo being thrust deep in and out of her own sex! The lovely slavegirl just couldn't bring herself to let the button go for more than a few seconds!

"My, those tits look sore," Abigail said contentedly, patting her sweat-slick, gasping, property on a trembling buttock.

The heavy globes, swaying into the stinging nettles each time the hooded girl pushed back to meet the thrust of the fat invader that penetrated her, were in fact an angry, agonised, scarlet. Unbearable pain! Little white blisters covered the tortured melons, and in places, many blisters had spread together to form larger irregular shaped bumps.

Unable to hear Abigail, the earplugs under her hood ensuring that nothing distracted the corseted pet from her nightlong ordeal, it was the pat on the backside that told the exhausted girl she had an audience. The unnamed slave whined plaintively, pleading for mercy, and even managed to take her thumb off the button of the rod strapped to her right hand for a moment. Panting heavily, heat radiating off the naked, gleaming, body Abigail stroked, pussy still stuffed to bursting point with the heavy shaft that impaled her — but now deliberately holding herself still — the British slave with her hood chained to a hook pushed into her ass, was trembling with exhaustion.

"Mistress?" the exhausted slave asked in a soft hesitant whisper. The ring gag making her question an almost unintelligible gurgle.

Abigail ignored her, resting her hands on her toy's corset-nipped waist a moment. Perfect! A wasp waist set off the generous curve of the unnamed brunette's firm haunches just beautifully. Born to be whipped. Gentle sobs rocked her property's body, ringed nipples quivering beautifully, and it was obvious the girl could take a bigger dildo.

"Please mistress," the girl chained down on all fours whispered louder, pleading now.

With an irritated sigh, Abigail turned the tap on the suspended bottle of semen open from its steady drip. The hooded sex toy, mouth forced open by the steel ring forced behind her teeth, spluttered, and was then forced to frantically swallow and swallow again as a steady stream of thick, slimy, gelatinous fluid, filled her mouth. Abigail forced her helpless property to gulp down a full pint or so of come — milked off agricultural slaveboys to keep them docile — before resetting the tap to a steady drip.

Testing, Lady Abigail handled nettle-stung breasts. The hooded brunette groaned in soft pained lust, but had learnt her lesson and was silent apart from a few understandable whimpers. Abigail squeezed and pulled harder, her fingers twisting painfully deep into heavily enlarged tits, but the velvet-skinned slave just mindlessly thrust herself back onto the dildo that impaled her, not a hint of protest in her cry of mingled pain and pleasure. Abigail patted her property's behind in approval again. She had tortured many girls before, but this really was the slave she'd dreamed of.

Gently stroking one of her own nipples, Abigail ran a finger down the juices thickly coating the hooded slave's dildo and tasted. Pure nectar. A throbbing scarlet breast spilling out of one hand — so heavy, so many stings — she lightly plucked at the clit chain that indented the impaled girl's belly with the other. Big Tits would have to get used to a permanently champed or chained clitoris. The torment obviously brought out the best in her.

Abigail turned the plant pot around, so that the worn out leaves now faced away from the bound slave, and fresh stings faced her trembling tits. A few whip strokes across her presented hindquarters soon set the lovely plaything in motion again — just like winding up a clockwork toy — and with a despairing cry, thumb stabbing down on the red button, the British sex toy set the vibrating dildo that filled her pussy into motion again.

Abigail's lovely new pet moaned in deep, mindless lust, thrusting herself back onto the dildo harder and faster as the piston picked up speed. Her breasts swung back and forth with each harder thrust; and then brushed up against the stinging nettles! The tightly corseted sex toy cried out in agonised despair, semen spraying out of her mouth and speckling the tight, form-fitting, black latex that was moulded to her face. With a happy laugh, Abigail tugged the curtains aside from the breeze and returned to her bed.

The slavegirl's panting as she fucked herself was music to Abigail's ears. Chained helpless on all fours, the corseted brunette probably thought she was being punished. But really her exertions were for no other reason than to further break her in, and provide a soothing backdrop for Abigail to sleep to.

Undoubtedly, the panting, groaning, grunting, plaything thought she'd long since reached the end of her tether, but Abigail knew the sweat-gleaming sex object had many more hours use in her yet. Owners, as the brunette would learn, were often a far better judge of a sex slave's stamina that the slave herself. By ten in the morning when Abigail's alarm clock was set to squeal, the unnamed sex object, as well as being utterly shattered, would be quite desperate to please her. A few weeks of nights like this, and she'd be a blank-eyed living doll with no thoughts in her head that Abigail didn't put there.

She pulled up the sheets and snuggled back up to her human pillow. It had been a good first day, but then you always went a little easy on a new slavegirl. Tomorrow, now that her doe-eyed, beautifully submissive, big-breasted, pet was broken in, she could really have some fun.

CHAPTER SIX

According to reports, the new British Ambassador was thoroughly enjoying the young married couple provided for his amusement. Doing a little background research on the man before the embassy reception she was hosting, it had occurred to Queen Victoria to wonder how he would react to sex slaves from his own world being put through their paces.

Unlike a true noble party, where the guests were friends and equals, and the humiliation, torture and use of sex slaves was the main-course entertainment, an embassy reception was a rather more sober, formal occasion. The traditional embassy reception was a forum for introductions, the negotiation of treaties, the arranging of royal marriages and occasionally the business of commerce, trade tariffs and the like; maintaining the complex web of allegiances and obligation that kept the peace between nations. A duty as well as a social gathering, but still requiring a few slave toys. There was after all, no reason business could not be combined with pleasure!

Quite naturally the reception would require a few slaves to wait on the guests, provide decoration and a little light entertainment when they were enjoyed in parlour games. Only unlike a real palace party, most of the guests would still have their clothes on by the event's end.

After some thought, the idea growing on her, she had decided to staff her little get together entirely with British slaves. She'd had no trouble rounding up enough; most, after all, were owned by the family. And as she'd made it quietly clear she was seeking to help her son Samuel, and not being in any sort of mood to be crossed she had made it clear that obstruction would be regarded as suspicious! — her assorted in-laws, siblings, cousins, nieces and nephews had all fallen over themselves to be helpful. In addition, her friend Lady Franklin still owned three, and the Grand Hotel owned a pair of British girls used for room service, which they'd been persuaded they'd be delighted to hire to her for the day. More than enough!

Princess Alice was currently in the neighbouring Kingdom of Scotland, one of her British slaves having been entered in a mud wrestling competition there, but had assured the Queen over the phone she'd put the girl on the night train, first class post, just as soon as the competition was over. She had also told Victoria to help herself to her other British slaves, the two pillow slaves already in the palace kennels; which only left Prince Alfred's pair.

Victoria found Samuel's cousin in his chambers, stripped to the waist, swinging a broad strap across a naked girl's behind. The lovely young sex slave stood with her legs tied wide to ring-bolts set in the floor, a single rope around her wrists pulling her arms high up above her to a ceiling winch, body pulled taut. A cute little redhead with a dusting of freckles over her entire body, the copper-haired slave gleamed with sweat, large green eyes tear-bright. Leather landed on flesh with a solid, satisfying, thwack, the helpless toy jerking with a gasp, big tits bobbing nicely as a new, wide, red blaze marked her buttocks.

Little spring-loaded metal clamps decorated the pretty sex toy's large tits, pulling and nipping the firm globes into strange pinch-distorted shapes. Both full mounds were also cruelly dragged up with a length of string tied tight around each nipple, the strings running up to each end of the rubber-coated bit strapped into the girl's mouth. With nothing to force her head up, no posture collar, only a thin gold jewel-set band with a nametag around her throat, the naked plaything had to torment herself. Obediently holding up her head, teeth tight on her bit, she pulled the full weight of both big breasts up high with the strings tied to her tortured nipples!

Prince Alfred swung his strap across the freckled buttocks again, the tit-tormented sex slave's gasp becoming a desperate shriek of agony. She'd jerked forward a little too much. In a final ingenious torment, a wire carrying an electric current — the same wire and voltage farmers used on electric fences — ran diagonally up between the girl's legs. One end set onto a terminal in the floor behind her, the other mounted on a post at waist height in front of her. The wire was only an inch or two clear of the redhead's clean-shaven pussy, and if she didn't lean back into every blow, or jerked forward a little too much when the leather strap landed on her backside, a bolt of agony seared her sex as the wire was pushed between her plump sex lips.

Leather licked across the bound toy's buttocks with a stinging crack again, the lovely little slave squeaking, head jerking up, the sound becoming a rising wail as she was forced to drag her own breasts higher and put even more weight on her tightly tied, now purple, nipples.

The copper-haired sex object had rings set through the base of each crushed nipple, the twisted, stretched, areolae pink, but strangely no other body piercings. A little quirk of Alfred's. She had lovely long eyelashes though, and of course Victoria always appreciated the sculpted hourglass figure and heavily enlarged tits of the New Ones. She was tanned a little darker gold than her own tastes ran to, but on a redhead, always best viewed totally naked, a nice deep tan did bring up her freckles beautifully. Her nametag said the girl now answered to Puppy.

Noble Lords and Ladies were not overly concerned with privacy. Victoria would have knocked before entering a private space like a bedroom or playroom, but felt quite free to enter another's chambers. The Prince wouldn't have been playing with his property in a study if he were worried about being disturbed. Alfred politely paused and asked her if he could be of assistance, but Victoria told him to go on, assuring the young Prince they could talk while he enjoyed himself.

The gasping redhead took good whip — a nice ripple running across her haunches each time her master's strap landed — usually managing five to six strokes before her concentration slipped, and the heavy leather strap biting into her scarlet, throbbing buttocks jerked her pelvis forward enough for her dripping pussy to touch the wire again and she registered the shock between her legs with an agonised squeal!

Wearing only a pet's five-inch-stiletto heels, almost hanging from her roped wrists with legs spread wide, the naked girl's nipples and breasts stretched beautifully each time a bolt of agony delivered to her sex made her throw her head back. Clearly a very powerful electric shock! A plea in her eyes when the wide green orbs met Victoria's, the freckled girl was slavering around her bit, saliva running down the front of her body between her breasts. Gasping for breath around the bit, her stomach swelling and flattening with every breath, the sweat-gleaming sex toy was lashed again.

Precious, naked in her own bonds, having dropped to her knees at Victoria's feet on the end of her lead, was clearly quite indifferent to the lovely girl's torment, taking the opportunity to look around the Prince's quarters, but Victoria was entranced. Quite delicious! It came as no surprise to find the redhead was one of the British girls she'd come to borrow.

"Punishment or pleasure?" she asked, admiring the deep, angry, red blush that decorated the panting, trembling slavegirl's deliciously curved rear.

The lovely girl could twist her body from side to side under her roped wrists, swinging heavy clamp-pinched breasts back and forth on their tethers and giving her pretty tail a delightful wiggle. Victoria herself thought she would also have probably chained a nice big uncomfortable ass-stretching butt plug inside a girl she was whipping standing, but otherwise she approved.

The Prince's strap was the perfect instrument for prolonged relentless teasing. Less severe pain than a whip, but without the possibility of eventual damage, a firmly swung strap could be applied to a bound girl's ass almost indefinitely. True, a few little purple dots and splotches now marked the twitching hemispheres, showing where blood vessels had broken under the skin, but this was normal on any protracted spanking. The Prince swung his strap hard across his toy's ass again, the redhead's gasp inevitably following the crack of leather on her firm flesh.

"Oh, just enjoying myself. She's actually very

obedient," Alfred replied to her question with a happy smile.

The Prince swung his lash harder across Puppy's scarlet buttocks, his property squealing in pain as she jerked forward and touched her pussy to the wire running up between her legs again.

"Feel free to have a closer look," he urged.

Victoria caught the young Prince's eye a moment, an unspoken but clear question passing between them. All slave owners were well aware of how good the human body was at conducting electricity. You could have hours of endless fun with a cattle prod, and a shock did not just have to punish one slave, but could be transmitted through any plaything the first slave was touching or tied to. But if you didn't want a nasty shock yourself, a slave owner also quickly learnt not to touch a slave wired up to the mains, without insulated gloves. Prince Alfred nodded reassurance.

Victoria slowly scooped up clamp-decorated tits, squeezing the firm full mounds together and letting their heavy weight settle into her palms. The pretty redhead groaned in a helpless mix of pain and pleasure as the lust-swollen melons were squeezed and the weight came off her tied nipples; but sharp-jawed little clamps were pushed even harder into her flesh. The clamped globes Victoria held, quivered as the sex toy squeaked again, her lovely tail further reddened. The green-eyed girl cried out in pain as Victoria deliberately let both full mounds drop, to be yanked to a stop by the lengths of string knotted tight around each tortured nipple.

Very nice! She let a hand stroke down the gasping girl's belly, the velvet flesh under her palm hot and sweat slick. Another stroke with Alfred's strap made the bound toy jerk, stomach muscles fluttering under her hand as Victoria let her palm stroke up. Straddling a firm velvet thigh, Victoria stroked down a hip, grasping a hot, throbbing, buttock, Alfred carefully avoiding her hand with his strap. The freckled plaything's skin was toned muscle overlaying soft padded satin. Perfect white teeth bit hard into the bit through the girl's mouth.

The large heavy tits hanging from stretched, tortured, nipples rose and fell faster as Victoria's hands roamed over the bound slavegirl. A cute little thing of about five foot two, the doe-eyed redhead was very clearly a show pony. As well as big tits and a surgically nipped waist, she had the just slightly heavy hindquarters and gently curved belly typical of the breed. Although pillow slaves were also typically cute and top heavy, a flatter stomach, firmer ass and a couple of extra inches of height were more the fashion at the moment. There were many different breeds of slave, the differences between some quite subtle. And as Queen Victoria so very well knew, a noble could always indulge in the type of slave that most pleased them! If enforced exercise and force feeding or diet couldn't give you the face and figure you wanted, then a cosmetic surgeon could.

Hanging naked from her wrists, still being strapped as she was handled, legs spread wide, the British girl cried out in forced ecstasy as her tied, crushed, nipples were licked. Body gleaming as if oiled, clamps biting all over deep into the ample weight of her humiliatingly enlarged tits, probably not even knowing who the woman handling her was, Victoria looked into dazed eyes as she stroked the girl's spine.

Alfred was right. The lovely sex slave had taken strap stroke after strap stroke to the tail, each a painful, burning bite, that added to previous pain, intensified it, with every crack of leather on flesh. And she hadn't jerked forward onto the wire and shocked her own pussy once. Probably the panting, sweat-gleaming, slave slut was not even consciously aware of what she'd done, would quite truthfully say on a lie detector that pain, not secret desire, had forced her onto the wire; to shock herself between the legs! But when Victoria handled her, she had instantly, if unconsciously, realised that she must not allow the current to transmit through her own body and shock the noblewoman touching her, and had endured the punishment without jerking forward. A genuine submissive, desperate to please!

Suddenly Victoria realised that here she had the perfect bribe to get Abby to part with her British policewoman. Even if the young aristocrat wouldn't consider a straight swap, offering her the title to this lovely redhead in exchange for a few weeks' loan of her new plaything, would surely sway her. In harness and bridle, pulling a pony trap in the arena, this girl and Abby's new pet, side by side, could surely take an Olympic gold for England easily. Nobody had put two British slaves together in competition yet. They were too rare.

"A pet?" she asked.

"Of course."

"But you're not in love or anything?" Victoria pressed.

Alfred paused in mid swing, and gave her a questioning look.

"No," the Prince allowed cautiously, "though she's the best butt fuck I've owned in years, and a delightful tit fuck."

A blush, excited shame, touched the girl's cheeks as she drooled around the thick bit strapped into her mouth. Eyes sparkling, Puppy proudly and deliberately lifted her head a little higher, groaning in pained pleasure as more of the weight of her own over-large breasts came onto her tied nipples.

"I may need her," Victoria said, thoughtfully hefting a clamp-decorated tit in her palm. She saw Alfred open his mouth in protest and added, "To help rescue Samuel!"

Alfred closed his mouth, and gave the redhead another abstracted flick across the backside with his strap. His property squeaked around her bit.

"Rescue?" he asked. "I've heard some rumours..."

"That's all I can say," Victoria said firmly. "I'll get you full market price for her of course."

"It's not the money," the young Prince said. "Though the supply of New Ones does seem to have dried up."

He stroked his plaything's tender behind a moment, the freckled girl sighing in pleasure and again deliberately raising her head proudly, so that she put more weight on her dragged up nipples. Victoria let her tongue flick across the now deep purple nubs again making the trembling sex toy groan in delight.

"If it helps Samuel, then okay," Prince Alfred finally decided. "But I will expect you to tell me how it helped when you can."

Victoria nodded agreement. "Thank you," she said sincerely.

The Queen pushed her palm hard into the bound girl's belly to keep her off the wire, fingers indenting firm flesh, and then let her lips close over first one nipple then the other. Free hand twisted into the young pet's hair, she slowly pulled the girl's head back until both breasts were dragged up into tortured cones, the areola around each crushed nipple stretched beyond endurance. Puppy wailed in protest, a clear plea in her desperate cry, the sound becoming a strangled moan of pleasure as Victoria bit and tongued the tightly tied nubs while her fingers stroked in and out of a dripping pussy; teasingly light across the squeaking, gasping, whimpering, sex toy's clitoris. Alfred's strap cracked across the green-eyed plaything's buttocks with a steady thwack, thwack, thwack, each stroke making the slave yelp, snorting through her nose between strokes, teeth digging ever tighter into her rubber-coated bit.

The redhead was forced to come in moments, Victoria holding the velvet-skinned girl off the wire a moment, until she was sure; and then she stepped away, letting the wild gyrations and bucking hips of orgasm touch the helpless slave's sex to the wire again and again. With bolt after bolt of agony delivered directly to her pussy as she came, still torturing her own nipples as she helplessly threw her head from side to side, the pretty little pet's orgasm seemed to go on for ever.

Finally sobbing gently, still almost hanging under the rope biting into her wrists and with legs tied wide, the wire stretched taut diagonally between her legs from behind her to waist height still just under her sex, a fresh blow with the strap refocused the sweat-gleaming, gasping, slave. With a helpless groan, Puppy raised her hanging head, again obediently dragging up the full weight of her heavily enlarged tits with the strings tied tight to her nipples.

Intrigued, Victoria scanned the green-eyed girl's bar code and then briefly unbuckled her bit, questioning the panting toy about her past while she scrolled through the young sex slave's pedigree. Puppy had apparently once been called Alice. So she'd have been renamed, even if she weren't a pet. No slave could be allowed to share a name with a Royal Princess.

The British girl was a nineteen-year-old medical student, drugged and kidnapped by the boyfriend she'd just met, a market researcher, older than her, with an accent she hadn't quite been able to place. After submitting to a spanking and then performing oral sex with her wrists bound behind her back, her handsome new boyfriend had given her a drink to wash away the taste, and suddenly she had become dizzy, fell to the floor and woken up to find herself here! A bar code and serial number had been tattooed on the underside of her breast and she had been branded high on the right buttock with a letter A. She was Prince Alfred's property, quite legally owned in a strange almost-England. She had no idea where she was, where her home was or how she had come to be here.

Obviously the girl could not be allowed to return to her homeworld, but Victoria saw no reason she could not finish her medical studies once she'd served her sentence. Thirty five years, for illegal entry to the Kingdom and vagrancy. Ex-slaves made the best vets. They understood the owners' needs, requirements and point of view, as well being realistic and not too easily shocked about the uses a slave could be put to. As a doctor, her children would be exempt from slavery, if she so chose. But for the present she had her betters to please. And Puppy had been persuaded she very much wanted to please!

Queen Victoria and Prince Alfred took turns disciplining the girl, both finding it easy to make her jerk forward onto the wire and deliver an electric shock to her pussy. The most delightful thing was the way she always managed to hold off the wire when one of them was handling her, and didn't even realise she was doing it. Her unrelenting torture making her hotter and wetter, unable to do anything about her arousal, after only two hours, the nineteen year old former medical student had been taught to firmly and deliberately push her hips forward and shock herself between the legs whenever she was whipped to orgasm, the wire that delivered the agonising shocks pushed deep between her own sex lips digging into her belly.

Pausing to lick sweat off a heavy clamp-decorated breast, Victoria noticed Precious, lying hog-tied on a sheepskin rug on the balcony now, was looking daggers at the copper-haired plaything. The tall, powerful, but normally placid brunette, fearing being replaced, always passionately hated any slave Victoria found interesting or attractive. The Queen of England laughed happily, taking up her lash again. Young obedience-trained women made just simply the best toys in the world!

Susan was bent forward from the waist, her head and wrists locked into a set of heavy wooden stocks, ankles chained wide. She moaned behind her gag as her young owner twisted a fat ribbed dildo deeper into her sex. Occasionally the pretty aristocrat would give a buttock a stinging slap, or reach under her and add another weight to the collection hanging from her nipple clamps. Susan's breasts were pulled down into cones, nipples throbbing painfully, ass burning hot, but she now knew Lady Abigail well enough to know she was just being teased, not punished. The nipple clamps had blunt teeth, not the sharp little metal ones she was growing used to, and she'd always enjoyed a good spanking. She groaned helplessly as the huge dildo was twisted deeper still. The now customary waspie-corset that nipped Susan's waist down to the pretty eighteen inches her young mistress liked, made the ribbed invader she thought she could otherwise have probably managed, an uncomfortably tight fit.

After only a week as Lady Abigail's property, Susan had been trained to appreciate the decorative restraint ever more with every second she wore it. First and foremost, simply because she was always laced and padlocked into the waspie-corset during sex, but also, there was pride. Susan knew from snatched glances at mirrors and from her owner's compliments, how spectacular she looked with a tiny wasp waist, in a collar and five-inch stiletto heels. Her already over-large breasts appeared even heavier, the flare of her hips equally dramatic, buttocks spankably plump. Already it seemed quite normal to become a little breathless when forced to exert herself during sex, unable to take a deep breath.

The corset's built in clit chain, digging into the swell of her belly and linking the base of the waist cincher to her piercing, was something she didn't think she would never get used to though; her dragged up, stretched, clitoris was, as always, a throbbing nub of torment. But like so much else that gave her young mistress pleasure, Susan now placidly accepted the necessity. The clit chain kept her, a dripping wet, desperately hot, bitch on heat. Permanently!

Just the way the young, pretty, Lady Abigail liked her.

"Darling, are you decent?"

"Sure, come on in Mummy."

The young aristocrat was barefoot, wearing a snug lilac T-shirt and soft white calf-length jeans-like trousers that Susan thought superbly complemented her slender figure. Falling in love, every day she was more and more aware of how truly beautiful her haughty, spoilt, aristocratic, mistress was.

Of course, nobody cared if Susan was decent! She felt herself blush, teeth biting deeper into the ubiquitous red ball tightly strapped into her mouth, imagining the older woman's eyes on the heavy dildo penetrating her and projecting from her pussy, sex lips tight around the invader, the heavy shaft dripping with her juices. Her owner's mother walked slowly around Susan's naked form, stroking her back, reaching under her to pluck her clit chain and heft a breast. Bent forward from the waist, locked naked in the stocks with ankles chained wide, looking up into the older woman's eyes, Susan groaned in forced, pained, pleasure again as Lady Abigail forced the dildo even deeper into her body.

Lady Abigail's mother looked about forty or so, hair swept up in an elegant braid behind her head, wearing an ankle-length skirt and a high-necked blouse with a single string of pearls. Graceful, refined, back home you could imagine her as a magistrate, or chairing the local Conservative association. The cool grey eyes inspecting Susan regarded her in the same manner an aristocrat back home would look over a new racehorse, or best of breed at a dog show.

Panting gently as the dildo was forced home, uncomfortably filling her — brushing her tonsils! — pussy stretched tight around the heavy shaft, Abigail's mother brushed Susan's fringe out of her eyes, looking into her face with mild interest. It was moments like this that most forcibly reminded Susan that she was not playing a game, voluntarily submitting to a lover for a night; but was quite legally owned. Sometimes, immensely enjoying the uses Lady Abigail put her to, she forgot she had no rights. Whatever her own wishes, tomorrow she would be used and enjoyed again, and then again, for years to come, perhaps bought and sold without her consent, passed from one noble to the next.

The situation she had put herself into thrilled and terrified her whenever she allowed herself to think about it.

"You have an invitation to an embassy reception tomorrow," Lady Abigail's mother told her. "At the Ministry of Offworld Affairs, whatever that is."

The woman reached under Susan on either side of the wooden stocks' central post, thoughtfully hefting and squeezing her slave breasts. The Lady's hands were cool and dry, her fingers strong. The grip of the wooden stocks still tight around her neck and wrists, Susan sighed behind her ball gag as the heavy mounds, still dragged and stretched down by clamped nipples, were roughly kneaded. She wondered what the Slaveworld etiquette on having sex with a son or daughter's slave was? Surely Lady Abigail wouldn't let her own mother use a sex slave she herself was currently enjoying. Yuk!

"Never heard of it."

"Somewhere on the North bank," Abigail's mother told her, sounding a little puzzled herself.

"Is the invite from anyone important?" the young aristocrat asked. "I'm busy tomorrow!"

"By Royal courier! I'm afraid you'll have to find time for this one," her mother said. "And the courier specifically said you should bring your new pet."

"Really? That's strange."

"A little," her mother agreed.

"Oh okay, I'll go," Lady Abigail sighed.

The young aristocrat's mother twisted her fingernails deeper into Susan's breasts to make her groan.

"But you're not getting bored with your new toy yet?" she pressed.

"Oh no!" Lady Abigail said positively. "She's lovely."

The elegant woman nodded approvingly, and settled herself into a wing-backed chair to watch her daughter tormenting her property. Still locked into the stocks, Susan was very conscious of the woman's eyes on her naked body; clit chained, bundles of weights hanging from clamped nipples, her ass spanked scarlet and impaled with a fat dildo! Not a person, but legally and in reality, a sexual plaything.

Her beautiful mistress cupped Susan's sex to hold the dildo in place and gave Susan's behind a couple more stinging slaps, her palm cracking loudly on flesh. Panting harder, inevitably drooling around her ball gag, Susan yelped as something was forced into her anus.

Oh no. An inflatable butt plug!

She gasped as a squeeze bulb forced air into the plug, a groan as it was inflated further becoming a rising squeak as the butt plug expanded, the intruder in her back passage becoming bigger and bigger. It hurt! Her chained clitoris, as always, throbbed as more air was forced into the plug, making it bigger still. Waist nipped down to a breathless eighteen inches and already filled with a giant dildo, she just couldn't take it. Whining, not a protest, just a soft plea for mercy behind the red ball that stretched her mouth wide open, Susan squeaked in pain as Lady Abigail pumped the plug up bigger still.

More weight was added to her nipple clamps, breasts surely dragged down to the floor. Spanked again and again, stuffed to bursting point by dildo and plug, a dull throbbing pain in her belly — watched by her owner's mother — it took only the lightest strokes across her tormented, stretched clitoris to make Susan cry out in pleasure, the wooden stocks creaking as she ecstatically bucked and twisted in the solidly-built restraint's grip. Lady Abigail was still a far better judge of what her pet could endure than Susan was herself!

Gasping, panting heavily, the twin plugs that filled her still a dull heavy ache, her eyes unfocused and juices running down her inner thighs, Susan heard her owner's unmistakable, sweet, clear and innocent sounding voice.

"See Mummy," the girl said happily, patting Susan on a reddened buttock. "She's perfect."

"Oh my God, look at these two!"

Annette had come through the Gate only that day, the latest addition to the new British Embassy's expanding staff. Inevitably, not a lot of work was being done by the new, mostly young, staff at the moment. Annette's office was supposed to face the inner courtyard, but along with most of her new co-workers, she had found an excuse to be in a room with an outside window. The Ambassador was being quite understanding, realising that it was going to take his small staff a while to settle into the Slaveworld, when you could look out of a window and see public sexual slavery.

Marie, the Ambassador's p.a./secretary, with the experience of five days on the Slaveworld behind her, did not dash to peer around the curtains as quickly as her colleagues. Although she hadn't been expected to touch them, her new boss had already matter-of-factly asked her to take. She had of course refused, but it had been a salutary introduction to the way this world worked, and how the embassy was going to operate. Marie peered around the heavy drapes.

Prancing proudly, erections bobbing, a pair of harnessed and bridled pony boys being driven by a young Lady, pulled a pony trap past the embassy at a brisk trot. The crack of her whip on flesh was clearly audible over the light traffic noise, the embassy being located in a quite suburb. Mark, clearly hoping for pony girls started to turn away in disappointment, and suddenly pressed his nose longingly up against the smoked one-way glass of the next window along. The elderly, now familiar, Lady of the House on the opposite side of the street, a white haired but sprightly Baroness, waved her front door closed behind her, leading her favourite pet down the steps to the pavement. An elegant fashion model type, tall with small, rounded breasts and long, long legs, the blonde had her arms strapped tightly behind her back. Sparkling pendants hung from pierced nipples.

"Oh wow," Mark whispered.

Heels tip-tapping, following collar and lead, the ball gagged sex toy was of course completely naked, breasts bobbing and jiggling with each step, hips swaying enticingly. Marie found herself admiring the lovely slave's thick waist-length mane of golden hair. They had some treatment here that could make hair grow faster and longer than normal, as well as the in colour you wanted.

"Poor cow. Can you just imagine being led around naked like that?" one of her new colleagues whispered.

Marie couldn't actually, but she'd been imagining herself holding a slave's lead in public all day. Wondering what it would have been like if she hadn't refused the Ambassador's request to exercise his sex slaves?

"Can you imagine having to have sex with someone that ancient?" another whispered, not sounding quite as horrified as she should have to Marie's ear.

"Oh yummy," Mark breathed.

The group twisted around to look up the street with him. A pretty young Lady with a map or notepad clipped to her bicycle handlebars was making her way slowly down the street, clearly counting off house numbers. Slender with short brown hair, wearing white calf-length jeans and a lilac

T-shirt, she appeared cool and unruffled in the humid, sticky, midday heat. Marie's blouse was already sticking to her.

But then, the young aristocrat wasn't actually pedalling. The tandem bicycle's power was provided entirely by the naked slavegirl chained to the seat behind her. The Lady was just enjoying the breeze, steering, braking, with her feet propped up on pegs. The front seat of the tandem bicycle didn't even have pedals.

The aristocrat brought her bicycle to a halt just off to one side of the breathless group huddled around the embassy's first floor windows, outside the archway that led to the central courtyard. Up closer, she was more than just pretty, quite stunning! She should have turned heads, probably did usually, but to the newly arrived embassy staff, the aristocrat's human motor was hard to ignore. For a variety of reasons.

"Look at the size of those tits!" Mark sighed.

The beautiful young Lady's power source, pedalling from the rear seat, was an especially heavy-breasted brunette, absolutely lathered in sweat, gasping for every breath. Her harsh panting carried clearly to the first floor window. The slavegirl was hooded, a featureless form-fitting latex restraint tight over her head, broken only by a ponytail projecting out of a hole in the back of the hood, and a large breathing tube from the front. Her mouth clearly stretched wide open by the tube pushed behind her teeth, the gasping girl was slavering helplessly down the tube as she panted.

"They can't be real!"

That had been Marie's first reaction too, but the heavy sway of the bicycle motor's huge breasts certainly looked real enough. And she knew from the British-side Gate crew, asking why they kept calling her new posting Titworld, that the Slaveworld had a simple injection to make breasts grow larger. They all knew that now.

She hadn't imagined the treatment was so effective. Marie shivered in horror, trying to imagine the humiliation of being so substantially 'improved', and trying to ignore the guilty thrill of pleasure she experienced at seeing another woman so publicly humiliated. The hooded brunette was locked to the bicycle's rear handlebars and pedals at wrist and ankle, nipple rings securing her bent forward to the frame with heavy chains. Some sort of padlock on the front of the seat also secured her to the bike. A ring set through her pussy lips? A broad leather band with a row of three padlocks down the spine, gave the voluptuous sex toy a dramatic, cruel, wasp waist.

"Is that a padlock on her pussy?" Mark whispered.

"Where?"

"No, can't be."

"She's got wires pushed up her ass!"

"And you thought the Baroness's pet had it bad," Marie whispered thoughtlessly, earning herself one or two strange looks.

A thick bundle of red wires, a dozen or so, did indeed disappear into the hooded sex slave's anus. Probably running up inside some sort of fat anal dildo with electrode studs on it, Marie guessed. Used to shock the brunette into pedalling faster, the pain graded and controlled by the aristocrat's twist-grip throttle on the front handlebars. Big heavy breasts, tethered at the nipple ring, swayed back and forth on their chains as the naked plaything panted, and sweat had plastered her ponytail down her back.

"I want, I want!"

"Mark!" Annette whispered, shocked.

Blind under the skin-tight latex hood moulded to her face, Marie wondered whether the poor slut realised total strangers were lusting after her displayed body? Of course, she had to. She must know she'd been pedalling along busy city streets. Perhaps for a none-too-bright, semi-literate peasant girl, brought up with sex slaves all around, it wasn't as humiliating as it would be for a real person like Marie and her new colleagues.

The trooper at the archway gate stepped forward and politely asked the aristocrat if he could be of assistance. Their voices carried easily up to the breathless embassy staff crouched around the open window.

"No thanks. I've been invited to a reception here tomorrow. Just making sure I had the right place. This is the Ministry of Offworld Affairs?"

"Yes, My Lady."

The trooper, perhaps currying favour, or maybe genuinely admiring, complimented the aristocrat on her pet's figure, and was graciously allowed to run his hands over the chained-down girl's naked body. With a happy laugh still propping up the tandem bicycle with one leg on the ground, the young aristocrat twisted the throttle full back to the stop. The heavy-breasted brunette squealed, her hooded head jerking up, instantly pedalling madly, shocked and shocked again through the bundle of wires penetrating her back passage. She would continue to experience bolts of unimaginable pain until the road speed matched the throttle setting.

The trooper yelped as the suddenly pedalling girl was pulled from his grasp, a shock briefly transmitted through the over-sized, chained-down, breasts he was handling. Aristocratic humour! A brief look of anger on his face was instantly wiped away, replaced by a careful look of rueful amusement when the rapidly receding young Lady looked back over her shoulder with a grin.

"Spoilt bitch," Marie breathed, silent envy as well as proper condemnation in her tone.

She'd give anything for that sort of confidence.

Thighs pumping, sweat-gleaming as if oiled and slavering down her breathing tube the hooded sex slave took her young mistress out of sight, her buttocks rolling, and Marie found herself wondering if the tandem bicycle's rear seat had a built-in dildo. Probably!

She couldn't imagine having that sort of power over another person, and imagining being in the total power of another was even harder. Probably not one in a thousand born in Britain, stepping through the Gate between alternate universes, could ever really fit in here, Marie thought. It was certainly the most interesting post the diplomatic corps had to offer though, no doubt about that.

Perhaps she would exercise the Ambassador's slaves in

the park for him, after all. Just to see what it was like. To understand these people better.

CHAPTER SEVEN

Britain's new Ambassador to the Slaveworld's Kingdom of England was enjoying the small party Queen Victoria II was hosting for him, very much. Without a doubt, the best embassy reception of his life. Not entirely unexpected — they did things delightfully differently here — but still doubly welcome on what was usually an occasion of tedious work for him. In fact, thinking about it he'd never had as much fun at an official reception, but had never actually realised that the solution was so simple. Amongst the laughter and chink of glasses, the perfect backdrop to the witty, cultured, conversation of the formally-dressed embassy guests, was the occasional squeak of female pain.

And who would have thought the odd slavegirl or two, displayed naked, in restraints, would so enhance a dignified, formal, reception's ambience? As well as the entertainment and service, several of the Ladies had gorgeous poodles on leads. But far from distracting from their owners, the contrast between displayed, nude, sex object and richly dressed noble, just made the Lords appear sharp, stylish; their Ladies more chic and elegant. The Slaveworld formal fashion of hat, gloves and big-breasted poodle had puzzled him up until now — in his experience women rarely deliberately distracted attention away from themselves — but now he totally got it.

From the Ministry side of the former townhouse, he looked across the sunwashed courtyard at his half of the building, his unexpected new embassy. You just never knew how life was going to turn out! Three months ago his world had been crumbling, crashing down around him, and now he had the job, not of his dreams — that was his last post — but way beyond his wildest fantasies. The Slaveworld was, purely, heaven on Earth!

Below, parked beside luxurious hand-built limousines, naked pony slaves standing between the shafts of pony traps, or hitched in pairs to small carriages, stood hobbled, sweat gleaming on bare skin. Directly below him, in elaborate harness and bridle, was a superb pair of matched blondes, big strap-bound tits heaving as they panted and slavered around the bits buckled tightly into their mouths. Just his type. The lush-bodied playthings stood placidly motionless, looking obediently ahead, blinkers restricting their vision, as three uniformed drivers discussed them and their tack. After a leisurely inspection, the chauffeurs wandered on to inspect a team of four brunettes.

He let his eyes roam over a pair of pony boys — not really his thing — and on over more luscious bound female flesh. On display, utterly helpless; naked and exactingly trained. He chuckled to himself. Perhaps not quite heaven on Earth, for all.

An aristocrat, late for the party, lashed her young mount through the archway, steering one-handed with reins clipped to nipple rings, her free hand viciously swinging a long flexible carriage whip back and forth across juddering, bouncing, scarlet buttocks. Chauffeurs scattered as the hard-lashed pony girl was driven straight through the group of men at a desperate sprint. Lathered in sweat, big heavy strap-bound tits bouncing and thighs pumping, the harnessed and bridled slave's high-pitched yelps echoed around the enclosed courtyard as she was mercilessly whipped across the last few metres; a firm pull on her reins dragging up both breasts by her nipple rings. Pierced nipples brutally stretched, the reins running through the rings on either side of her bit, the lovely pony girl wailed in a mixture of pain and pleasure as she was cruelly pulled to a stop.

The Ambassador felt his cock stir again, even though he'd spent half the night tormenting and shafting the female half of the married couple he'd been provided with. God, what a great post. What an embassy!

Some embassies are naturally more important than others. When you're the British Ambassador to Washington or Beijing, then you're an important man, on first name terms with the Prime Minister. But most Ambassadors were just medium-grade civil servants, doing an unforgiving job, hopefully nine to five, but more usually seven to ten. The main task was trying to persuade the host country to buy British.

And all that applied double when they assigned you to some forgotten third world toilet; his last embassy had been in a tiny African country the Prime Minister probably hadn't even heard of, let alone cared about, run by the usual ex-general dictator.

The Ambassador had liked his little embassy. A career cul-de-sac true, but he'd been very happy there. He'd got on splendidly with the President; they both shared a taste for the subjugated female. And back in London, his superiors couldn't have been more delighted with the military hardware and industrial projects he'd persuaded the dictator to invest in. When they both had their pricks in the same bound women, the general had always been very accommodating, easily persuaded of the need for a half dozen APC's or a couple of jet fighters.

Some idiot British tourists occasionally thought that British Embassies existed to help them out of the trouble they stupidly got themselves into, but the truth was, the Foreign Office couldn't give a damn as long as trade didn't suffer. At least that was how it was supposed to work. So when some British pro-democracy protestors had got themselves thrown in jail, he hadn't concerned himself too much, just asked his friend the general to see they didn't get beaten up too badly before being deported. They'd been inspecting a new batch of political prisoners at the local women's jail at the time. The President liked to personally select those assigned to his special chain gang.

Unfortunately, the father of one of the arrested young Oxbridge do-gooders, turned out to be a newspaper editor. Outraged at his son's treatment, Daddy had done a hatchet job on the Ambassador. With pictures! There they were, the British Ambassador and the African dictator, side by side on sun loungers, being waited on hand and foot beside the general's private swimming pool, while British subjects rotted in a vermin infested jail, etc, etc. Shock horror! Fortunately the reporter with the telephoto lens hadn't been close enough to realise that the blonde in the skin-tight French maid's outfit serving them, was an Australian freelance journalist whose interview technique and questions the dictator had taken exception to the year before. She'd been caught going through customs with a bag full of heroin.

Her fellow journalist, mostly concerned with getting a good shot of the Ambassador's face, hadn't noticed or been close enough to catch the collection of weights and bells hanging on fine chains between the woman's legs, sharp-jawed clamps biting into her pussy lips. The butt plug's harness didn't show in uniform, and you'd have to squeeze her tits before realising she wore a pin-lined bra, but it had still been a close call. The sprayed-on French maid's uniform had barely covered the woman's crotch and had displayed a lot of cleavage, but then a few scantily clad bimbos about a dictator's playground were only to be expected. If the journalist with the camera had realised he was seeing a colleague being obedience trained, not a mistress or call girl, he might not just have snatched the few quick shots he had. Half an hour later, he could have seen the blonde naked and bound, with two cocks — one black, one white — in her mouth at once.

A very close call but even the pictures the paper did get, innocent of sexual slavery, splashed across the front page, made the Ambassador look bad enough. Career in tatters, expecting to spend the rest of it in some forgotten office filing C eleven hundreds, out of the blue an unknown branch of Intelligence had offered him a secret job. It was the best thing that had ever happened to him!

He couldn't have refused anyway. The general liked to make home movies, had thousands of tapes, and some copies of his collection had obviously got into the Spooks' hands. At his first interview, playing on a television in the waiting room, the Ambassador had watched himself and the general racing pony girls around the presidential palace, a sport he personally had introduced the dictator to. The President had been driving the wife of one of his political opponents, a lovely voluptuous coffee-skinned creature, the

Ambassador's own harnessed and bridled mount, an almost jet-black girl, the daughter of the owner of the local TV station.

During the interview, while a stern looking woman named Ms Carson had briefed him on the Slaveworld, and the rather muddled contact history between the two alternative realities so far, it had been taken quite for granted he would accept the job. Another widescreen TV, playing a video, ensured his co-operation. The sound was muted, just occasional grunts, gasps and sobs being audible, but the picture was in perfect focus and showed the general thrusting his cock deep in the Australian reporter's ass while the Ambassador simultaneously came in her mouth. The attractive young woman had her arms bound behind her back, breasts in tight rope bondage, and whip marks clear on her body.

When you thought about it, a dictator and an aristocrat had a lot in common, especially in the way they regarded ordinary people; but they did things even better here! They had more practise! Below him, the young Lady clipped her gasping pony girl's ankle straps together, patted a dildo-stuffed belly, gave huge sweat-slick breasts an approving squeeze and kiss, and then hurried into the Ministry, skipping lightly up the entrance steps. With a grin, the Ambassador turned away from the window. The view inside was just as good.

On a pedestal in the centre of the palatial ballroom, three slaves were putting on a live sex show. Against the far wall, forced to stand on their toes, jerking and twisting as little steel tipped darts embedded themselves in flesh, a pair of naked, hooded, slavegirls were the target for a game played with blowpipes, Lords verses Ladies. A winch chain connected to a ring on the top of their leather hoods held each human target in place, and the hood protected her eyes. The darts had coloured flights, red for the men and yellow for the ladies, and they clustered heavily on the target circles drawn on breasts, belly and buttocks in thick black ink. Chained on their knees to stout wooden posts in curtained alcoves, male and female slaves provided oral sex for those in need of a little light relief.

To the Ambassador, the amazing thing was that the curtains were only waist high, many Lords and Ladies amiable chatting with friends standing around them, standing themselves, while a naked slave fellated them! For the frailer, older nobles, there were stools set in front of some slaves. There were about thirty or so nobles, and perhaps forty slaves attending the reception.

Four serving-slaves pulling little trolleys loaded with snacks, treats and drinks made their way between the guests, one personally assigned to the Ambassador, following him as he circulated. He'd been given a bracelet, some sort of proximity sensor or GPS system, which would automatically deliver a shock to the girl if she strayed more than ten feet away from him. The nametag on the beautiful little redhead's collar said she was called Puppy.

Puppy wore only five-inch stiletto heels with a built in hobble chain, a heavy orange ball gag was strapped tightly into her mouth, and her arms were crossed behind her back, her wristcuffs chained to her nipple rings. Eyes sparkling with excitement, the chains looped around the girl's body swayed gently back and forth as her big tits rose and fell, nipples standing out hard. Saliva dripped down the heavy freckle-dusted mounds; her ball gag making her drool.

She pulled the small but clearly heavy four-wheeled trolley with a dildo prong that curved up from the front set of steering wheels. The lovely girl groaned every time she had to lean into her burden, juices running down her inner thighs. The dildo was quite huge, a real pussy stretcher, but the redhead was perfectly docile when he'd stroked between her legs, investigating the heavy shaft, her sex lips stretched tight around the invader penetrating her. She moaned softly when he pressed a palm into her belly, hard up against the dildo; sighing in contentment when lightly stroked, clearly a slave quite happy with her lot.

Other guests felt themselves free to handle the top-heavy girl as she pulled her burden around after him, hefting big breasts, rolling swollen nipples between finger and thumb and patting her pert backside; and they were barely even aware they were doing it. Just as naturally as the Ambassador himself would have reached down to scratch a dog behind the ear on another world, his homeworld, here nobles petted slaves. A slave existed only for their class to enjoy, after all.

It was truly wonderful to be able to — expected to — reach out and fondle, grope and tease a naked helpless woman as he wished. Pet owners would actually feel slighted if he didn't compliment them on the weight of their plaything's breasts, the softness of her skin, the cruelty of her bonds or the collared, gagged, poodle's docile demeanour.

There were also tray slaves, tongue-clamped with their arms strapped down their backs, circulating throughout the reception, collecting empty plates and glasses. Fitted with a tray supported on one side by a tight belt or corset, and on the other by two chains from each ringed or clamped nipple, the attentive tray slaves ensured a guest always had somewhere to put an empty glass.

Pushing away from the windowsill he'd been half sitting on, the Ambassador strolled across the grand ballroom, seeking his hostess. Connecting archways led to equally ornate rooms, a mud wrestling pit set up in one, a small crowd wagering on a slavegirl tug-of-war in another. With a helpless groan, Puppy followed, pulling her heavy burden by the dildo that curved up into her. The Ambassador had been formally introduced to Queen Victoria II when he'd arrived, but hadn't had a real chance to talk to her yet.

He nodded with a knowing smile to his deputy. The inevitably named Humphrey, a rather camp but very experienced career diplomat, was happily handling the erect cock of a male tray slave, the boy toy's genitals bound in a tight arab strap. The Ambassador had brought five of his embassy staff to the reception with him. All of course had been warned to be on their best behaviour, which meant no obvious pity, sympathy or disapproval of sexual slaves. No problem with Humphrey there. John, his security advisor, would also be around somewhere, the Spook making little attempt to hide the fact he was Ms Carson's eyes and ears, but he was at least quite at home with sex slaves.

The junior staff were another matter. Watching the three formally dressed young women was quite entertaining. Clustered together for safety, wine glasses and plates held protectively in front of them in both hands, so that they wouldn't have to pet slaves when invited to admire a noble's property, the trio were watching the blowpipe competition with fascinated horror. They'd gasped and whispered in proper disapproval from behind the embassy curtains at the sights you saw on an ordinary Slaveworld street, but this was up close and personal! Protected by diplomatic immunity themselves, young attractive men and women their own age, were all around them, displayed naked in cruel, humiliating bonds. And it would not be diplomatic to disapprove.

The Ambassador had found many of his new embassy's staff were young and female, university graduates who had applied for the civil service, and had been diverted into Security's project. He wondered if it had occurred to any of them that if the sinister Ms Carson ever needed a way to quietly silence them, a Slaveworld auction block would be ideal and profitable. Maybe he was just naturally cynical, but it had been his first thought, when, apart from a scattering of experience like Humphrey, he'd realised how many young graduates he had on his staff.

The latecomer who had just so expertly lashed her top-heavy little pony girl across the courtyard, a slender, very pretty young Lady, bounded up the grand staircase to the reception suite, and snatched a cool drink off another dildo-pulled trolley. She exchanged warm greetings with a pair of aristocrats, one Lady about her own age, perhaps a little older, the other a face the Ambassador recognised from his briefing photographs. The older woman was Lady Franklin, the former professor Phillips-Webber, and inventor of the original British Gate. Himself, he was easily recognised in his official sash, and Lady Franklin looked up with a welcoming smile as he approached the group.

"Do forgive my intrusion, Lady Franklin," he said. "I just had to tell you how much I admire your work. The team

Security assembled were amazed at what you accomplished with such limited resources. Just university funding, and a few students working for you."

Lady Franklin preened. The plump jolly-looking woman had two exquisite blonde slaves on her lead, a male and female. Slender, delicate, but both quite beautiful. The girl followed a split chain clipped to her nipple rings, the boy toy following her, a ring set through the tip of his penis linked to the ring set through the girl's clitoris. Both bound, gagged, sex objects were quite placid under his appraising gaze.

"Why thank you, Ambassador. So how are you enjoying my adopted world?"

"Very much indeed!" he said honestly.

The three aristocrats laughed at the obvious sincerity in his voice.

"May I introduce my stepdaughter, Lady Isobell, and Lady Abigail, my husband's goddaughter."

The Ambassador nodded politely. They took godchildren a lot more seriously here than back on his own Earth, almost on a level with legal adoption. A goddaughter would be one of the family.

The petite Lady Isobell had a huge-breasted brunette on a lead, the lovely young slave quite tall, a viciously tight waspie-corset giving her a dramatic wasp waist. A high collar held her head up, fresh whip stripes decorated her buttocks and her arms were pulled up high behind her back, wrists chained to the back of her collar. Her slight owner's head barely reached her shoulder, but it was clear the girl was under complete control.

Lady Abigail was the latecomer who had almost run the chauffeurs down with her pony girl. After exchanging polite greetings with the Ambassador, the slender aristocrat nonchalantly ran a hand over the corseted slave's marked behind. Lady Isobell's brunette trembled as the whip stripes on her buttocks were stroked, her huge breasts quivering beautifully, tears welling in her wide blue eyes. A head harness held a broad strap tight across her mouth, a cock gag no doubt filling her mouth.

"New toy, Issy?"

"Yes. The last British girl brought through the Gate before the treaty was signed. Victoria made sure I got her."

A British girl! The Ambassador realised there was a plea in the naked girl's eyes, directed at him. She must have heard his title mentioned or recognised his accent.

"I see your tastes haven't changed," Abigail teased.

"No, you know I've always loved big, dumb, animals," Lady Isobell replied quite seriously, leaning over to plant a light kiss on a rapidly rising and falling breast.

"Do I get a ride?" Lady Abigail asked.

Isobell laughed. "But of course, though she's not fully trained yet. And you might have to be quick. She's appealed against her sentence. The hearing's next week, so I might have to let her go."

All three Ladies laughed together. Local girls knew better. Pleading Not Guilty got you an extra ten years. Appealing against a court's ruling, usually doubled a sex slave's sentence. The clearly inexperienced sex slave groaned in a mixture of pain and pleasure as Lady Abigail scooped up her breasts from behind, twisting her fingers deep into the heavy melons. All the slavegirls on display had full, firm, breasts, but some, like Puppy and now this girl, were quite truly spectacular. The sex slave's wide doe eyes were tear-bright, a sob muffled behind her cock gag, but she held obediently still with her head up and her ankles neatly together, while her impressive udders were mauled.

"She's not used to having such huge tits yet," Lady Isobell said offhandedly. "They only finished growing to the size I wanted last week."

A first tear ran down the tightly-corseted girl's cheek, pooling against the strap tight across her mouth. The Slaveworld's breast enlarging injection must have come as a horrifying surprise to her. And now on collar and lead, paraded naked in front of strangers in humiliating bonds, she had just been told that the beautiful young aristocrat handling her would be allowed to use her as well. Fat ringed nipples swollen hard, when Lady Abigail stroked her fingers down between the British girl's legs and back up from behind, the trembling brunette's juices matted her neatly trimmed pubic hair.

The Ambassador surprised himself, momentarily considering sympathy for the delicious sex object, as she discovered the hard way that reality had a far sharper bite than any of her secretly harboured submissive fantasies. A perfectly normal girl one day, with the usual dull little hopes and dreams, boyfriend, studies; then the next, transported to a world of masters and slaves, finding herself quite legally owned, purely for the sexual gratification of others.

The sex toy's nipples were a little darker than the Ambassador liked, but she had a nice plump pussy. His eyes lingered on the lust-swollen mounds Lady Abigail was squeezing and kneading a moment, just long enough to let the slave know he was admiring the size and weight of her newly enlarged tits, and then he met her eyes again. He saw understanding in her helpless gaze, tears running down both cheeks, as she realised the Ambassador had no intention of interfering with her service. He let an appreciative eye trail down long legs, starting at hip and working down to toe. Like Puppy, the top-heavy brunette had a manacle chain built into the five-inch stiletto heeled pumps she was padlocked into.

"But wait a minute. Didn't your long-suffering father just buy you a new toy of your own?" Lady Isobell belatedly protested.

"Sure," the younger Lady replied with an impish grin, "and you must give her a ride. She's lovely! But variety is the spice of life."

"It's a trade."

Where the general had occasionally been quite possessive, here, young aristocrats shared their playthings with each other as a matter of course. An act no more significant than letting a friend ride a horse in the Ambassador's own reality. Lady Franklin watched indulgently as Lady Abigail lifted a breast by a nipple ring, inspecting the tattoo on the firm globe's underside. The first six figures of her serial number were the collared brunette's date of birth. Lady Isobell graciously allowed the Ambassador to handle her property, superb heavy tits spilling out of his grip, nipples hard against his palms, before proudly leading the cock-gagged girl off to show to other friends and acquaintances. Viewed from behind, her hobble making her take small neat steps, the almost naked brunette's ass had a truly delicious sway. With her arms pulled up high behind her back, wristcuffs secured to the back of her collar with a short length of chain, there was nothing to distract from rolling whip striped haunches and beautiful long legs.

The Lady's younger friend Abigail, paused to run her hands over Puppy's naked body, and then wandered off to watch the tug-of-war. Lady Franklin then invited him to pct her pair as well, and although a little skinny for his sexual tastes, it would have been impolite to refuse. The blonde couple were also familiar from the briefing photographs, two of the professor's own former students!

"That's one of mine as well," the aristocrat said proudly, pointing to the waist-high pedestal.

The black girl was chained down on all fours, the white cocks rhythmically pumping into sex and mouth a nice contrast with her darker coffee skin tone. The Ambassador stroked and petted her as the two hooded slaveboys, wrists cuffed to a chain around the slavegirl's waist, continued in their duty. The one-time physics undergraduate was a champion racing pony now, smoothly muscled, ass and thighs very toned and with small firm breasts, but quite magnificent all the same. He found himself suddenly reminded of some of the general's toys, mostly local girls, the odd European descended journalist or aid worker the exception rather than the rule in the dictator's stable.

Very nice. He had of course allowed his hands to roam over the bodies of the many bound slavegirls he'd enjoyed or shared, but he'd never handled a girl being shafted by someone else without being involved himself before. It was remarkably pleasant. The way she rocked back and forth, gasping in time with the slaveboys' thrusts, was delightful; and pressing fingers into her belly or stroking her throat, he could even feel the pressure of the two huge surgically enhanced cocks pumping into her.

To use the Slaveworld vernacular, he really wouldn't mind giving her a ride. The Ambassador had always thought his type was a cute little blonde with big tits; and it was, it was! But now he realised, you only had to have a type, when you were limited to choosing just one girl. The female half of the married pair he'd been provided with was a fantasy come to life. She took everything he did to her without a hint of protest, and could be forced to enjoy it. Three months ago, he couldn't have asked for more, but now...!

Everyone should have the occasional revelation. Puppy was at his side, huge freckle-dusted tits rising and falling as she panted gently. He let his eyes roam over the other poodles and serving slaves on display. Slim, curvy, tall, short, brunettes, blondes and a scattering of Asian and Oriental. Why limit yourself to a type when you could have the variety of a totally different girl for breakfast and lunch every day of the week, and still have a top-heavy blonde for supper. He wondered if he'd be allowed to retire here?

Resting his hand on the black girl's rump as she was shafted, lips tight around the cock in her mouth, brown eyes a little glazed but placid, he was reminded again of a thought he'd had earlier. If the supply of British slaves became a problem, and a Gate could be opened into the Africa in his world, he was sure his friend the general would be more than happy to sell a few eighteen to twenty year olds that no one would miss, for hard cash. The Ambassador intended to keep the idea to himself until he was sure he could personally profit from it.

He imagined the dictator's favourite toy, the once pushy, opinionated, Australian journalist, in the black girl's place, and it was easy to do. She would fit in just beautifully here, he thought. Again, when you thought about it, a dictator and a King, and their style of government, were really not that far apart at all. There was an urgent tugging at his elbow.

"Excuse me Sir," Marie, his secretary hissed in an

urgent whisper.

"Yes Marie?"

"That girl, that, that.... the Lady you were talking too, had on a lead! The one with.... The one with the dark hair," she stammered.

"You mean the one with the huge tits," he teased. "Lady Isobell's pet?"

"I know her!" Marie hissed. "We were at university together!"

"Are you sure?" he asked, his secretary too agitated to notice his fascination.

"Her name's Ruth. She was studying Law."

They both looked around just in time to see Lady Isobell deliver a series of hard slaps to her corseted, head-harnessed, pet's heavily-enlarged breasts. The ring-tipped globes swung and quivered deliciously with each stinging crack, both melons quickly splotched a burning red. The inexperienced slave had pulled away from an old man stroking her between the legs.

"You have to help her!" Marie hissed.

Heads across the room turned, in most cases briefly, to watch the former law student's public punishment. The lovely girl held position quite easily, just little twists and flinches, her cock gag muffling her squeaks. It was humiliating and painful, but by now Isobell's toy surely knew there were far worse things that could be done to her. The Ambassador supposed that once a slavegirl had been whipped a few times, and sat on a shock dildo or two, she would find it easy to stand still, with ankles together and head up, while her breasts were slapped.

"Please!" Marie pleaded, as the brunette's big breasts were slapped again.

"There's nothing I can do," the Ambassador told his young secretary softly, trying not to let on how much he was enjoying the show.

There were the beginnings of tears in Marie's eyes as she watched her university friend's public humiliation. Lady Isobell used a borrowed whip to give the tit-slapped sex toy two whip strokes across the belly, and then a flurry across the backside. Two perfect horizontal welts marked creamy skin below the corset, the British girl squealing loudly at each new stroke, her ass soon criss-crossed with lines of pain. But although her hips jerked forward with every stroke, bound hands fluttering, her ankles still stayed neatly together.

"Are you sure it's your friend?" the Ambassador asked, very much enjoying this unexpected turn of events.

"It's Ruth!" Marie insisted. "Her father's a vicar. She never even had a boyfriend at university."

Perfectly docile now, the lovely brunette moaned in pleasure as her slapped, reddened, tits were licked by the old man she'd pulled away from, trembling, wrinkled, liver-spotted hands twisted deep into the big heavy mounds. Lady Isobell stroked the new welts criss-crossing her buttocks. Perched on her stiletto heels, wearing only a brutally tight corset and high collar, hands bound behind her, the former law student's eyes widened in horror as she recognised Marie. She still couldn't help herself gasping in pleasure as the old man bit her nipples.

"Nice haunches, hasn't she?" the Ambassador said, nudging Marie. "You don't always get a good ass with long legs."

He was just curious to see how Marie would act, teasing her, but his young secretary must have thought it was part of the embassy's mission, and rose to the challenge. Over the strap tight across her mouth, the naked brunette's eyes were riveted on her one-time friend. First the Ambassador, and now Marie, were proof that her homeworld was not out of reach.

"Nice heavy tits on her too. Do you think she'll have back problems in later life?" Marie replied with magnificently feigned indifference.

"No, they'll just do a spine transplant on her."

The brunette's head harness was secured with two padlocks, one on each side of her collar. Fitting a key into one padlock, Lady Isobell smiled cruelly, realising that her inexperienced new sexual plaything had obviously known the young diplomat in her previous life. The Ambassador performed introductions, Marie promoted to Lady Marie, and Lady Isobell politely invited Marie to pop around to the family estate some time, to give the girl a ride! The old man's thumb penetrating her anus now, free hand between her legs, the helplessly aroused, deeply humiliated, sex slave gasped softly in time with fingers stroking in and out of her sex, slap-reddened slave breasts heaving. Mortified, cheeks scarlet, her blush spreading down her chest, the intelligent young law student clearly realised almost at once that behind Marie's polite, half-hearted, decorous, refusal, her former university friend was just a little tempted.

Head harness removed, at a barked command Ruth dropped to her knees in front of the old man she'd pulled away from, the Marquis settling himself into a chair. Directly under Marie's avid gaze, she licked and kissed a wrinkled flaccid cock into stiffness, her public apology for her initial misbehaviour. The old boy had a large, vein-swollen and eventually very hard shaft, surprising on such a wrinkled, shrunken old man. Lady Isobell impishly invited the Ambassador's secretary to hold her pet's lead while she went to the loo.

Marie looked down helplessly at her once virginal friend, on her knees with a cock in her mouth, with dozens of people watching. She looked around for her co-workers, a wide-eyed shrug denying responsibility for the lead pressed into her hand. Arms bound behind her, whip stripes on her buttocks, a corset cutting her waist down to a breathless but attractive eighteen inches, the former law student groaned around the huge veined shaft in her mouth as her over-large breasts were firmly and cruelly squeezed.

"How does she get it all in her mouth?" Marie blurted.

The question was probably directed to the Ambassador, but the old man sitting in front of Ruth answered amiably.

"She's trained to relax her throat muscles," the Marquis explained, quite unconcerned at his audience.

He squeezed his fingers deeper into the collared pet's big breasts, the British student's lips sliding down the length of his cock, until her nose brushed white pubic hair.

"See, I'm right down her throat now. I have to let her

come up for air occasionally of course, but a healthy young animal like this, can hold her breath a long time."

Ruth was looking a little red in the face by the time the grip on her breasts relaxed, and she was allowed to raise her head, but she was perfectly docile. A quick tit slapping in public, followed by a few whip strokes, had settled her down beautifully. Marie was looking a bit flushed herself, still holding her one-time university friend's lead as if it might bite her.

Marie's genial new friend, the Marquis, clearly appreciating a young girl's interest in his expertise at oral sex, went on to explain that the brunette was tit trained. Twisted nipples made her lick and nibble his penis, nipples squeezed, and she would kiss and lick the Marquis's balls. Otherwise her head would bob, lips tight around hot meat, in time with her breasts being squeezed.

Sympathetic tears long forgotten, Marie watched in increasingly rapt fascination while the white-haired aristocrat demonstrated. The sex slave on her knees in front of the old man moaned in pleasure as fingers twisted deeper and harder into her heavily enlarged breasts, docilely letting her user's grip control her mouth. With a grin, the Ambassador moved on, the faithful Puppy following with a soft moan.

He circulated, introducing himself, aristocrats and royalty being introduced to him in return, just like the usual reception round except that here he couldn't go ten paces without being invited to admire and inspect the human pets the invited dignitaries had on leads. Several Lords and Ladies offered him the use of their property; the lovely young women in chains offered to him, of course given no say in who would have sex with them, or what would be done to them. And there were full firm tits everywhere! He'd never imagined getting his hands on so many superb jugs. In public.

By the oil pit, watching two naked oil-gleaming girls grappling — mud wrestling a popular Slaveworld sport — he was invited to judge a wager.

Squeezing yet another pair of big heavy tits together, a

beautiful dark-eyed poodle moaning in pleasure as her nipples were rubbed back and forth across each other, the Ambassador found himself looking into another face he recognised. The Asian woman was older than most of the other sex toys on display, late twenties, maybe early thirties, but as foreign slaves were rare, her exotic looks probably made her more valuable than the younger run-of-the-mill blondes.

The plaything was tightly harnessed, thin silver-studded leather straps digging deep into her mocha tinted skin, arms secured behind her back, a crotch strap pulled up hard between clean-shaven sex lips holding in place a buzzing vibrator. Near her, you could hear a constant steady hum, feel the buzz through the panting sex toy's flesh when you stroked her belly. The naked woman's eyes were totally glazed. Punjabi Indian descended, originally a data analyst at MI5, he didn't remember her name, but even with much bigger and heavier tits, put on a serious diet and drooling around a ball gag, the Ambassador still recognised one of Ms Carson's captured British secret agents. Code name, Ms Violet.

It had to be more than a coincidence. Encountering some of Lady Franklin's five original students, naked on leads, was not entirely unexpected. According to reports, she and Queen Victoria were now firm friends. But Ms Violet made two faces he'd recognised from Security's 'Missing' files now, and Marie had identified a third. The Queen, making the not too subtle point that superb slaves were all his world had to offer the Slaveworld, had clearly chosen to provide some British entertainment.

Proudly holding the forcibly aroused woman's lead, the young Prince who owned her, idly stroked a buttock. Unconsciously, his fingers stroked back and forth over the brand set high on his property's right buttock, almost on the hip. A slight youth, he looked no more than eighteen, the dark-skinned beauty towering over him in a pet's five-inch heels.

Asked about the vibrator, the young Prince earnestly explained it was a permanent control, along with twice daily punishments; electric shocks to the Asian slave's heavily enlarged tits. Reading between the lines, the Ambassador guessed the former British agent, horrified and upset to find herself a bitch on heat with huge udders, and far too proud to properly submit herself to a teenager on her first day of service had been a less than satisfactory first ride. Perhaps she'd insulted the Prince, belittled him sexually, refused to perform oral sex or let him urinate in her mouth? The Prince didn't go into details, but the Ambassador got the idea the young virgin riding his first slave had ended up running to his mother in tears, and King Philip's furious sister had quickly devised a regime to break in her only son's unsatisfactory new sexual plaything.

The Ambassador felt himself grin again. The young Prince now owned a beautifully responsive mount, a joy to own and screw, but didn't realise the older woman was now thoroughly and totally broken in, probably within two or three days of his mother's intervention. He didn't realise the top-heavy sex toy no longer needed a permanent vibrator turning her into a mindless sexual animal to make her eager for degrading sex. Didn't realise that the lovely pet would be perfectly obedient now even if her breasts weren't locked into a tit clamp twice a day and repeatedly shocked with electrodes clamped to her nipples. In just one moment's unthinking defiance, the former secret agent had made her own life a living hell! And now she was too well trained to speak without permission, and tell the boy how much she longed to please him, how devoted she was to him, until he thought to ask her. The boy's unforgiving mother, who surely also realised the former agent was completely docile now, had advised her son to keep his slave permanently gagged, except for oral sex. To never allow her to speak in his presence.

The Ambassador turned away from the Asian beauty to an equally well-endowed blonde, and scooped up another pair of firm heavy tits. Warm, weighty, velvet, mounds tipped with pink nipples, settled into his palms and spilled between splayed fingers. The tongue-clamped blonde with elbows and wrists strapped together behind her back was the property of an eighty year old duchess. A good girl, quite placid, she clearly accepted without any reservations his right to handle her in public and was obviously quite delighted to find herself the centre of attention.

"Well, there's not a lot in it," he decided. "Blondie's tits look just slightly bigger because she's shorter, but I'd say the Prince's girl's are just a little heavier."

There were good natured groans and cheers from the group around him, money changing hands, wagered on his estimate of which slave had the weightier breasts. Truly Titworld had been well named.

"Sorry, what was that?"

He turned to find himself facing his hostess, the Queen of England, Her Most Gracious Majesty, Queen Victoria II, and swept her a formal bow.

"Sorry, just thinking aloud, Your Majesty."

The Queen gave him an enquiring look, and the Ambassador explained that the British Gate crew and Intelligence staff had informally christened her homeland, Titworld.

"Ah yes, I'd heard," she nodded.

Had she indeed. From where?

"You like big girls?"

"Oh yes," he agreed happily, taking the time to let his eyes roam over her own pet's chest.

Another face he recognised from the briefing photographs; Jenny, another of Lady Franklin's original research team. Tall, powerful, top heavy, Lady Isobell had once owned this girl he remembered. Glancing back at Ruth on her knees, head bobbing in time with her big breasts being squeezed, there was a clear resemblance. It seemed he wasn't the only one who had a preferred type.

The tall slave had an almost featureless metal band around her waist, practically cutting her in two, padlocked clamps swinging from her clamped nipples, breasts hugely and painfully milk swollen. Topping out at well over six foot tall in five-inch stiletto heels, the statuesque beauty was hobbled, her wristcuffs chained to the pussy lock threaded and padlocked through the rings set through her sex lips. Whip marks criss-crossed her buttocks, a few curling around hips.

"Feel free," Her Majesty waved him forward.

The former British student whimpered in helpless pain when her amazingly distended udders were handled, but was otherwise quite placid when the Ambassador handled her. The look in her eyes was the same regal disinterest you saw in the eyes of a caged lion at a zoo. The Ambassador realised that being owned, displayed bound and being handled by strangers, had become normal for her, that only what Queen Victoria — the mistress she adored and loved — wanted from her was of any consequence to the tall brunette. If Her Majesty gave him the proud girl to play with or ride, the Ambassador was sure she'd be perfectly responsive, the best screw he'd ever had, but only because the Queen wished it. As an individual, he was of no interest at all to the chained pet.

The padlocked clamps screwed down on the bases of her nipples looked incredibly painful, and the polished steel look — pussy lock, collar, chains, and wrist, ankle and elbow cuffs all in shiny silver chrome — was very attractive. Her nametag, swinging on a short length of chain from a pierced earlobe, said the naked girl answered to Precious now.

With smaller tits he could easily imagine the powerful beauty cast as an Amazon warrior type in a Sword and Sorcery style film or TV series back home. She had a real presence. He'd always liked cute little things for preference, but that was limiting himself to a type again. First Lady Isobell, the young Prince and now Queen Victoria clearly got an extra kick out of subduing and riding a slave bigger and more powerful than themselves. He let his hand stroke slowly up a firm inner thigh. Imagining the magnificent brunette chained down under him during sex, bucking and fighting her restraints, did make a very nice image actually.

Queen Victoria mistook his daydreaming for hesitation.

"You know my pet's pedigree of course. Is it different for you, with a girl from your own world?"

"A little," he agreed anyway.

"But if you didn't know?"

Suddenly suspicious, he looked around at the lovely slave flesh on display with new eyes. The naked girls in the oil pit, squirming together as they tried to anally screw one another with strap-on dildos! The two blondes with their arms strapped behind their backs, facing away from each other in the tug-of-war competition. Pulled forward with strings tied to their nipples, whipped forward with lash after lash across the ass. Tits bound, the rope running down between their legs to the other breast-roped girl, the two girls strained against each other. All young, beautiful, expensive and mostly top-heavy.

There was Puppy, still obediently following him; and the blonde whose tits he'd compared to Ms Carson's captured agent, Lady Isobell's brunette. There were the blowpipe competition's human darts targets, the slaves on their knees in the alcoves providing oral sex for the guests, and every pet on a lead. Each and every one of them was from his own homeworld!

Set up! The Ambassador let a grin of appreciation slip across his face.

"Point made. British girls make stunning sex slaves," he agreed, "but our system of government has to look on their harvest as a hostile act, I'm afraid."

"Harvest? A good word, but discussing your world with my good friend Lady Franklin, I came across another word. Conscription!"

Oh, she was good. How was he going to argue that one? If a democratic government could call up young men against their will and send them off to die in war for the greater good, then why not sex slaves. The technological benefit to Britain would be just as great.

"A fascinating suggestion, I'll have to raise it with my superiors," he said honestly.

Conscription was actually a neat solution to the thin ice the Slaveworlders found themselves on. For as the Ambassador had pointed out, while their own working class could be quite legally sentenced to sexual slavery under

Slaveworld law; most of the British slaves, no matter how submissive, had been kidnapped, and were guilty of no crimes here.

In all honesty, British Intelligence didn't really care, but it did give Britain a legal claim to reparations. An out of court settlement. The Ambassador had already negotiated free youth treatments for the five elderly members of Gate Project's Civil Service executive. Keep the boss happy was a motto that had mostly served him well and he definitely didn't want to get fired from this job.

The middle-aged monarch, leading a helpless, young, naked and cruelly bound British girl on a collar and lead, nodded amiably. The Ambassador was well aware his hostess wanted something from him. The Slaveworld's Queen of England might attend a reception for a new Ambassador, but would not normally personally organise one. And personally select the sex slaves! What it was she was after, he might or might not find out today. But patience was the name of the diplomatic game.

First and most urgently, the two countries had needed an agreement, 'an understanding,' and now that the treaty was signed, an embassy established, they could get to know and accommodate one another. Patience again. Realistically, British Intelligence wanted the technology, medical advances and youth treatment the Slaveworld had to offer and wasn't about to let its hooks out of the alternative reality any time soon.

It was in a large part the Ambassador's job to persuade the Slaveworlders that even with the supply of the new superior sex slaves officially cut off, their visitors still had more to offer than the threat of unexpected nuclear annihilation. Officially, the kidnapping of British citizens to turn into sex slaves was not acceptable. But what he had to get across was, unofficially, say for helping us build a fusion reactor, we might look the other way, if, say ten girls and two boys went quietly missing. The Privy Councillors he'd dealt with so far were mostly having trouble with the concept of being seen to do the right thing, without actually being too concerned about doing it.

Politically, they were quite naive! The Ambassador had been obliquely explaining the concept of "deniability" at some length but the concept still seemed to puzzle his hosts. They'd owned slaves for over two thousand years, and even the serfs and workers had long ago accepted sexual slavery was the way things were, always had been and always would be. No one here saw anything in the slightest wrong with sentencing shoplifters to a few years of sexual slavery. And as for a government signing a treaty because it was the right thing to do, but not actually intending to abide by that treaty. Who concerned themselves with what the lower classes thought of one to that extent?

They were certainly going out of their way to be hospitable though. They'd even agreed to the return of some of the older British secret agents under arrest, and asked nothing in return. It had been politely and apologetically explained to the Ambassador that there was no chance of the younger agents being returned. They had already been sold, or were in pet shop windows all over the Kingdom. Parading Ms Violet naked in front of him in her bonds, had again been a rather unsubtle way of making the point, he thought. But it showed that the Queen at least, unlike some of the Royal Privy Council, seemed to be able to think in more than just two dimensions. Rule by inbred aristocrats, he was discovering, really did seem to limit your choice of talent.

In due time, seeing how the new official relationship turned out first, Queen Victoria would let him know how he could help her. Stroking the stripes on Precious's backside, the Ambassador nodded approvingly to himself. It was the way the game should be played. You didn't put all your cards on the table at once. Toned muscle flexed under the velvet buttock he was stroking as Precious shifted her weight from one foot to the other. The tall dairy slave really was just magnificent, and Queen Victoria didn't miss his stirring erection. On another world, the parallel universe he called home, nothing would have been said, but here, it was different!

"You should do something about that," the middle aged

woman said solicitously. "It doesn't do to keep these things in."

Suddenly flustered, feeling pushed, events slipping beyond his control — probably what the clearly intelligent woman intended — the Queen took his arm and led him to the nearest pair of alcoves. Straps tight around their bodies, arms and ankles secured behind stout tree-trunk-thick posts, two lovely girls looked up at his approach. Almost automatically, he selected the big-breasted blonde. The Ambassador pulled the waist-high curtain closed, fumbled his flies open, and a hot, moist, mouth instantly enveloped his cock.

To his utter amazement, the Ambassador found himself chatting to the Slaveworld's Queen Victoria about the weather, while a naked girl strapped to a large pole on her knees, fellated him. The alcove's curtain provided privacy from the other reception guests, but the Queen standing beside him could look over the curtain and down, watching soft lips sliding up and down his penis. She occasionally did.

Victoria, out of curiosity, and perhaps with other reasons as well, had questioned many of the British sex slaves about their former lives. Stroking Puppy's freckled belly, she casually informed him the girl pulling the dildo trolley was a medical student. She confirmed Lady Isobell's new pet, the brunette with the newly large breasts, was a former law student. The blonde sex toy slowly licking up the Ambassador's cock from between his balls was not actually British, she was a Hungarian exchange student who had encountered the RSP's trap questionnaire.

Queen Victoria patted the bobbing blonde's head. The fantasies the young closet submissive had never confided to anyone but had hesitantly put down on a supposedly confidential questionnaire — assured by the charming market researcher that the psychological profile she'd been paid twenty pounds for was completely anonymous and just for marketing research — had meant her first sexual experience had been a three into one, in chains, on a public stage in front of an audience of twenty.

“Does your government object to us harvesting foreigners?” Victoria asked.

“Officially, it’s not our concern, as long as they don’t disappear inside our borders,” he replied carefully.

The Queen nodded thoughtfully. They were both thinking the same. Could the British government be blamed if French or Irish girls went missing in their own countries? Especially, when officially Britain knew nothing about their disappearance. The Ambassador smiled. He was probably going to be able to charge a ten per cent agent’s fee for each African girl his friend the general sold to the Slaveworld!

“She’s got a great mouth on her,” the Ambassador changed the subject with a sigh, thrusting his cock hard into the back of the top-heavy blonde’s mouth with handfuls of hair now.

“Yes, I’ve used her,” Victoria agreed. “That one,” she waved to another deliciously top-heavy poodle, “takes good whip. A former Sunday school teacher I believe. Now that one there, he’s a gymnast. Very flexible!”

The Ambassador nodded helplessly, close to coming now. He wasn’t as good at carrying on a normal conversation while having sex as his practised hosts.

“We’ve even got one of your police officers in a collar,” the Queen added. “Would you like to see her?”

“Sure,” he groaned, come pumping into the bound girl’s mouth in spasm after spasm.

Looking up at him with wide baby-blue eyes, the young slave obediently swallowed his semen, a look of momentary revulsion on her face at the task she had to perform, not quite concealed. With a chuckle, the Ambassador gave her breasts an approving squeeze, the blonde moaning in pleasure as the lust-swollen globes were squeezed. Giving pleasure to many but permitted none herself, she was quite clearly desperately aroused, dripping wet with aching hard nipples. The well-trained sex slave he’d just enjoyed then placidly licked his cock clean, the Lady taking the alcove after him quite matter-of-factly hitching her skirt over the top of the post the young Hungarian philosophy student was bound to.

"Yes, I think I'd quite like to see a cop sex slave," the Ambassador said contentedly.

The Queen nodded and led him to the ballroom's grand staircase, collecting Lady Isobell and Lady Abigail on the way. Both young Ladies were clearly on intimate terms with the Queen's tall pet, Precious, handling the big girl's naked body and milk-heavy breasts with an easy familiarity. The group paused beside the Marquis in his chair.

"Hold this for me a moment would you, dear?" Victoria asked, holding out her pet's lead.

Marie, down on one knee, a hand between her one-time university friend's legs, working her fingers deep into the corseted law student's pouting sex in time with her bobbing head, looked up with a guilty start. The brunette on her knees before the Marquis, lips obediently sliding up and down his cock in time with her breasts being cruelly squeezed, was now forced to gasp in pleasure around the hot meat shaft in her mouth with each squeeze, as cruel fingers were thrust hard into her sex. She was gasping for breath now, hips twitching as Marie teased her, her hands pulled up high behind her back and secured to the back of her collar, were desperately fluttering but she still obediently let her user's cock slide deep down her throat with every firm breast squeeze.

The Ambassador's suddenly flustered secretary found herself helplessly holding a second naked, chained, slavegirl's lead in one hand, her free fingers glistening with her bound, tit-trained, abjectly humiliated, university friend's juices. Precious whined in soft protest at being abandoned, and was carelessly punished with a quick slap across the behind by her owner. Oblivious to the shocked looks of her embassy co-workers, with a dreamy look Marie ran an admiring palm over the handprint on the tall, dairy slave's, buttock.

They strolled down the staircase four abreast. Puppy following, pulled her trolley to the edge of the staircase and then whined softly, squeaking loudly as a sensor detected she was out of range of the Ambassador's bracelet; and shocked her with the dildo prong she pulled her trolley with.

The Ambassador paused halfway down the staircase, looking back up at the naked girl's freckled body. Wristcuffs chained to nipple rings, orange ball gag nicely complementing her ginger hair, the lovely serving slave in stiletto heels twitched, breasts bobbing, as the dildo that impaled her shocked her again. He laughed, and continued on his way. A former medical student should be bright enough to figure it out.

In the entrance hall, as the group paused to admire the sex slaves on display in glass cases, the service elevator's doors opened with a soft chime. Eyes wide, heels tip-tapping in a frantic staccato on the marble floor, a sheen of sweat on her flanks, yelping behind her gag, Puppy burst out of the lift and raced to the Ambassador's side. The ease with which the naked girl could pull the heavy dildo trolley at a trot in a hobble was quite impressive.

Queen Victoria took a moment to soothe the trembling redhead, stroking her belly with one hand, her free hand twisted into the girl's hair, pulling her head back and making her look up. Big freckle-dusted breasts heaving as she panted, Puppy moaned in pleasure as a palm pressed up against the pussy-stretching dildo that had been shocking her. The action was as natural, and the sympathy as superficial, as that with which a noble woman on another world might soothe a frightened horse.

"I'm surprised she could operate the lift," the Ambassador said with a chuckle.

"Oh, an erect nipple is stiff enough to press the buttons, if the girl is properly hot." Queen Victoria explained matter-of-factly. She pressed her fingers deeper into Puppy's belly making the girl groan. "Though shocks deep inside the vagina are much more distracting than say, electrodes clipped to the sex lips."

"Much more," Lady Abigail agreed, playfully flicking one of the redhead's nipples.

The former British police officer turned out to be the top-heavy pony girl the Ambassador had seen the young Lady Abigail lash across the courtyard. Recovered from her previous exertions, the harnessed and bridled sex toy stood motionless between the shafts of her pony trap — just breathing steadily — looking directly ahead as she was inspected, handled and admired by Lady Isobell and the Ambassador. Lady Abigail watched proudly.

Her bridle secured to her harness, and her blinkers, didn't let the one-time policewomen look at anyone who was not directly in front of her but the Ambassador and the three noble ladies were free to view the cute little slave from all angles. She flinched a couple of times when her striped buttocks were stroked, but otherwise accepted up to four pairs of hands on her naked, bound, body at once, quite placidly and with evident pleasure. Clearly in the process of having her hair colour changed, the lower two inches was growing through a nice honey blonde.

The harness girth was as tight as Precious's metal waist cincher, or the corset laced and padlocked around Lady Isobell's brunette. It probably took the slavegirls longer, but the Ambassador thought he could get used to eighteen-inch waists very quickly. Top-heavy girls especially looked superb with an hourglass figure, tits always appearing heavier, buttocks plumply spankable.

The docile pony girl's delightfully enlarged breasts were very firmly bound, a tight strap looped around the base of each full globe, thinner criss-crossed supporting straps further squeezing the heavy mounds. Her reins were clipped to her nipple rings, running through a ring on each side of her bit, and a heavy metal bar with a screw-down clamp at each end linked the abused nubs. Asking about the nipple bar, Lady Abigail explained the cruel device was to weigh the top-heavy pony's breasts down, and make the over-large globes swing neatly together at a trot.

"So that she doesn't bounce about too untidily," the aristocrat said carelessly.

A hint of a blush touched the former policewomen's cheeks. The swell of her stomach above and below her cruel girth was more noticeable as excitement made her breathe faster and deeper, but otherwise the dark-eyed slavegirl was quite calm as two strangers handled her bound breasts, her teeth resting lightly on the rubber-coated bar buckled hard into her mouth. Two broad cuffs above each elbow, padlocked to her body harness, locked her arms to her sides, her wristcuffs double locked to the trap's shafts, in front of and behind her hands.

Demonstrating the nipple bar, Lady Abigail gave her property's breasts a few stinging slaps, her palm cracking loudly on squeezed taut flesh. Tightly bound, the harnessed globes just quivered a little instead of swinging back and forth, but the way the movement of one breast dragged excruciatingly at the tightly clamped nipple of the other, was clearly and painfully demonstrated. Still the helpless slave made no move to twist away, just closed her eyes in resignation, teeth biting tighter into her rubber coated bit, gasping softly as her huge tits were slapped forehand and back by her young owner. Again and again.

The pretty pony slave also had an unusual crotch strap. All the Slaveworld pony girls he'd seen so far had been fitted with a nice tight crotch strap pulled up hard between the sex lips. Even if the strap digging into the girl's belly didn't hold in place a fat dildo, butt plug or both, it looked attractive. And a light pressure against the clitoris kept the slave hot and bothered! But this pony girl had a Y-shaped crotch strap down her belly holding the usual fat dildo and butt plug in place, which also allowed a chain running from the girth to pierced clitoris, to drag up at the ring-set nub. It was a permanent torment, Lady Abigail explained, the chain also usually padlocked to a corset or belt, as well as today's girth. The clit chain lying taut across her belly apparently made the satin-skinned sex toy a better ride in bed.

Tightly gripping the twin carriage shafts her hands were secured to, knuckles white, the pony girl cried out in desperate obedient pleasure around her bit as her owner stroked her cruelly stretched, chained, clitoris. It was clear to the Ambassador that the slender young aristocrat was absolutely delighted with her cute new plaything.

The Ambassador scooped up both breasts. Squeezing the bound melons hard enough to make the placid slave moan in pain, he thought her tits were probably the equal of the spectacular brunette Lady Isobell owned, though squeezed out into perfect pink spheres by the tight harness straps, it was hard to be sure. Certainly quite huge! Not quite as large as the Queen's pet, Precious, but they might be, if allowed to become as painfully milk-swollen.

She was a walking wet dream, but to his faint disappointment, only marginally more sexy than the many other naked, bound, sex slaves he'd seen today. Though he'd occasionally fantasised about seeing a lady cop like this, ever since being written a speeding ticket on the M25 by a pretty but officious WPC, now he found that humiliating and teasing a former British policewomen — while thoroughly enjoyable — didn't give him the extra buzz he'd expected.

The problem was, she was just too perfect a pony girl. He decided he needed to at least see a picture of her in uniform, before she'd been collared, to really believe that this docile, voluptuous, quite perfect sex object had ever once wielded authority. At the Queen's suggestion Puppy was stood alongside the naked pony girl. Once the padlocks on her shoes' ankle straps were unlocked and the redhead was stood alongside the bridled brunette in bare feet — the pony girl fitted with trainer-like running slippers — they were all agreed that if Puppy's breasts were grown a bit larger to match, the two would make a beautiful dressage team. Perfectly matched!

"I thought her pedigree said she had a pussy lock, like my Precious," Queen Victoria said.

"I had the rings cut off," Lady Abigail replied carelessly. "Too much protection when I whipped her between the legs!"

The carefree young Lady, proudly displaying her top-heavy mount, didn't realise it, but the Ambassador suspected the Queen also had an agenda for her, or for her pony girl. Why else would the Monarch look up the British slave's pedigree? The Queen had also deliberately manoeuvred the two slaves side by side, and the match was more than coincidence. Perhaps Victoria just wanted to buy

Abigail's new girl, or perhaps it was something more. Probably not his concern, but there again, perhaps it might be. All would be revealed in good time.

It never even occurred to him to refuse, when Lady Abigail offered to let him take her property for a quick drive.

"Actually, do you mind if I use my own whip?" he added quickly.

"But of course."

"Please excuse me a moment."

A perfectly normal Slaveworld request, though to be honest, he didn't really have enough experience with a carriage whip to have a preference. The Ambassador was actually dashing up to his office to check his files. He'd suddenly realised the cop might be on file. He half remembered a policewoman's file in amongst the collection listing missing Britons, agents and Phillips-Webber's five original students.

Yes. It was her! Fantastic. Some bright spark had even clipped WPC Barncroft's warrant card to her Security file. Even better, she wasn't just a former cop, she was still serving. Officially just listed as seconded to the Intelligence Service. Delighted, he slipped the I.D. into his pocket, grabbed a carriage whip, and in moments was apologising to the three noble slave owners for keeping them waiting.

"Quite all right," the Queen assured him.

She had to want something. Even Lady Isobell was starting to look a little thoughtful at how accommodating Queen Victoria was being now.

"Enjoy." Lady Abigail said as he settled into the pony trap's comfortable seat, helpfully unclipping her property's hobble for him.

Idiot! What an elementary mistake. More cautiously, he took up the slack on the reins, slowly pulling up both heavy strap-bound breasts, feeling their substantial weight through the reins he held. Both nipples pulled, the harnessed and bridled sex object obediently walked backwards. Very neatly, more luck that judgement, he backed his docile mount off the grass and onto the driveway around a limousine.

"Walk on," the Ambassador ordered firmly, punctuating the order with a firm whip stroke across both buttocks.

The police officer secured naked between the shafts of the carriage gasped and obediently moved off. His lush mount had a strap pulled up hard between her buttocks, secured to the back of her waist-nipping girth, both whip-striped hemispheres criss-crossed with raised welts and red lines. Almost mesmerised by the delightful roll of the wonderfully obedient pony girl's haunches, it took Lady Abigail's encouraging call to remind him to whip his gorgeous mount into a trot.

"Trot on!"

Leather licked across flesh with a harder stinging crack. With a grunt of effort, the big-breasted pony girl moved into a smart trot. Obviously quite a fit little beast under her puppy fat, she quickly settled into a brisk pace, pulling the sprung pony trap very smoothly. Her ass, right in front of him, just a whip's length away, had the most beautiful wiggle to it at the trot. With a happy grin he remembered his mount's dildo, imagining it flexing and thrusting inside the cop as her firm satin thighs pumped.

Even without his whip stinging her buttocks, a soft squeaking gasp was forced from her with every step. Lovely! If there was one thing the Ambassador knew about slavegirls, it was that making a girl trot with a large dildo strapped inside her was a wonderfully cruel torment. The archway approaching, he gave his naked mount a couple more whip strokes to keep her focused on obeying him.

The prancing pony girl could not turn her head, her bridle secured to her harness at the shoulders, blinkers further restricting her vision. She had to trust the Ambassador totally to look left and right, and not to drive her out in front of a car on the main road. She didn't falter by even a half step as she was driven through the archway, a firm yank on the left nipple with a rein turning her down the street past his embassy, and no doubt, his watching staff.

The pretty little pony girl was breathing harder now, but

a steady flurry of firm whip flicks across her beautifully curved haunches easily kept her pace up. Her squeaks and gasps became gradually louder as the Ambassador's whip left new red lines across bouncing buttocks, pushing her faster; but without the slightest hint of protest. A well-trained pony girl accepted the necessity of being firmly whipped if her driver was to get the best out of her.

As soon as he was out of sight of the divided former townhouse, the Ambassador pulled his human mount in beside the curb and parked her. The few other aristocrats about ignored him, a street sweeper quickly looking down at his work when he dismounted. He ran a hand over a hot, further reddened buttock, and stepped over the pony trap's shaft. His pony's tightly bound, strap-supported breasts were rising and falling rapidly now, the first rivulet of saliva running down one of the bulging mounds as the well-whipped police officer panted around her bit.

He stepped in front of the pony slave where she could see him. In a bridle and blinkers, her eyes now dyed a dark violet and with a bit buckled tight into her mouth, it was actually a little hard to tell from just the police I.D. card's photograph if it was the same person. But the way the pony girl's eyes widened in surprise when she saw her own warrant card, and then a mortified, horrified, deeply embarrassed, blush spread across her cheeks, were all the confirmation he needed. Now he was getting the buzz he'd anticipated! The Ambassador wedged the naked cop's I.D. under her clit chain, and let his hands rest on huge heavy tits, the harness straps really making the full mounds balloon.

"Officer Barncroft. You've been a very naughty girl!"

There was fear in the pony girl's eyes, the tips of her clamped nipples — supporting the heavy steel nipple bar that linked the abused nubs — hard against his palms. She moaned in helpless, forced pleasure when he squeezed her bound breasts, but he could feel a little apprehensive tremor run though her.

"I gather a certain Ms Carson would very much like to discuss your defection with you."

His plaything shivered.

"But don't you worry," he soothed, "I'm not here to take you home. You're obviously quite happy where you are. I'm just going to enjoy you."

A wave of palpable relief washed over the helpless slavegirl. Standing naked between the shafts of a small carriage on a public street, with a happy moan she gratefully leant into his grip, thankfully pushing her bound swollen breasts harder into the Ambassador's hands to be further abused. A key hung from the British WPC's left earlobe like an earring, and curious, he unlocked the two padlocks the sex slave's Y-shaped crotch strap.

"Jesus Christ!"

Lady Abigail was clearly an exacting mistress. The dildo he slid halfway out of the heavy-titted pony girl, and then forced back into her, was absolutely huge. Bigger than anything he'd ever strapped into one of the general's playthings. The bridled slave flinched minutely when she heard the padlocks snap back into place, the giant intruder now locked deep inside her body again. She was panting faster still.

"Can you run in that?" the Ambassador wondered.

Eyes sparkling with excitement, eager to please now that she realised she was just going to be cruelly used and enjoyed, not rescued, his borrowed pony girl responded with an obedient whinny, nodding her head as far as her bridle would allow. She groaned, eyes closing, when he pressed his palm into her belly.

"Uncomfortable?"

Another obedient whinny.

"Very uncomfortable?"

Again, yes.

"And the butt plug? Just as big?"

The docile little show pony again responded with another soft whinny. Pausing to nod politely to a Lady driving a pony boy, the Ambassador squeezed his desperately aroused mount's bound breasts again and gave the welts on her behind another stroke. Squeezed out of her body when he'd forced the fat dildo back into her, the helpless police officer's juices welled around her crotch strap, running down her inner thighs.

Slowly and deliberately, the Ambassador pulled the strap around the base of each big breast a notch tighter, the heavy globes squeezed out even bigger, skin now shiny-taut and drum-tight. The panting pony girl of course could not look down, but she must surely have thought her tits were going to burst. Fishing in his pocket for one of the little sharp-jawed, spring-loaded, metal clamps he'd got in the habit of carrying around since being assigned here, he carefully applied it to the helpless slavegirl's clitoris. The ring-set nub was easy to clamp, already cruelly stretched, pulled up hard to the whimpering sex toy's brutal eighteen-inch girth with a length of chain

The helpless plaything's eyes went wide, teeth biting down hard on her bit as she squealed in agony. Snorting through her nose, tears welling in her beautiful wide violet eyes, she did a desperate little dance, twisting this way and that, knees buckling! She took a step back, back again, forward; and then realising there was no escape from the atrocious pain, forced herself to put her ankles neatly back together and stand still again. Panting hard made her drool all the more on her bound breasts.

The Ambassador was impressed. His married blonde had screeched and thrashed about helplessly; had eventually had to be gagged as well as tied down tightly spreadeagled on his bed, when he'd put one of the same clamps onto her clitoris before shafting her. Perhaps acclimatised by the permanent cruel clit chain Lady Abigail kept her in, the still-serving British police officer was enduring a tortured clitoris almost placidly by comparison. A few nearly silent, heaving, sobs, gave the trembling pony girl's bound tits a nice additional quiver and she was leaving teeth marks in her bit, wide eyes swimming with tears, but she still didn't make one sound of protest. He let his tongue flick across the tip of clamp-crushed nipples, and clearly desperately aroused, his harnessed plaything cried out in ecstasy.

He looked around the street, wondering if his pony girl's heart-rending cry of pain or shriek of pleasure had attracted untoward attention, but this was the Slaveworld! As an honorary aristocrat, he was legally quite free to publicly torment, tease and torture the big-titted slave hitched to his small carriage, as he wished. To anyone watching, the naked girl in harness and bridle was just a convicted criminal, atoning for her crime.

As her juices continued to well around her crotch strap, he wished he had another sharp-jawed clamp or two to put on her clitoris. He realised that the gasping pony girl was not only forcibly aroused, but was just as intoxicated by her surroundings as he was. But he still couldn't resist rubbing her situation in still further.

"I've always wanted to whip a cop," he whispered in the pony girl's ear, big breasts rising and falling faster as he toyed with clamped, weighted down, nipples. "Ever since some tight-ass bitch on the M25 gave me a ticket."

Happily, he settled himself back into the pony trap's seat. His docile mount moved off at an obedient trot from a standing start, encouraged with braided leather licking back and forth across bouncing buttocks. Her squeaks as she was lashed were louder, had a nicely desperate edge to them; now that the pretty little sex toy was forced to trot and prance with sharp little metal jaws biting into her clitoris. Wanting an audience, he drove her to the nearby High Street, a row of shops serving the local area, busy enough to justify four sets of traffic lights.

Lashed into a sprint away from traffic lights, his human mount became even more shrill, needed a lot more whip, but the Ambassador was amazed she could even walk, let alone run, stuffed to bursting point, front and rear with dildo and butt plug as she was! Just thinking about the huge twin shafts she had strapped and locked inside her, made him hard.

Racing other pony slaves away from the lights, or just politely trying not to hold up faster limousines, he was raising welts on the slave's ass now. Lathered in sweat and panting harshly around her bit, to use another local phrase, his pony girl definitely took good whip. Juices running down her inner thighs, ass surely on fire, nipples excruciatingly yanked with reins and the weight of the nipple bar that made her breasts swing and bounce neatly together — not to mention sharp little metal teeth biting into her clitoris — she was beautifully responsive to his commands, whip and reins.

Probably sweat blind and with her lungs burning, forced into a sprint whenever the Ambassador wished, the big-breasted sex toy could not actually see the pony-pulled carriages alongside her with which she was being competed with her vision restricted. It took more whip each time, but lashed hard, without respite, the sweat-gleaming pony girl with a bar code and serial number tattooed on her right buttock, would obediently lunge forward against her burden with a maddened, agonised wail, giving every race everything she had! Her desperate cries, the crack of the Ambassador's whip on her haunches and the bounce of her huge tits, turned many appreciative heads.

The Ambassador was in heaven. It still amazed him that the lovely creature he drove had once worn a police uniform, but her warrant card safely back in his pocket had left no doubt in his mind now. She was terrific fun to torment and humiliate!

Besides, tit straps, a pussy full of dildo, a bit to bite on and a firm hand, clearly suited her. He was actually being very fair with her, he thought. He had been entirely honest when he said he wasn't going to attempt to set her free. Ms Carson would probably enjoy making the twenty three year old defector's life unpleasant, but in all honesty the Ambassador thought Ms Carson probably wouldn't be nearly as good at it as the angelic looking Lady Abigail.

His dildo-stuffed, clit-clamped toy eventually collapsed exhausted to her knees, and had to be whipped back to her feet. Pony girls, unless they were big powerful animals like the Queen's Precious, were usually worked in pairs or four-teams, not alone. The Ambassador parked his harshly panting mount outside a small café while he sipped an espresso, to allow her to regain her breath. Admiring the sweat-gleaming police officer's harnessed body, bound tits now nicely purple, he did hope she realised how much he was enjoying her.

Finally, prancing smartly back through the townhouse archway that led to the British Embassy and the new Ministry of Offworld Affairs, his gasping, slavering, sweat-lathered little pony girl managed not to drop to her knees again, until after the Ambassador had dismounted. A beautifully trained animal.

He returned to the reception, and profusely thanked Lady Abigail for the loan of her plaything, Puppy with her shock dildo again switched on, once more following him. A slavegirl he barely even looked at provided more oral relief in one of the curtained alcoves.

It was a good hour or so later, happening to glance out of a window and down at the assembled pony slaves below, that he remembered he'd forgotten to take the clamp off his borrowed slave's clitoris and loosen her tit straps after his drive. He chuckled, hand closing around the police warrant card in his pocket. No matter. It wasn't as if the heavy-titted sex object was allowed to complain!

CHAPTER EIGHT

Perhaps out of a warped sense of humour, or more likely a genuine desire to see justice done, the Magistrate dealing with Ruth's appeal had decided the former British law student's case had some merit – contrary to the opinion of the majority of nobles who really did believe that their legal system was fair and that sexual service was a just punishment for many crimes — and should be heard by a judge in a full Court of Law. Ruth, perhaps suspecting the Slaveworld's legal profession might not have her best interests at heart, had opted to represent herself.

A bailiff showed the British Ambassador, accompanied by his secretary Marie, to a plush bench seat outside the courtroom. Ruth had called him as a witness.

Settling himself comfortably, legs stretched out in front of him, the Ambassador allowed himself a smile. Quite clever of the girl really. The former law student was making it obvious she was going to bring up the existence of other worlds, and that travel was possible between them, in the hope that the authorities on either side would rather see the case quietly settled instead of having the invention of the dimensional Gate made public.

It wasn't going to work of course. The British girl had forgotten the Slaveworld media was state controlled. Her hearing, which had attracted some interest, would still be broadcast on the Slaveworld's 3V, but suitably edited of all references to Britain and alternative universes. The hearing was in all the news feeds, Ruth's pedigree and information on whether she was for sale, suddenly being accessed from the public central data base as often as some champion competition slaves. A convicted sex slave's appeal taking place in a proper court happened once in a decade. By making herself interesting, the British girl had actually added a good five thousand Crowns to her auction value. Several floating news cameras had been overhead on the courthouse steps when Lady Isobell had stepped out of her limousine leading the naked slave.

Inside, looking around the central hall, the petite aristocrat gave the Ambassador a brief smile of recognition, and led her helpless property over to their bench. The tall sex toy was looking particularly fetching today, wearing nothing but five-inch stiletto heeled sandals and a nice light gold tan. Her arms were firmly secured behind her back, folded wrist to elbow, a body harness's straps tight around wrists, elbows and upper arms. Thin straps, cutting deep into the brunette's stomach, criss-crossed between her over-large breasts, over her shoulders and a single strand ran snugly around her neck. Large matching sapphires hung from each nipple ring and a third swung between firm thighs on a short length of chain from the naked plaything's clit ring.

A matching black-leather head harness, similar to the one the British slave had been fitted with at the Queen's embassy reception, held a broad strap tight across the doe-eyed brunette's mouth. The difference here was an opening over the mouth, which was stoppered with what looked exactly like a bath plug on a short length of chain. Presumably so that, if necessary, the girl could speak for herself in court. There were fresh whip stripes on the naked sex toy's belly and big breasts, the heavy mounds jiggling and quivering quite delightfully with every step. More angry red lines curled around and over the firm swell of the former law student's hips, her buttocks undoubtedly well marked.

Under Slaveworld law, you were guilty until proven innocent!

After a casual hello, Lady Isobell reached out and pulled out her slave's gag. What had looked like a bath plug on a chain, linked to Ruth's chinstrap, was actually the base of a short fat dildo, no doubt stretching the helpless girl's mouth wide open. At a barked command, Ruth dropped to her knees, slave breasts squashed into the cold marble floor and only minutes away from the hearing that would decide her fate, tongue projecting through the steel ring in the strap across her mouth, began placidly licking her owner's shoes clean.

The Ambassador's guess had been right. Her ass was covered in the criss-crossed welts of a severe whipping! Lady Isobell looked around impatiently.

"Well how long are we expected to wait?" the aristocrat demanded.

"The bailiff just said to wait here."

The aristocrat had clearly never had to deal with the British Civil Service, and was obviously not used to being kept waiting. Recognising Marie, she gave the Ambassador's secretary her kneeling slave's lead to hold again, stuffed the chain-hanging dildo back into Ruth's mouth, and went off to find out what was happening. Ruth swayed upright, sitting on her heels, thighs spread obediently wide to expose her pussy. Naked, on her knees, firmly gagged and with her arms strapped tightly behind her back, the beautiful slave looked calmly into the eyes of her one-time friend. Her heavily enlarged breasts rose and fell gently, the girl's breathing slow and calm, the Ambassador quite liking the way her waist strap dug deeper into her stomach with each breath. The brunette's nipples were very hard, juices glinted on her pussy rings and on the chain suspending a sapphire from her pierced clitoris, but there was not a hint of panic in her eyes. Under Marie's avid gaze, she held her head up proudly.

She'd obviously had time to get used to the idea that her one-time university friend, now holding her lead, would not only make no attempt to rescue her, but was actually turned on by her humiliating servitude! Marie, obviously delighted to be given charge of her former friend — naked and helpless — but still wrestling with a residue of guilt, fidgeted in her seat, fiddling with the lead she held. Her gaze on the rise and fall of Ruth's over-large breasts was rapt with wonder.

"Oh give them a squeeze. You know you want to," the Ambassador chuckled.

Ruth, kneeling naked and bound at Marie's feet, groaned in soft, helpless, forced, pleasure as her one-time friend's fingers sank deep into her hugely enlarged breasts, the weighty mounds lifted and squeezed together. Eyes sparkling, licking suddenly dry lips, Marie squeezed harder, making the former law student moan in mingled pain and pleasure. Marie held up both heavy globes by their nipples a moment, and then gave each breast a few experimental slaps.

"She can take more than that," the Ambassador said in soft encouragement.

"Yes?" Marie breathed.

The following blows were hard, then harder, stinging slaps that left angry red splotches all over the gold-tanned, whip-striped melons. Ruth gasped and squeaked behind her gag as slap after slap rained down on her tits, heavy flesh bouncing this way and that. She blinked away tears, but apart from little involuntary twitches as Marie's palm stung her breasts, held herself mostly still, looking directly into her tormentor's eyes — her one-time friend — as she'd been trained to.

"Ow," Marie shook her hand. "That stings!"

The kneeling sex toy's deliciously big tits soon glowed an angry, throbbing, burning, scarlet. She was panting around the dildo that filled her mouth now. Marie let her fingernails trail over the abused melons, plucking swollen, aching nipples and laughed in delight when the bound sex slave she'd punished involuntarily shivered.

Finally Marie pulled the dildo out of her one-time friend's mouth again, and waited breathless for the former law student to beg, to plead. To protest! Panting gently, eyes sparkling bright, Ruth was obediently silent, just groaning softly when the Ambassador's secretary squeezed her slap-reddened breasts again. Clearly slightly disappointed, Marie ordered the naked girl to lick clean her own shoes. The bound slave obeyed without hesitation.

"I made her come three times at the party when she was sucking on that old Marquis's cock," Marie said with shy pride.

She leaned forward, fingers briefly exploring the straps that bound her former university friend's arms securely folded behind her back, and then on, stroking the welts on the brunette's backside.

"I almost can't believe she really is the Ruth I knew," Marie breathed, clearly fascinated by the whip marks she stroked. "The Ruth I knew was always so polite, so helpful, and so shy. We didn't think we'd ever find her a boyfriend."

Naked on her knees, no doubt listening intently as she was discussed, slapped scarlet breasts squashed into the marble floor, the former law student's tongue left saliva gleaming on Marie's shoes.

"I mean, when you see a slave like this, naked, bound, obedient and they've grown her tits so big, then yes! It's obvious she exists to be enjoyed, and needs a touch of whip to get the best out of her."

"But it was never obvious before?" the Ambassador asked.

"Yes!" Marie said in frustration. "Doesn't Ruth get a say?"

The Ambassador yanked the kneeling slave's lead to get her attention, the sexual plaything gasping as the leather strap around her neck was tugged, and then ordered her to her feet. Ruth obeyed instantly, her dildo hanging between her breasts on its chain from her chinstrap. He stood and pulled the British girl's head back with one hand twisted into her thick dark hair, free hand stroking her belly.

"Your problem is, why you feel guilt, is you still see her as a person even when you're enjoying her. You should really look on a sex slave like this as just a vibrator. Nothing more."

The lovely brunette, head pulled back by her hair so that she was looking at the ceiling now, was still perfectly docile. She moaned, gasped and squeaked in soft pleasure as the Ambassador's fingers stroked in and out of her sex while he gave her slap-tender breasts little licks and nips between his teeth. People coming and going between the courts paid little attention to the naked, bound, girl's public teasing.

"Just think of her as a vibrator on legs," he coaxed. "You use a vibrator as often or as little as you wish, purely for your own pleasure. When not in use, it goes back in its box, and can be forgotten until you want it again. You of course buy the size and shape that suits you. And the more money you spend on your sex toy, usually the better the quality it is."

The girl he teased sagged, knees buckling, and cried out in desperate, agonised, pleasure; the Ambassador squeezing and twisting the helpless sex object's pierced clitoris as she was forced to come. Still holding the girl by a handful of hair, he pushed her limp body facedown over a table, unclipped her gag-dildo from its chain, and thrust and twisted the shaft into a dripping pussy. He pulled Marie's bound friend upright again, and held out the short fluid-glistening shaft to his secretary.

"Just a vibrator on legs," he reminded.

Marie's grin mirrored his and slowly, teasingly, obviously quite intoxicated with her power, she pushed the dildo firmly into her one-time friend's mouth. Then she twisted the fat shaft back and forth to thoroughly coat the naked girl's tongue in her own juices before clipping the end of the dildo back onto its chain. The base of the dildo now looked like a bath plug again.

Marie, reservations finally set aside, handled the bound girl as if born to it now — a noble's right! — one moment making her naked plaything cry out in pain, the next forcing a low growling moan of pleasure from the helpless, forcibly aroused, sex slave. The Ambassador watched indulgently, surprised at how easily he'd been able to corrupt his new assistant.

"I thought your file said you were hetero?" he commented.

Marie, a nipple between her teeth, paused, looking thoughtful.

"I think I still am, but I'd still love to own her," she finally said seriously. "I could have her fucked every day; three, four, ten times a day, while I watched!"

"And even if you didn't want to have sex with her yourself, she'd still be fun to obedience train?" he prompted.

"Oh yes!" Marie breathed, one hand between her naked friend's legs, the other resting on one of the bound sex slave's whip-marked buttocks.

Ruth was panting with lust now, her juices glistening between her plump ring-set pussy lips. Marie, using the leather strap of the aroused girl's lead to rope the placid sex slave's over-large breasts into two tight bulging pink balls, skin shiny taut, was delighted when a single tear of shame ran down one of the brunette's cheeks. All too soon, the bailiff returned, and took her wonderful new toy off her.

Marie, practically dragging her boss the British Ambassador into the courtroom, secured two front row seats. Watching Ruth secured in placc, she waited with bated breath to see what further humiliations the Slaveworld had in store for her one-time friend. She'd never imagined, even suspected, how much of a turn-on it would be for her to see little Miss Goody-goody treated so cruelly.

"All rise for his honour, Justice Taylor-Forth."

Those assembled in the courtroom came to their feet while the red and black robed judge, wearing a white wig, settled himself into his chair behind the raised bench. Ruth was already on her feet, held in place by a choke chain from a ceiling winch. On the left side of the court was the prosecutor's table, the naked slave standing to the right. Slaves were not permitted to sit in the presence of their betters, only to kneel. Guilty until proven innocent or acquitted! The various witnesses, reporters and the just plain curious sat behind a railing behind the naked, bound, gagged appellant and the robed State prosecutor. Only nobles got a jury.

Marie was surprised at how normal it all looked. Apart from Ruth in her birthday suit and bonds, looking just a little out of place, the hearing otherwise could have been taking place in an ordinary British courtroom.

"The Prosecution requests leave to protest these hearings," the State prosecutor opened.

The judge, taking a moment to admire Ruth's naked

body, nodded amiably.

"On what grounds?"

"My Lord, it is unseemly that I should have to argue with and be contradicted by, a mere slave," the prosecutor said.

"Disallowed," the judge decided. "If she is to get a fair hearing she must be able to state her case."

"Then assign someone to defend her," the prosecutor suggested.

"No," the judge decided. "It's rare, but she has to the right to speak for herself. Bailiff, bring me the appellant."

Ruth, still gagged, was released from her choke chain, and frogmarched over to the judge's bench. She was made to stand with her big breasts resting on the edge of the judge's desk. The old man in wig and robes — clearly a tit man — gave their ample weight a good long moan-producing groping before removing her sapphire pendants and attaching a bell to each nipple. The naked brunette squeaked as the spring-loaded clamps drove sharp little metal teeth into each fat nub.

"Bailiff, you may secure the appellant again."

The winch whined once more, the one-time law student again held firmly in place by a choke chain.

"Now listen to me Big Tits," the elderly judge said, not entirely unkindly. "If you wish permission to speak, or protest against the prosecutor's statements, you may ring those bells, and I will direct the bailiff to remove your gag. Be aware that for the duration of this hearing, you are the legal property of the court, and I will not tolerate any argument or insolence from a bed toy. You will at all times show me, the prosecutor and the witnesses proper respect, or I will have you punished. Understood?"

Ruth nodded obediently, her choke chain cutting in deeper under her jaw. Standing on her toes in five inch heels, ankles neatly together, arms firmly strapped behind her back, her head secured in a complicated harness and the marks of sexual abuse clearly visible on her naked body, Marie wondered if the former law student knew her hearing was being televised, and suitably edited, it would go out on the Slaveworld's 3V that evening. God, she hoped so!

The bailiff scanned the bar code tattooed on the underside of Ruth's left breast so that her pedigree and criminal record could be entered into the court's records, and then took a seat behind the naked girl. Marie thought she looked quite calm, considering. The big heavy breasts that only moments ago Marie herself had been squeezing, kneading, roping and licking, now decorated with bells, were heaving a little, but nothing like when the helpless slave had been made to come - and she was secured with a choke chain now, making her pant a bit.

Marie realised that for the first time in her life she was looking at another woman, not just to compare with herself, but with actual hunger; sexual lust! With her huge tits, twenty two inch waist, long legs and firmly curved haunches, Marie now found the bound, helplessly displayed, sex object she'd once known as Ruth, absolutely delightful. She wondered if the shy vicar's daughter she had once befriended partly out of pity could still taste the juices, her own, that Marie had smeared across her tongue.

Ruth had undoubtedly imagined herself arguing a case in a Court of Law one day, but surely never like this.

"The State may make its opening statement."

The prosecutor stood, and walked around Ruth's naked form. The man gave a buttock a squeeze, weighed a breast in his palm and yanked the tall slave's pubic hair. Ruth, by now well used to such treatment, was quite placid in her humiliating restraints.

"My Lords and Ladies. What we have here is a total waste of the court's time." He gave Ruth a careless slap on the behind. "This top-heavy fucking machine, distressed to find herself owned by a women instead of a man, or unhappy at the physical improvements her owner has made to her, at quite considerable expense I might add — or some such similar trivial reason — has maliciously chosen to try and escape her legal owner's quite legitimate enjoyment of her, by the only means open to her."

The man squeezed Ruth's sharp-jawed nipple clamps deeper into her flesh, making her cry out in pain, and then turned away from her in feigned disgust to face the judge.

"As she is already youth treated and will serve the maximum possible sentence, I request that if her appeal is found to be without merit, then any future daughters and granddaughters be given an automatic twenty year sentence on reaching eighteen."

The judge nodded to himself and made a note on his pad.

"So noted in the records," the judge agreed. "I will consider your request."

Ruth shook her shoulders back and forth, breasts swinging and bouncing nicely as she made the bells attached to her nipples jingle madly.

"The appellant may speak," the judge decided.

With a sigh, the bailiff stood and removed Ruth's dildo gag. Ruth, speaking softly, respectfully argued that punishing someone simply for appealing against a sentence could not be fair as it might deter the innocent from going to court. She'd obviously realised hysterics would get her nowhere.

Perhaps it was the strap buckled tight across her mouth and having to speak through a steel ring, but Ruth's voice sounded very different now than Marie remembered from university. Soft and husky, very sexy. Most likely the cosmetic surgeon who had made her other more obvious improvements, had also tweaked the British student's vocal cords too. It was all just too yummy. Marie realised she had to get herself a slave. She wanted, craved, the power to have another human being altered to her whims. To be able to say to a Slaveworld cosmetic surgeon, I want a little off the hips, legs a little longer, bigger tits and dye its eyes blue. Oh yes, and make her voice husky!

"You have a point Big Tits," the judge allowed kindly, addressing Ruth, "but the law does allow punishment for peasant stock bringing malicious court actions and wasting the court's time. Bailiff, stopper her mouth again, and give her a couple of strokes."

The bailiff, looking interested in the proceedings for the first time, unhooked a short crop from his belt, and gave the bound brunette three firm cuts across the backside. The crack of leather on flesh was very loud in the tall echoing courtroom, Ruth gasping in pain at each blow, eyes bulging, as three new horizontal lines marked her buttocks. Marie found she was hugging herself in delight.

"And the specific charges?" the judge asked.

"My Lord. This slave was convicted three months ago on three counts; vagrancy, debt and trespass i.e. illegal entry into the Kingdom. The RSP later added the charge of Enemy of the State."

"And the slave will contest all these charges?" the judge asked.

Ruth nodded her bridled head. Admiring the lush curves of the nude girl's hindquarters, the new whip stripes that decorated the firm hemispheres of her buttocks, Marie wondered idly what it might be like to have a harness buckled and padlocked tightly around your head? To be on display, naked, a strap tight across your mouth and a dildo stretching your mouth wide open. She herself would hate it, but clearly a well-trained vibrator on legs didn't mind.

The prosecutor ran a hand up Ruth's spine, free hand again hefting a breast, slowly squeezing until the helpless slave moaned for him. He clearly found the leggy brunette sexually attractive, but was justly irritated at having to argue a case against a mere sex toy. Just for the moment, technically, the naked and bound girl was legally his equal. Ruth, quite sensibly, made no move or sound of protest as she was handled.

"As was proved at the first hearing, this slave has no assets, no abode, is not a subject of the Kingdom and could not account for how she entered the Kingdom."

Ruth shook her breasts back and forth to make her bells jingle and was allowed to speak again. She did not deny the charges but claimed that she had extenuating circumstances. Before she could continue the prosecutor was on his feet and had rammed her dildo back into her mouth, the fat shaft hanging between big breasts on its chain, when not in Ruth's mouth.

"The slave admits her guilt. Ignorance of the law is not

an extenuating circumstance. I move to end this ridiculous hearing. Further I would..."

Ruth swung her shoulders back and forth to make her breasts swing and bounce harder, the bells the judge had clamped to her nipples making an urgent jangle now.

"Order!" the judge barked, striking down with his gavel. "Let the prosecutor finish!" he commanded.

Ruth made the mistake of allowing her bells tinkle again, though Marie thought it might just have been that the former British law student was gasping for breath around her choke chain, tits heaving. The judge didn't give her the benefit of the doubt, and ordered the bailiff to whip her, five strokes across the tail, three across the belly and a half dozen to each breast. The tennis-ball sized news cameras that had been hovering around the ceiling moved closer.

Marie hadn't expected to see her former friend punished in a courtroom, and again watched in delight as the bailiff's short, thick, crop landed on beautifully curved buttocks with a solid satisfying thwack; once, twice, three times. Then four and five. Ruth squeaked at each stroke, whipped harder this second time, a ripple running across her magnificent haunches each time the crop struck, breasts bobbing as pain pushed her up onto her toes.

Marie, entranced, had never seen anything so arousing in her life, experiencing both thrilling, non-sexual excitement — a powertrip! — as well as sexual arousal. Her own nipples were hard, breasts lust swollen and she could feel a heat in her groin like never before. She was actually wet! That usually took utterly ages of foreplay.

Ruth's cries had a plaintive, quite heartrending plea to them, as three perfectly parallel lines marked her belly, but she didn't become really shrill until the bailiff started whipping her big breasts. Viper fast, again and again, the uniformed man's lash darted in, and left behind an agonising blaze of pain. The heavy melons, quickly tear-splashed, quivered and danced beautifully as the British girl twisted and jerked. She'd managed to hold position, facing forward with her head up and ankles together so far, but this was too much for her! The bailiff waited patiently between whip strokes for the sobbing former law student to compose herself, and turn herself back to face his crop again for further punishment. To Marie's utterly entranced, delighted amazement, the trembling, gasping, brunette did time and time again.

Ruth's hands, secured behind her back, fluttered helplessly, sweat suddenly gleaming on her flanks. The vicious crop added line after line to those already decorating her heavy udders, and every time Ruth would squeal and twist away. And then, trembling, sobbing, force herself back around for the next whip stroke.

"Look how wet the slut is," the Ambassador whispered to Marie. "See, her juices are running down her inner thighs. A few more strokes and she'll come."

He was right! God, he was right. But just too soon for the whipped girl, her punishment was over. The judge ordered a short recess while the defendant composed herself, and the bailiff again frogmarched the former British law student over to the judge's bench. With Ruth kneeling under the bench, the judge sitting with a vacant, happy look on his face, arms rhythmically flexing; ten minutes passed in silent communion, punctuated by the occasional jingle of the bells clamped to Ruth's nipples. He was tit fucking her, Marie realised.

The elderly judge finally struck his gavel and brought the court back into session. The whip-stripe-decorated brunette he had enjoyed was led back to her place and secured with her choke chain again, the judge's semen now gleaming all over the inner surfaces of both huge breasts and up her throat. Marie found herself grinning widely. No British courtroom was ever this entertaining. The Lords and Ladies who tuned in to see the hearing on their 3V sets later that evening were in for a treat.

"The hearing will resume. The slave may now make her point."

With the prosecutor handling her breasts from behind, the heavily enlarged mounds, lubricated by come, sliding easily together, Ruth was finally allowed to have her say. Her defence was actually quite well thought out and coherent, considering the distractions she had to contend with Marie thought. But then Ruth always had been bright. It was easy to forget when you were absorbed in enjoying her that the magnificent sexual animal, so proud in her bounds, had a brain. Ruth's contention was that she was not a debtor or a vagrant as she had assets and a home in another world. As the British Ambassador could testify. She maintained her position was that of a shipwreck survivor, a victim of circumstances beyond her control, and with help she could contact her homeland for funds. Having the prosecutor thrusting his fingers deep into her sex and squeezing and twisting her cruelly clamped nipples was clearly very distracting for the lovely young sex slave, and gasping and panting, she occasionally forgot what she was saying or repeated herself, but the judge didn't seem to mind.

After Marie's boss, the British Ambassador had reluctantly confirmed on the stand that Ruth was not actually destitute or homeless and did have assets in another country, the prosecutor requested another short recess, declaring himself too stimulated to think clearly. The judge graciously allowed him to use Ruth for his sexual relief.

In moments, the body-harnessed and bridled slave was bent forward over the prosecutor's desk, practically right in front of Marie and the Ambassador, and Marie found herself happily watching her one-time friend being used for sex again. She had a ringside seat. Perhaps the prosecutor had simply needed a moment to think, seeing his open and shut case getting away from him, or maybe he was genuinely horny. He certainly thrust his large cock into Ruth's body with commendable enthusiasm.

Her huge tits squeezed almost flat under her, gasping behind her dildo gag each time the prosecutor thrust his cock deep and hard into her from behind, the man's hands tight on the generous flare of her hips, Ruth's glazed eyes met Marie's. No plea for mercy or help in the wide baby-blue orbs this time, just the docile acceptance of a sex toy who knew her use was being enjoyed by more than one person.

"Just a vibrator on legs," Marie whispered, hoping the former law student would be able to read her lips.

Bent forward over a desk, a fully dressed man in a lawyer's robe and white wig who had opened only his flies to use her, Marie realised that the now bucking and squirming brunette looked perfect with her arms strapped behind her. A slavegirl just wouldn't look right without her arms firmly secured behind her back. And the head harness holding the dildo in the gasping plaything's mouth was also just perfect. Even if it had been in her power to set her one-time friend free at this moment, Marie realised she would want to change nothing. Set such a prize free? Not a chance! Ruth twice cried out in forced pleasure as she was made to come.

Dazed and gasping after her perfunctory but hard use, but still somehow thinking clearly, Ruth was allowed to question a representative of the Royal Security Police when the hearing resumed. Her case was further strengthened by reluctant official admission that she had in fact been kidnapped, so was not only on the Slaveworld through no choice of her own, but was here because of the actions of the State that had convicted her! Despite vigorous protests, slapped breasts and a few pubic hairs yanked out by the prosecutor, her point was allowed. The judge formally dismissed the charges of vagrancy, debt and illegal entry to the Kingdom.

"However," he concluded, "the fact that you are not knowingly a danger to the state, does not eradicate that danger. I will have to deliberate on the question of whether you can safely be set free."

Ruth, gagged again, shook her bells urgently to object, but the judge did not allow her to speak further; and having already been thoroughly whipped once, she now knew better than to press the point. The judge called a lunch break while he deliberated, and to Marie's disappointment, had the bailiff take Ruth into his chambers behind the bench. Occasional squeals of pain, the crack of a whip on flesh, the buzz of a cattle prod and desperate, forced cries of pained ecstasy drifted out through the open door into the courtroom as the elderly judge 'deliberated' with a bound, helpless and quite gorgeous girl only a quarter his age. Marie listened avidly, but it wasn't the same for her as seeing her newly top-heavy, amazingly compliant and submissive one-time friend, used, abused and enjoyed, up close and personal.

Lady Isobell reappeared, asked how the hearing was going without much apparent urgency and told the Ambassador someone wanted to see him in the adjoining court. Marie, answering the Lady's questions in monosyllables, and trying to imagine what the kindly looking old judge was doing to Ruth, barely even noticed him go.

The British Ambassador wasn't surprised to find Queen Victoria waiting for him in the empty courtroom, two silent plain-clothed men closing the door behind him. He'd thought they'd be meeting again soon. Small talk was quickly steered onto more serious topics.

"I see you brought your little friend with you again," the Queen said, suddenly changing conversational tack.

"Yes. Our Security has insisted we do not travel alone from now on I'm afraid. We all carry recording devices as a matter of course, so that expert analysis will pick up any points the wearer might have missed in conversation as well as for personal security, and they didn't seem to work at your reception for some reason."

Actually Security knew damn well their wires had been jammed, though they were not sure quite how. And they were far more worried about betrayal by their own personnel — defection — than they were about the British Embassy staff's safety. If they couldn't record every word their people made, then they didn't want them alone with any Slaveworlders. He and Marie shouldn't really be apart now, but Marie was enjoying her one-time friend's humiliating day in court far too much to notice his absence for the moment.

"Yes, sorry about that. It seems our personal computers jam your recording devices, no matter what frequency you use."

Clever! She was telling him he could talk freely, but letting him make the first move. Might now be a good time to mention his source of African slaves? It was breaking the rules, true, but it was hardly full-blown treason. And after being blackmailed into a job he'd willingly have taken anyway, he wasn't feeling too loyal to Intelligence anyway. If he gave the Queen a little hold over him, while he got rich, then she might tell him what she wanted from him.

Yes, go for it, he decided.

A quiet way into his dimension turned out to be exactly what Queen Victoria wanted, though she didn't tell him why she wanted to return two formerly British slaves to Britain, via his African connection. He didn't see any real harm in it. The deal was done!

"And if you ever need to be alone, letting your little friend Marie play with her former acquaintance, might be a good way. I'm sure I can persuade Isobell," Her Majesty said.

Perfect. Marie would think he was covering for her with Security, when actually she would be his alibi.

"You don't think Tits is going to win her appeal then?" he asked.

Queen Victoria laughed. "She might, but she's had a taste of the lash and a collar now. If she's set free today, she'll get herself arrested and sentenced to slavery by the end of the week."

"You're sure of that?" he asked.

"I've enjoyed the girl myself. Trust me, I know what goes on in the head of a slave," the Queen told him positively.

She was right. The judge, after having given Ruth a long hard ride in his chambers, while she was still legally the property of the court, had acquitted her after the recess. The Ambassador found his secretary comforting her sobbing university friend on one of the benches in the hall outside the court, a robe hastily wrapped around her. Freed of her bonds and gag, though still padlocked into her stiletto heels the Ambassador noticed, Ruth clutched her robe closed in front of her.

"Then why did you appeal?" Marie was asking, clearly exasperated.

"I was scared, confused, at first," the brunette snuffled. "You can't expect someone from my background to agree to be owned for sex! I had to say I wanted to appeal."

"But you argued your case so well."

"But I never expected to get a fair trial," the lovely girl wailed.

The Ambassador smothered a grin as Marie looked up helplessly, clearly not knowing what to do with her one-time friend. Though whether her irritation was at Ruth not knowing her own mind, being stuck with having to comfort the inconsolable, now-freed slave or that there was now no chance of having slave sex with Ruth now, he wouldn't like to put money on. Probably a large measure of each.

Lady Isobell strolled down the corridor, not looking too put out at losing her new plaything. She would undoubtedly be financially compensated for the sobbing brunette's original price as well as the cosmetic work she'd had done on her, so she wasn't going to be out of pocket. Ruth looked up, and bolted forward, dropping to her knees in front of the aristocrat. Her robe fell away, revealing bare flesh as her hands clutched at the Lady's skirt.

"Please Mistress, take me back. I'm sorry, I'm sorry, I'm sorry!"

"Well it's done now," the aristocrat said coolly. "No hard feelings for the uses I put you to I hope? If it's any consolation, you were a great screw and one of the nicest pony girls I've ever driven. Now cover yourself up, and you really ought to get yourself a veil as well," she said, tugging her former property's robe back up over her shoulder, and then deliberately catching Marie's eye. "We don't want you getting arrested for indecent exposure, do we?"

Ruth sagged back down on the bench, huge, almost silent sobs racking her body, her head down. Marie put a comforting arm around the sobbing girl's shoulder, an understanding smile lighting up her face. She whispered softly in her friend's ear.

The distraught brunette's head came up slowly, hope lighting her tear-streaked face. She stood, stepped forward, and slapped her former owner across the face!

It was the lightest of blows. Barely even left a mark. The Ambassador had seen Lady Isobell, the State prosecutor and even his own secretary, slap the blue-eyed girl's big heavy slave breasts, far far harder. But it was enough. By striking an aristocrat, in front of witnesses, Ruth had just sentenced herself to at least thirty five years in a collar. And as Lady Isobell was the injured party, she would get first refusal to buy the top-heavy British girl. Probably at a discount, as a slave convicted of an assault on a noble would normally be sold cheap.

The British Ambassador nodded to himself as a bailiff was summoned to arrest Ruth. No doubt about it, the Queen certainly knew her slaves.

CHAPTER NINE

Without warning or explanation, Susan's beloved mistress had packed her in a pet crate and had her delivered to the palace, by first class post. She was apparently on loan to Her Majesty, Queen Victoria II. The following four weeks in the palace cellblock were a taste of a house slave's typical servitude. Susan was horrified! After a taste of life as a prized, exotic, pet, she was now being treated like just one of the pack. An ordinary slave. Her Majesty the Queen had enjoyed her three times, which had been fun, and she had the household troopers — the men who groomed, exercised and punished her — to serve, but quantity was not quality!

Any trooper could pet and grope her as he wished, a corporal was allowed to tit fuck her, sergeants could come in her mouth as well as between her breasts and officers were allowed to have intercourse with slaves. but it was still a tame existence, a pale imitation of her service to Lady Abigail! It was mostly long periods of waiting, sexually frustrated, looking up with eager lust and longing, heart pounding, at the sound of footsteps or the jangle of keys. Longer hours spent on public display in a glass display case in the palace halls while whip marks and rope burns slowly faded from her body, and more often staring blankly at the bars of her tiny cage-like cell. She was frequently kept hooded, gagged, and in earplugs between obedience training, exercise and being fed.

Slavery was like the old definition of war, ninety per cent boredom, ten percent terror. Except sexual service was ninety per cent boredom, ten per cent terror, passion, joy and ecstasy!

Then suddenly, always without warning, like pulling the hood from a hunting hawk, or delivering a racehorse to the track, the monotony of her placid, trooper-controlled routine would be shattered. A Royal Prince or Princess wanted to play with her and anything in the cellblock without a brand or pussy lock was fair game. Once again permitted to experience pain and forbidden thrilling, arousal, pleasure beyond anything she could have imagined before being given a serial number and bar code brand, her Royal users had put her to bound, degrading, humiliating, sexual use!

The young Royals who sampled her had clearly enjoyed themselves, because only one, Prince Gregor, had ordered her punished for inadequate sexual performance afterwards. But Susan was aware she was just a novelty, a bit of variation, not a prized, exotic, pet. To Lady Abigail she was special. Delightful! Here, mostly she was being treated like some lowly serving scrap or table slave. The grooms would be fitting her with four-inch heels next!

Susan didn't know why she was in the palace cellblock, apparently it was on the orders of Her Majesty, Queen Victoria II, but she hoped it wouldn't last much longer. Queen Victoria didn't seem to have any urgent use for her. And the way Susan reasoned, if the Queen didn't appreciate her, then she should be sent back to someone — young, beautiful and cruel — who did!

She hadn't been sold. Her reassurance that she would be returned to her young mistress was the pet's nametag now hanging from a fine ring set through her right earlobe. After a long night's sex and sexual torture, Lady Abigail had pierced Susan's earlobe herself, and snapped the self-sealing ring into place, before putting Susan in the post. PROPERTY OF LADY ABIGAIL DIANA GRACEFORTH, was clearly engraved on the reverse side of the silver disk, Susan's new name, HONEY, on the front. She'd been renamed on her birthday, apparently for some connection with a slave she was going to be teamed with.

Her best birthday present ever! Lady Abigail's failure to name her or put a pet tag on her straight away had been a gnawing worry.

Today, freshly groomed, exercised and fed, Susan knelt up against her cell bars on the plain padded plastic surface that was her bed, wrists handcuffed to ankles, her breasts squeezed and pushed between the metal bars. Her nipple rings were padlocked to each other to hold her in place, squeezing the big heavy mounds together. A pear-shaped pendant on a fine chain hung from her pierced clitoris, and for the first time in two weeks she'd been fitted with a matching collar and corset set, waist trimmed down to an owner-pleasing eighteen inches once again. Clearly she'd been prepared for something, but as usual, she had absolutely no idea what.

The clincher was the Sergeant of the Guard writing on the upper surface of her right breast in neat block capitals with a marker-pen, signed underneath in an untidy scrawl, THESE TITS ARE NOT TO BE BRUISED. But no one ever told slaves anything! Her body had been used as a notepad before, and Susan knew the ink could be either waterproof or permanent, and would wipe off cleanly with an alcohol soaked cloth if the sergeant wished. Today's ball gag was pink, which Susan was only too well aware, best suited fluffy blondes.

Her beautiful long dark waist-length mane had been cropped, new dark gold hair shoulder length now, growing through thick and fast thanks to the pills they gave her. In a couple of months, if Lady Abigail wished – and didn't prefer the short fluffy look on a Honey — her hair would again be the long, thick, shiny, cascade that most owners preferred. Inevitably, the pink ball gag was making her drool.

A passing trooper paused to give her a friendly grope. She wasn't quite sure why, but somehow she seemed to have become a favourite amongst the rank and file, often being stroked, petted, admired and sometimes even given little treats, chocolates, sweets and the like. The NCOs, who had sexual rights, agreed she had a delicious mouth and was a superb tit fuck, but were businesslike, even perfunctory in their use of her. While on the other hand the mostly young troopers were positively spoiling her, to the extent that sometimes she was almost surprised to be spanked instead of stroked, or when sharp-jawed electrodes were attached to flesh instead of body piercings on the gym's exercise machines.

That she was the cellblock pet had become noticeable to the extent that many of her fellow slaves were now giving her the cold shoulder. And a few were even expressing their resentment and jealously more physically. She'd had her breasts cruelly squeezed and twisted a couple of times now, her pussy lips and clitoris viciously pinched with fingernails, and pubic hairs ripped out on the rare occasions her fellow sex toys managed to get their hands on her. The troopers protected her and punished the offenders when they caught them, which only made her more of a target. The Duty Sergeant had just laughed, and as far as she knew, had made no real attempt to find the culprits when Prince Alfred had set him to discovering why he'd had trouble controlling a very frisky pony girl one morning. Somebody had smeared something like ginger or pepper sauce all over Susan's butt plug! On the capital's streets she'd been maddened, quite frantic, constantly fighting her reins and bit, twice trying to bolt through red traffic lights; only finally brought under control with a lot of whip after she'd come many times.

Now she thought about it, there had been a troopers pet on a slave farm she'd worked on once; a tall, elegant, blonde. Susan had never taken part in any of the physical mistreatment herself, but remembered once watching with a certain amount of satisfaction, four other slaves squeezing the bound and gagged sex toy's breasts against a hot water tank, savouring her cries and the tears that welled in her wide blue eyes. There too the Regimental Sergeant in charge had been aware of the situation, but allowed it to continue. In fact, now that she thought about it, the girl's punishments had often been public events, a small crowd of slaves usually permitted to watch the blonde's humiliation and experience her cries of pain. An air of staged entertainment about the occasion. Towards the end, Susan had even looked forward to the shows herself.

She shivered, belatedly realising that her pet's five-inch heels and nametag, but no Royal brand burnt into her flesh, had made her different, an outsider, and she'd become the 'teachers pet' of this cellblock. She'd been a bit slow on the uptake there. No wonder the other slavegirls were being so mean to her. And it did explain why the various Sergeants of the Guard kept having her mounted on the dildo pole and tit whipped so often, and why there always seemed to be so many other slavegirls about to witness her punishments as she thrashed, squealed and came.

If you thought about it, it made sense from the guards' point of view. Allowing the slaves to have one underdog, a focus for resentment, to know that there was someone beneath them in the pecking order, inevitably meant the troopers then had a much easier time controlling the cellblock. Susan was the perfect whipping girl, because she was what every ordinary slavegirl aspired to be. Not just a spare body, but a named pet, chosen and cherished by one particular noble.

She moaned in soft pleasure as the uniformed young man reached between the bars and cupped her sex, middle finger stroking softly into her.

"Hello beautiful, I brought you a treat," he whispered softly, ducking his head to nip at her big breasts bulging between the bars of her cell with his teeth.

The trooper's bites were light, just teasing, carefully not hard enough to leave a mark for more than a few seconds. Another sign some Royal had plans for her in the near future. His hands stroked up and down her body and then dropping to one knee, with a firm handful of buttock in each hand, he pulled her body hard up against the bars so that he could taste her sex.

Susan moaned in delight around her ball gag as a tongue penetrated her. Another and more concrete reason for her newfound popularity, her juices were reckoned to be the best aphrodisiac in the whole cellblock. One enterprising trooper had even been caught, and disciplined, a vibrator in one hand, a dozen small bottles ready, with Susan herself tied, legs wide, across the Sergeant of the Guard's desk; planning to go into business.

It was a bit bizarre to hear the way the troopers who teased and tormented her to make her juices flow, talked to one another about how much their wives and girlfriends appreciated their newfound sexual stamina. And while she loved being popular, Susan wasn't actually sure if the phenomenon was real or in the mind, though it was theoretically possible that the aphrodisiac surgically implanted in her body was secreted in body fluids. She'd seen and experienced Lords and Ladies savouring 'The taste of submission,' licking sweat, tears and juices, often enough. Perhaps stimulating themselves?

Susan groaned behind her gag as the man's tongue probed deeper, reaming her out. The soldier nosed aside her clit pendant, and then suddenly, in a cascade of sensation, she was wailing in helpless pleasure. The trooper scrambled to his feet, his hand over her ball gag, looking guiltily from side to side.

"Quiet you noisy bitch!" he hissed. "You know you're not supposed to come without permission."

Susan lowered her eyelids in silent apology, actually not in the slightest contrite. The young soldier should have realised he was too inexperienced to be licking her, and just worked his fingers into her pussy to scoop up some of her juices.

"Bad girl!" he hissed, as fear gave way to anger, squeezing her breasts to punish her. "Are you trying to get me into trouble?"

Susan whimpered in pained arousal as fingers sank into her trapped flesh. Pain flared in her nipples, the man's pulls and twists trying to pull apart nipple rings firmly padlocked together. Collared, breathlessly corseted, kneeling upright and pressed against the bars of her cell with wrists chained to her ankles, naked and gasping helplessly, she gave a little whimper of relief as the sudden, brutal, punishment ended.

"Bad girl," the trooper repeated again, softly, grinning now.

He plucked at her swollen, stretched, locked-together nipples, hefting her breasts and then lightly stroking the over-large globes. Susan moaned in obedient pleasure.

"You can't help it can you, beautiful?" he laughed, patting her belly.

Susan made a soft noise that might have been assent,

knowing her keepers didn't really want her to communicate, just to pet her as they wished, and expect her to enjoy it like a family dog. The man unbuckled her ball gag for a moment, placed a mint on her tongue, and then pushed and strapped the huge pink ball back into place. Held in place by a handful of pubic hair, Susan made appreciative noises while the trooper looked cautiously around.

"Keep your cunt pressed up between the bars," he ordered.

She watched apprehensively as he furtively pulled a small, lighter-sized aristocrat's shock device that he shouldn't have had, from a tunic pocket, and began amusing himself touching the instrument of torture lightly against her pussy. Susan squeaked, hips twitching convulsively at the first shock, a jolt of pain delivered directly to her clit ring. He shocked her again and then again, and then made her press her pussy up against a cell bar so that her sex lips were spread to either side on the cold metal bar. And so that he could shock each pussy lip individually. Agonisingly!

"You like it don't you?" her tormentor pressed, more an order than a question.

Gasping and snorting around her gag, lungs heaving, Susan groaned obedient assent. She sighed thankfully when boots crashing down the corridor made her tormentor put away the illicit device. Another uniformed man, leading a hooded, whip-striped girl back to her cell from some Royal's playroom, rope marks on her breasts, grinned companionably at the man handling Susan's naked, bound body.

"I wonder how long you're going to be here," her tormentor mused, thoughtfully hefting her breasts again. "I make corporal next month, and I can't wait to get my cock between these!"

Susan groaned obediently once more as her over-large breasts, still bulging between the bars with nipple rings padlocked together, were squeezed and kissed one last time. And with a little pat on the hip below her rigid waspie-corset, her abuser then strolled away, whistling cheerfully to himself. Panting with lust, heavy breasts still aching with a deep throbbing after being so cruelly squeezed, pussy dripping wet and pulsing with every beat of her heart, a mint dissolving on her tongue, Susan found herself again desperate for more. She whined plaintively, eagerly pressing herself up against the bars as the next uniformed man approached.

The new trooper, a corporal, was unfortunately all business and just gave her a quick grope. Breasts freed from between the bars, her wrists were unchained from her anklecuffs and locked behind her back, a second set of restraints above the elbows making her elbows touch together. The scrawled note in black ink was carefully wiped off her breast, a short chain between the ankles quickly hobbled her, and in minutes she was out of the carpeted cellblock and tip-tapping down the marble floored corridor of a Royal-used part of the palace in the proper pet's five-inch stiletto heels she knew she deserved. Hips swaying and breasts jiggling, as she'd been trained to walk in restraints, she did her best to keep up with the man leading her, a chain lead clipped to her collar. The heavy gold pendant swinging between her legs, gently but implacably teasing and stimulating her pierced clitoris as it bounced and bumped off her thighs, was driving her to distraction.

The palace was huge, and Susan was soon totally lost. Somewhere above the main hall she thought, she was finally led to a large and very grand reception room, a half dozen seated dignitaries in best tails, top hats on laps, waiting to be seen. A pair of identical twin slavegirls were serving refreshments, a slave-receptionist sat behind a glass desk. The waiting Lords' eyes roamed over her helpless nudity, curious but not intent, Susan was pulled aside by her lead to allow another worthy to pass. There were a pair of troopers in dress reds flanking the doors leading into the next room, and gold crowns were embossed on the wood. Susan felt her heart suddenly pounding faster. Oh God! These were the Royal Chambers! What could the King want with her?

The pert-breasted blonde behind the desk looked up

politely at the approach of the white-haired Lord who Susan had been pulled aside for. At first glance the bound slave looked about thirty years old, but Susan was getting used to people who were older than they actually looked, and there were little give-aways if you knew what to look for. Faint crows feet around the eyes, the casual grace and lips that almost, but didn't quite, have the lustre of youth. The receptionist slave had been given the youth treatment, and was probably twice the actual age she looked.

The blonde plaything was naked, with firm high breasts, a slender waist nipped tight by a seamless shiny-leather band, and she was chained to her desk with delicate chains swaying from her nipple rings. Surprisingly considering her duties, a ball gag filled her mouth — Susan was right, pink did suit blondes — and her thick golden hair had been woven and plaited into a rope looped over the hook of a ceiling winch. The chain and rope of hair held her head up so that she was almost suspended. Under the desk the naked sex toy's feet had been pushed into impossibly tall stiletto heels so that only her toes and the shoes' heels touched the floor, ankles chained apart, spreading her legs wide. The shoes were surely impossible to walk in, just decorative Susan thought, almost like ballet pumps with stiletto heels.

The slave's fingers flashed across a keyboard and words scrolled across a large LCD sign on the wall behind her. Her wrists were secured to two of the four rings set through her sex lips with the same fine chain that linked her nipple rings to the desk. Also, looking through the glass surface, Susan couldn't help but notice the blonde's chair was a dildo stool, a fat shaft penetrating her. A second set of chains from the other pair of pussy rings chained her to the stool, so she was unable to rise up off the shaft.

GOOD MORNING SIR. MY NAME IS ANGELA. IF I FAIL TO BE OF SERVICE TO YOU, PLEASE PRESS THE RED BUTTON ON THE DESK TO PUNISH ME. HOW MAY I HELP YOU?

"Hello Angela. Councillor Gordan to see His Highness. I have a two fifteen appointment."

The blonde checked her screen, fingers rattling across

her keyboard again.

YES SIR, YOU ARE EXPECTED. I REGRET HIS MAJESTY IS RUNNING APPROXIMATELY 20 MIN BEHIND SCHEDULE TODAY. PLEASE TAKE A SEAT AND I WILL INFORM THE CHAMBERLAIN YOU HAVE ARRIVED.

The man sighed, and after a moment's thought, gave the red button on the desk an experimental press. Viper fast, a thin lash unfolded itself from a recess in the wall behind the blonde and licked back and forth across her behind with two vicious cracks. Angela squealed behind her gag. Probably given a shock through the dildo as well, Susan judged, from the amount of noise she made and the way she was gasping behind her gag.

Nipples chained to desk, hands chained to pussy, and pussy chained to dildo stool, legs spread, waist nipped and mouth full of ball gag, the blonde looked up to Susan's corporal and began typing again. One last chain wrapped Angela up into a nice, neat, integrated slave-receptionist package. The final fine chain ran from the ring set through Angela's clitoris to her keyboard and screen. The chain swinging deliberately loose, and the way the lovely toy was keeping her keyboard on the edge of the desk, was a clear indication of the restraint and obedience that had been trained into her.

YES CORPORAL, she typed, MAY I HELP YOU?

"Er yeah," the man stammered, clearly overawed by the surroundings he found himself in, yanking Susan forward with her lead. "His Majesty wants to look this over."

Every pair of eyes in the room suddenly found Susan's bound nudity vastly more interesting, she could tell, feeling their eyes on her displayed form. Calculating, appraising, cruel! Unable to help herself her breasts rose and fell faster, lust coursing through her.

THANK YOU CORPORAL. THE PRESENT MEETING WILL CONCLUDE SHORTLY. HIS MAJESTY WISHES TO VIEW HER NEXT. PLEASE WAIT A MOMENT.

"Huh, yeah thanks. I mean, good slave," the corporal

managed, slipping into a grateful parade-rest, and then belatedly remembering Susan on the end of the lead he held.

"You, Tits! Heel!" he barked.

Susan obediently dropped to her knees, thighs spread and head up, as she'd been trained. She could see clearly under the desk now. The shaft Angela was mounted on was huge, stretching her wide. The chains were pretty though.

A man exited, and with pounding heart and dry mouth, Susan was led into the King's audience chamber, trying to put an extra little sway and jiggle in her stride without being too obvious. She'd always done her best to appear sexy, desirable and attractive when on display, naked in chains — docile and hot — but before Lady Abigail had bought her, more out of pride and lust than out of any real fear of punishment. Now she had an added incentive. Lady Abigail could get quite irritated, and sadistically inventive, if her property didn't walk with a sexy sway, breasts jiggling and bobbing properly.

Tossing her head to flick her newly-long fringe out of her eyes, her clit pendant's teasing more insistent than ever, Susan was led across a broad expanse of carpet to a large desk. Mouth filled with ball gag, her hair now a honey blonde halo that framed her face, decorated with broad collar and tight waspie-corset, and perched on her toes in five-inch heels, Susan was at least confident she looked her submissive best. Perfect for whether she was being admired as a pet on a lead, performing in a live sex show, or simply being gently enjoyed in her owner's bed. If given a choice, it was the way she herself would have chosen to wrap a Royal present.

A man behind the broad, but strangely scuffed, scarred and battered wooden desk, looked up from his papers, eyes inspecting her naked body without much apparent interest and waved her guiding trooper to a hanging winch chain.

"Hang it from its wrists over there," he ordered the corporal.

Susan recognised the voice from the occasional Royal Proclamation on the 3V, the Slaveworld's three dimensional TV, but found that the portrait artists had used a little artistic licence on banknotes. In the flesh, the King of England was a slight man, much older than she'd expected, with thinning grey hair and a weary air about him. A lot older than his Queen, his true age was hard to judge because of rejuvenation treatments, but he appeared about eighty or so.

Susan suppressed a shiver as, arms released from behind her back, she was made to reach up, the rings on her broad wristcuffs clipped to the chain. The electric motor whined briefly as her toes left the floor. Spinning under the chain, the corporal's hands rested briefly on her hips to steady her, facing His Majesty. Most slaves had their 'thing'. Some hated being fed semen, being paraded naked in public — though Susan loved crowds, especially in a pony girl's harness and bridle — while some hated being made to lick shoes, feet or urinals clean. For some it was simply that they were not naturally bi-sexual, and they found themselves the property of an owner of the wrong sex. Susan's thing was old men! She hated being enjoyed by old men.

There were some slaves who liked the less demanding, less vigorous older owner, but Susan couldn't help herself. Just the thought of wrinkled, trembling, liver-spotted hands on her body filled her with revulsion. Experience told her she was usually okay after a few whip strokes, and responded well once she was actually being shafted by a Wrinkly, but to start with... Yuk! The very idea was just disgusting.

The next pair of dignitaries to see the King were shown in behind her, taking their seats, papers passed back and forth over intense, urgent conversation. It occurred to Susan that perhaps she was flattering herself. There were three other slaves in the room. A girl chained under the King's desk for when His Highness felt like a little oral relief, and a decorative male and female pair who were performing together on a small stage-like pedestal. The girls, who surely represented the King's personal tastes, and not forgetting Angela on the reception desk and the serving twins, were all svelte, almost skinny toys with small pointed breasts. Women more than girls! Perhaps King Philip just wanted to question her about some aspect of Gate travel or about her home reality?

The pair on the stage were a married couple, Susan spotting the wedding rings set through their noses straight away. Individually they appeared nothing special, but like twins, of which the palace had several sets, when matched they became rare and exotic toys and were valuable property. An inventive mind could find humiliations for the married pair that simply didn't exist with the ordinary sex toy.

The slaveboy was standing tightly strapped to an upright pole, the blonde kneeling in front of him licking, kissing and stroking his penis, her body free of restraints, but not going anywhere. Her tongue had been chained to his cock. A ring like Susan's was set through the tip of her tongue, and another was set through the tip of the male slave's penis, the two linked together with a short length of chain. He was groaning and moaning softly behind his gag, cock hugely swollen, and the petite blonde was certainly enthusiastic, so Susan didn't quite see the cause of his distress. Perhaps he wasn't allowed to come, or had been chastised just before she'd entered.

The girl under the strangely scruffy desk was also on her knees, sitting on her heels, wrists chained to ankles. Her control was quite ingenious, Susan thought, once she saw the girl in action. Her long blonde hair had been plaited into a thick rope that was pulled up through a hole in the centre of the desk, a bar woven through the end of the plait as a stop. The King could pull up on the rope, pulling the girl up directly under the hole and her lips off his penis, pushing a pencil through the rope of hair to hold her in place. A simple and clever system, requiring no orders. The pencil pulled out of her hair, the chained slavegirl had enough slack to reach his cock again, and knew what she was supposed to do. When pulled up she would sit still and silent, waiting until her mouth was required again.

"You needn't pant you know. I have noticed how big

your tits are."

With sudden horror, after being ignored for three meetings, Susan realised the King was looking directly at her, addressing her! She felt herself flush helplessly scarlet, ringed nipples rising, cheeks burning under the straps of her ball gag, heat spreading inexorably down her chest. Her corset suddenly seemed too tight to breathe in, the gold pendant hanging from her pierced clitoris so very heavy. She tried to calm herself, deliberately breathing slowly and deeply, but lust was making her gasp ever faster around her ball gag. Susan thought she saw a fleeting smile tug at the corner of his mouth.

"But I suppose my wife The Queen enjoys you, does she?"

Hanging naked from her wrists, Susan nodded obediently, nipples swollen painfully erect now, heat stirring in her groin, juices flowing. Oh God, the Slaveworld's King of England himself was talking to her, his eyes were on her! He nodded thoughtfully to himself, and then looked up to greet the next appointment. Three meetings later, lust still swelling her breasts and clitoris, Susan was finally forced to concede that the brief exchange had been just that. It was done. It really was unfair sometimes, the way nobles treated their sex toys.

The meetings went on and on. It should have been fascinating, listening in on the workings of a Kingdom, but Susan was simply too hot and wet to concentrate. She wanted to come! She'd been a really good girl these last four weeks. Why wasn't she allowed to come? A familiar voice dragged her thoughts out of her submissive and humiliating fantasies and back to the present.

"Hey!" His Majesty protested as Her Highness, Queen Victoria, having entered through an adjoining door, swept his papers up out of his hands and shuffled them into a neat pile.

"Enough for today My Love. You have staff for this remember?" she said, her eyes sweeping the room and alighting on Susan's naked form. "Oh really! You haven't even touched her. You promised me you'd give her a try."

"My love, you know I'm always willing to share one of your choices with you in bed," the King protested.

Susan, listening with bated breath, found herself if possible even hotter. The Lords' and Ladies' idea of sexual intimacy, making love, was sharing a slave together. After the usual torments and humiliations of foreplay, that usually meant being penetrated front and back with cock and strap-on dildo, or more often, enjoyed doggie style, the Noble Lord thrusting into her from behind, her head between the thighs of his Lady wife. Right about now, being the bound, blindfolded meat in a Royal slave sandwich sounded just heavenly!

"And we will," the Queen promised, "but first I want you to try her out. I've been trying to get you to give her a ride for three weeks. Now, she's on your diary — I've booked her in — so you don't have anything else to do this afternoon."

Toes swaying just above the carpet, her almost naked body stretched out on display under the winch chain, Susan's heart thudded louder in her chest as the thrillingly commanding woman approached her. She suspected being owned by the short, authoritative, middle-aged noble might be almost as delightful as kneeling at Lady Abigail's feet. The Queen of England ran an appreciative hand up and down one of Susan's buttocks with an easy, practised, familiarity.

"I'm busy, and she's not going back through the Gate, and that's final," the King muttered, his Queen grinning.

Susan squeaked, a tight grip on her neatly trimmed tuft of pubic hair used to pull her hips forward, body arched out into a bow. She sighed in gag-muffled delight as Queen Victoria's fingers stroked, lightly to begin with, between her pussy lips. Her moan of pleasure as the fingers pushed deeper into her sex, penetrating her, abruptly became a wail of distress as the pressure of thrusting fingers finally became more of a strain than her stretched, cruelly yanked, pubic hair could bear. Susan slipped out of the Queen's grasp, and it felt like quite a few of the newly blonde curls had been ripped out of her body too. Victoria patted her pussy, happily kissed both straining nipples, and then reached under Susan to push the gold pendant up into her anus, the clit pendant's fine chain now pulled through her sex.

"You really like her don't you?" King Philip asked, seriously but faintly amused. "Or is it just the huge tits?"

"Heavenly aren't they?" Victoria sighed, hefting one of the big globes, Susan's flesh spilling out of her small hand. "Don't you think?"

Susan felt saliva running down and between her breasts, the Queen's fingernails trailing down her spine, the fully-dressed woman's dress brushing across her legs.

"A bit short, a bit young and more prominent — curvy — than I'd like," he agreed. 'But I'm sure she's an adequate ride."

The Queen slipped behind her, Susan still hanging from her wrists facing the King. She groaned in pleasure as her breasts were squeezed and kneaded from behind, strong fingers sinking fingernails painfully, delightfully, deep into her heavy flesh.

"More than adequate! And her figure's the least of it actually," Victoria said softly rubbing Susan's nipples across each other, "though I admit, physically she's very much to my tastes. The reason I want you to shaft her, is then you'll finally believe me, that it's safe to let her return to her own world. She won't betray us, and she'll come back of her own free will. She's just like Precious, a perfect slave, born to be owned."

"So she's a natural submissive and enjoys her use," the old monarch agreed. "That still doesn't mean she can be trusted. I'm sure she could find someone to properly train and discipline her, back on her own world."

"It would still be a game, not real. She can't really be truly owned in her own reality," Victoria pressed.

"She likes it here that much?" the King snorted incredulously.

"Try her!" Victoria challenged, twisting fingers again making Susan groan in pain, nipples hard against her tormentor's palms. "Just give her a good shafting, then make your decision. That's all I ask."

Susan, still hanging from her wrists, was helplessly, desperately, aroused now, almost having trouble concentrating on the meaning of their words. How utterly humiliating! Naked, gagged and bound — a girl couldn't be more available — and the Queen was having to cajole and prod her reluctant husband into having sex with her.

"Alright, alright! I'll give her a try," the King of England surrendered.

"Promise?" Victoria pressed.

"I'll give her a good, hard, long, fucking," the greying King Philip assured his Queen.

Victoria kissed Susan lightly on the shoulder, and jauntily ordered her to "Be good!" with a little pat on the behind, before kissing her husband and leaving the room.

His most gracious Majesty, King Philip IV sighed, stood, and walked slowly around Susan's suspended body. He was clearly a little irritated at being pestered into having to agree to have sex with her, and Susan certainly didn't want to be enjoyed by someone so old, but by squeezing down on the pendant deep in her back passage, she dutifully made herself moan in lust. The fine chain from the pendant clipped to her clit ring cut painfully into her pussy, but dragged deliciously at the pierced nub.

At the sound, the King permitted himself a slight approving nod when he saw her hips twitching, but there was still a look of faint disdain on his face when he reached out and lifted a breast, his touch cold and clammy. He bounced her breast in his palm as so many others had done, though with a lot less enthusiasm than most, then reached out and hooked a finger through her nipple ring. With his free hand he slowly lifted the full mound out of his palm, peeling Susan's ample flesh up out of his hand, and then lowered her breast back into his splayed fingers. Susan panted harder behind her gag, an insistent heat in her groin, nipples aching harder still. She desperately wished for someone younger to twist, bite, squeeze or clamp the swollen nubs.

"Oh well, I suppose I'll have to," he sighed. "A promise

is a promise."

Clearly he would

Clearly he would have much preferred to be enjoying the charms of one of his own more mature, slender slaves. Hanging naked from her wrists and feeling somewhat slighted, Susan knew that even if her mouth hadn't been filled with a ball gag, she would never have dared to tactfully suggest to the monarch that he might perhaps be more appreciative. You didn't upset people who had complete power over you. His hands stroked up her thighs, over hips, following the lower edge of her crushing waspie-corset, and back down over buttocks, his groin brushing lightly against her crotch.

"Nice skin," he murmured, sounding pleased for the first time.

Susan preened, knowing full well how nice she was to stroke. Lords, Ladies and soldiers were always running their hands over her satin skin, though usually they also appreciated the weight of her over-large slave breasts as well. His fingers stroked lightly through her neatly trimmed tuft of pubic curls, and distracted by growing arousal, Susan didn't quite manage not to flinch as she suddenly realised — visualised — that his wrinkled, liver-spotted hand was on her belly.

"So!" he hissed with a grin, Susan having suddenly made herself more interesting.

She moaned in obedient surrender, juices flowing, the sound becoming a soft wail of pleasure as the King's fingers stroked deeper in and out of her sex to one side of the clit chain. But he wasn't fooled.

"Do I disgust you, pretty toy? My wrinkled old hands on your firm young body?"

God, he was sharp! She risked faking a louder moan, eyes closed, but he wasn't fooled. A hand in her hair to yank open her eyes, he again lifted a breast in one hand, this time to his lips. Susan couldn't help shivering in revulsion as loose, slobbery, old-man's lips closed over her nipple, the steel ring set through the swollen nub caught between yellowed teeth. Humiliated tears welled in her eyes as she was made to gasp in pleasure for real.

"I'm a hundred and twenty one years old you know," he told her conversationally, unbuckling her ball gag.

Susan felt a moment's nausea as his tongue was thrust into her mouth, but her training made her respond; and then she was forced to gasp pleasure into the King's mouth as fingers again probed inside her sex. A deeply shamed, shuddering sob racked her body. The familiar taste of her own juices, fingers thrust into her mouth calmed her. Her breasts were slapped, nipples twisted, clitoris pinched, and all the time fingers kept thrusting in and out of her, only to then be pushed into her mouth. Spinning gently under her chain, Susan was played like a musical instrument by the vastly more experienced monarch. He soon had her panting in desperate lust, eager to be ridden, even by a man who revolted her!

The King rummaged in a toybox a moment, considered a whip, and then tossed it aside. A rubber-coated steel bar, like a bit without a bridle, but with a chain hanging down from each end was pushed into Susan's mouth. The chains had little spiked metal spheres on their ends, which rolled over, and bounced off and between her breasts; sharp little pins prickling the heavily enlarged melons with every breath, or movement of her head. Padlocked into a familiar, broad, tight collar, she had no choice but to hold her head up and forward. She could not hold the pin-spiked little metal balls away from her own flesh!

Hobble chain removed, the King attached a length of chain to each ankle, and then one after the other, her legs were pulled up, the ends of the new chains attached to the same winch chain her wristcuffs were secured to.

Swinging gently back and forth as the King stepped out of his trousers, her legs now pulled up in front of her in a V, hips and pussy thrust forward, Susan waited breathless, to be used, shafted — enjoyed! The winch whined briefly as she was lowered fractionally, to put her pussy on the same level as the King's crotch.

"I want your eyes on mine throughout your fucking,

understood?" he ordered.

Susan groaned assent. Clearly not considering her worth the effort, just doing what he'd agreed to, her user didn't take off his shirt, even his jacket, or remove his shoes and socks. Just stepped out of his shorts. Susan felt her eyes widen in surprise. Swinging between skinny, bony legs, he was hung like a donkey! The aristocrats were rarely vain enough to indulge in the facelifts and the like they subjected their property to. But they were not above enhancing the sexual experience and their own stamina for themselves.

Her user unclipped the pendant-chain from her pierced clitoris, the chain now hanging out of her anus and the gold pendant functioning as a small butt plug, taking a moment to inspect the bar code on her ass. Then steadying her, he stood directly in front of her, raising his limp cock and letting it flop down on top of her invitingly thrust-forward sex. His flesh was hot on her pussy, Susan was so hot and wet herself, her helplessly twitching hips disguised her disgusted shiver. Slowly, with all the time in the world, her user rubbed his penis back and forth across her flesh, becoming gradually harder, his cock nosing between her sex lips as he became harder still. With a firm grip he grabbed twin handfuls of breast from underneath to pull her swaying, suspended body forward, the pin-lined spheres rolling down each breast into her armpits in a trail of little needle stabs!

"Twenty three years old?" he mused, rubbing his cock up against her.

The first six numbers of her tattooed serial number, under the bar code the old man had just inspected, revealed Susan's age.

"Do you realise I'm almost a hundred years older than you?" King Philip teased softly.

Susan's gasp of horror became a rising wail of pained ecstasy as the King's big, heavy, and now quite rigid shaft was brutally thrust into her sex, the huge meat pole rammed almost to the hilt in one savage thrust. She bucked and twisted, squeaking around her bit, tiny pins stabbing into her breasts, but hanging suspended under her winch chain the King held her easily in place with hands under her buttocks. Standing between the raised V of her legs, leaning against her thighs, he pumped his cock in and out of her with long, slow, deep, easy strokes. She was completely helpless!

Looking only into His Majesty's eyes as ordered, gasping in forced pleasure each time he thrust his massive erection into her, quaking breasts tortured with every thrust, wrists and ankles all secured to the same single hanging chain, Susan was quickly and easily ridden to her first unwilling orgasm, her squeal of ecstasy quite uninhibited. Being enjoyed while suspended from a single chain in this fashion, legs spread and nipples teased, was as she knew, actually very easy on the slave; her only discomfort the, lower front edge of her corset digging into her belly because her hips were lifted.

The old man standing in front of her thrust harder and faster, scattering stinging slaps across her outer thighs and behind now. Susan obediently helped by deliberately tossing her head, making the pin-covered spheres suspended from her bit swing out and bounce harder off her breasts. Reminded of her beloved owner, Lady Abigail, sitting on her face in the Grand hotel, she found she loved it! Gasping a little himself, quite energetic considering his advanced years, the King seemed a bit more intent now, earlier reservations forgotten. Susan bit harder into her bit, forcing her eyes open, as the remorseless, huge cock pumping in and out of her continued to be rammed to the hilt. She whimpered, another orgasm building.

Susan tried to hold back, owners liked it when she came as they did, but it was no use! As it happened, she'd misjudged the King, and after shrugging out of his jacket, he effortlessly rode her to two more breathless, all-consuming orgasms before coming himself. Desperately hot and dripping wet, Susan wasn't even sure she really had felt his semen pumped inside her until he slumped against her, breathing deeply.

He worried her for a second, panting so hard, but after a moment he looked up, giving her breasts a moan-producing squeeze. Susan was often treated in similar fashion after sex, though it had taken her a while to figure out why. She'd eventually realised, that with her eyes lust-glazed, her noble users were never quite sure if they had her full attention of not. His penis slowly softening, King Philip was still inside her.

"I've barely put a sweat on you have I?" he panted. "Ready for more?"

Susan moaned emphatically, eagerly nodding her head as far as her high collar would allow, pin-lined spheres bouncing off her boobs again.

"Like to lick my prick clean?"

She nodded eagerly again. The winch whined as she was lowered further, her bottom swaying just above the carpet, the King's penis swinging in front of her face. Looking up his body, a faint smile tugging at his lips now, she moaned plaintively again and was allowed to drop her bit. It had never occurred to her to do so without permission, even though the rubber-coated bar had not been strapped into her mouth.

His shaft glistening with a mixture of semen and her own juices, Susan ducked forward and took the softening shaft into her mouth without hesitation. It was a taste she'd been trained to enjoy, and sex with a noble Lord was not really complete without it. Knowing he'd like it, she relaxed her throat muscles and swallowed the heavy cock, nose eventually mashed into pubic hair.

"Good toy!" he breathed, the shaft down her throat slowly hardening again, forcing itself out of her throat as her user became stiff again.

His Majesty chose to withdraw, tossing aside the rest of his clothing. Clearly Susan had been a far more energetic ride than he'd expected. He lowered her to the floor, and released her wrist and anklecuffs from the chain. Waved to her feet, semen and her own juices glistening on sex and inner thighs, still in only collar, corset and five inch heels, she obediently slipped into the 'stand' position. Motionless, feet set apart, head up, and hands behind her head, fingers laced, the naked King walked slowly around her again. She quivered in pleasure as he idly stroked a slap-pink buttock.

A puzzled look on his face, he again stroked her belly, squeezing and licking her breasts, finally kissing her on the lips. Susan sighed in delight.

"You were horrified at the thought of being fucked by me, weren't you?" he demanded.

"Yes Master," Susan agreed honestly.

"And in heaven from the moment I started?" he pressed.

"Yes Master," she agreed placidly.

She wondered why he was surprised. She loved anyone who made her come, at least for a while. Didn't all slaves? Clearly intrigued now, His Majesty pulled hard down on the chain trailing from her anus, the heavy gold pendant popping out of her, and then re-attached it to her pierced clitoris. Curiously, he squeezed her corset-nipped waist with both hands, but the decorative restraint held her rigid as steel and there was no give. One hand under her jaw, fingers digging into her cheeks to force her mouth open, he pulled out and lifted her tongue.

Placidly still, slave breasts rising and falling gently, nipples still swollen, and the air on the moisture between her legs cool now, her clit pendant bumping lightly between her thighs as it swayed, it took Susan a moment to understand what he was looking for. She spent so much time in a ball gag, it was easy to forget the tattoo was there. But on the underside of her tongue had been tattooed, Susan, her birth name.

He ran his fingers over her teeth, tried to get a finger under her tight collar, and concluded the inspection with a palm pressing into her belly, fingers cupping her sex. Susan moaned in docile pleasure.

"Victoria's right! You are a hot little beast aren't you?" he said, still cupping her sex, ducking his head forward to nip at a breast with his teeth. "How tall are you in bare feet?"

"Five feet two, Master."

"Waist without the corset?"

"Twenty one and a half inches, Master."

"And so very placid."

Susan tightened her laced fingers behind her head, bracing herself into position as more bites were scattered across her big breasts. She whimpered, but held position easily enough.

"Tell me pretty toy, do you like existing purely for sex? For the pleasure of my class?"

"Yes Master."

"Being bought and sold? Hunted, tortured and fucked? Do you like pulling a pony trap through the city streets, naked, a bit buckled into your mouth? Do you like the whip, the dildos, the tug of the reins on your nipple rings?"

"Oh yes Master," she breathed. "It's wonderful!"

"Hmm," he nodded thoughtfully. "I'm beginning to understand the appeal of British slaves."

His fingers scooped wetness out of her sex, which he stroked and rubbed around and onto her aching nipples. Being helplessly bound was so much easier than having to obediently hold still. Her breasts held together and lifted to her lips, Susan was then ordered to lick her own nipples clean, a task she wasn't given often enough in her opinion. Happily, she closed her lips over the ringed nubs, tonguing her own flesh. Actually allowed to stimulate herself, and again allowed to taste mingled semen and her own juices, she obeyed the King's order with a contented sigh.

"Now I know you're a bright girl. And you heard what Victoria and I were discussing?"

Susan, tonguing a ringed nipple, mouth full of her own flesh, nodded.

"So you understand that Victoria wants to send you on a little task for her, back to your homeworld?"

"Yes Master," Susan agreed placidly, when her own nipple was at last pulled out of her mouth.

"Though of course there's no question of my allowing that! Do you still want me to enjoy you?"

"Oh yes, Master. That's what I'm here for."

The King chuckled.

"Kneel in front of my desk, tits on the table!" he barked.

Susan obeyed, folding her arms behind her back, wrist to elbow, her breasts on the edge of the desk flattening a little under their own weight, the heavy globes lightly squeezed together, touching. The naked monarch settled into his chair opposite Susan, pulling the pencil that restrained her out of the plait of the girl under the table so that she could lick him hard again. Her own nipples straining towards him like gun barrels, a raging heat in her belly, Susan realised she was almost pathetically eager to be enjoyed further. Her weeks in the cellblock had been mostly very frustrating.

The King lifted first one breast and then the other, squirting something out of a tube onto the desk. She felt her flesh bonding to the desk almost immediately. Some sort of superglue! She then obediently held out first one hand and then the other, at the King's order, pressing each onto her own hips. Skin bonded to skin even faster then her breasts had stuck to the table. Powerful stuff! She was totally helpless.

No wonder the desk's surface was so scuffed and scared. Restraint without restraints. The desk must have been sanded down and re-varnished countless times. No doubt this was how the King really preferred to enjoy his property, his use of her swinging under the winch chain had just been him keeping his word to his wife the Queen. Only now, Susan had caught his interest.

And thinking about it, as long as she was helpless, why not? There was no real reason why restraints had to mean just rope, straps, cuffs, and the like. The undersides of her breasts glued to the table, hands stuck to her own sides, Susan watched with growing arousal as the King, eyes half-closed in pleasure, allowed the girl under the table to lick and tongue him. He contentedly lit a small, dark, cheroot, probably a sexual stimulant as tobacco wasn't common on the Slaveworld. It was bad for the health.

"I suppose those big tits get whipped and shocked a lot?"

"Yes Master," she agreed placidly.

"That's going to come as a bit of a shock to future toys we collect from your dimension, isn't it?"

"Yes Master," Susan agreed, unperturbed. "They'll get

used to it."

He nodded, and reached out with the smoking cheroot. Susan squeaked in alarm and tried to pull away.

"Don't worry, the mark won't be permanent," he assured her. "A quick spray of new skin, ten minutes with the vet at most."

That the mark might be permanent had never even crossed her mind, but it was a natural enough first thought for an owner. Damage affected her value. She forced herself still.

Slowly the King pushed and twisted the glowing orange end of the cheroot down onto the upper swell of her right breast. Flesh hissed for a moment as it burned, Susan crying out in agonised distress as she was marked. The burn's pain, throbbing and pulsing, burrowed deeper long after the stubbed-out dog-end was removed. Swaying back — her glued-down breasts held firmly, just stretching — she saw black ash on the scarlet burn marking her breast. Susan realised she'd almost come on the spot. The possibility of being branded with a hot iron had lurked far beyond the limits of her pre-owned fantasies, but in dark moments, she'd still sometimes toyed with the thought all the same. The smell of her own scorched flesh in her nostrils brought it all flooding back, lust overwhelming fear.

"Lick it better, and think about what your docile obedience is condemning other girls from your world to," he advised.

Collar digging in hard under her chin, Susan tasted ash as she licked, pain pulsing each time her tongue trailed over the burn. It didn't really hurt more than a good shock or whip stroke, she decided. And while she'd much prefer to be licking semen off her large breasts, it wasn't anything she or any other well-trained slave couldn't take.

"No?" he probed when he'd asked for her thoughts. "But why should you care about strangers? Perhaps we should move a little closer to home. You have a sister I believe. Now, you tell me truthfully how you feel — and remember, before I made you come a couple of times you were recoiling from me, that you didn't want me to enjoy you in whatever manner I chose — and I'll personally spare your sister from any future cull."

Just for a moment Susan considered lying, but knew she could be checked up on later with a lie detector. There was really only one answer.

"It will be my privilege to be further enjoyed by you Master," she said softly.

"You really are quite delicious," he said, lighting a candle and pushing its base into her mouth. "Now coat those big tits in wax for me. All over!"

Susan bit lightly into the soft wax for a better grip, wincing as the first scalding droplet of hot wax dripped off the candle end onto her flesh. As always with hot wax, pain came as a delayed reaction, increasing, flaring, after the wax landed and dried. Another droplet splashed down onto her breast, and then another, each one a little delivery of molten agony. Susan gasping, moved the candle over her other breast, and then back, but there was no escape. The King was clearly enjoying her distress, especially when, forcing herself not to bite through the candle, she dutifully coated both ringed nipples in a thick, painful, layer of wax. He was sitting slouched back in his chair, having his penis licked, sipping tea he'd had one of the serving twins bring him, while she tortured herself for him.

He would occasionally give her a different coloured candle to hold in her mouth, so that the frozen rivulets of wax that had dried while running down her gasp-heaving breasts, were streaked different colours. White burned the hottest. Cracks appeared in the wax coating as she flinched, occasional sobs making the heavy globes quiver, but the undersides of her breasts were still firmly stuck to the desk!

Susan had once managed to stick her own fingers together with superglue, but it had been no big deal. Skin flakes off naturally all the time, and sweat secretes under an airtight coating. With a little patience, she knew the glue would peel off itself after ten minutes or so. The more generous amounts used by his Majesty would clearly hold her longer, and his superglue seemed to bond deeper into skin. Perhaps a formula especially designed for use on sex slaves, with a built-in antiperspirant to prevent the glue peeling away so easily? It was only after a good half hour of obedient, gasping, self-torture that she felt one of her fingers had come loose from her own hip.

Finally the King pulled the girl under his desk off his cock by her plait, pulling her head up under the hole in his desk with the rope of hair, pushing a pencil through the plait to hold her in place under the centre of the desk again, out of the way. Standing he walked around behind Susan, pulled her to her feet with both hands on her corseted waist, and without preliminaries or ceremony, rammed an again rock-hard cock deep into her sex.

Susan cried out in pained delight as she was taken brutally from behind, dripping pussy stretched wide. Wax cracked and flaked off her breasts as, forced to bend her upper body forward, their undersides still stuck to the desk, the heavy mounds were painfully twisted and squeezed up under her. The wonderful, firm, hot-meat rod filling her, pumping in and out of her sex was compensation enough.

Her clit pendant swung back and forth on its teasing chain, and in this position the King was able to land really hard, stinging, slaps on her backside. Squeaking as she was spanked, knowing His Majesty was leaving handprints on her buttocks, and lost in lust, Susan discovered she'd bitten through and dropped her candle. Her buttocks soon throbbing, no doubt quivering scarlet, Susan's own hands just millimetres away from the slaps cracking down on her behind. But there was no way to protect herself. Her palms were still firmly glued to her own hips.

This was a great way to be fucked!

No longer concerned with her user's age, and after a solid half-hour of delicious tit torture, breasts squashed and bottom burning, if anything Susan was easier than ever to make come. She was shrieking in ecstasy for the sixth time, up on her toes, legs locked rigid, the King's hands tight on her corset-nipped waist when his Majesty finally pumped a second load of semen into her. An orgasm in a really tight corset, cinched waist reinforcing and magnifying sensation, somehow confining pleasure to the groin, always made her loud. Except when being enjoyed orally, used to a ball gag strapped into her mouth during sex, Susan worried she might have been a little too loud, but the King just gave her an approving pat as he finally pulled his huge cock from her body.

"Silly!" she told herself after a moment's thought. What noble getting on in years didn't like audible proof of his sexual prowess echoing down the corridors and ringing out of the windows? She was too used to being enjoyed by women.

Panting heavily, breasts still squashed and twisted uncomfortably up under her, mingled juices and semen running down her thighs, Susan waited patiently in position, standing with legs spread, bent forward from the waist. The King's fingers scooped more wetness out of her sex, which he again pushed into her mouth. Trying not to be greedy, Susan slowly and sensuously licked and sucked all four fingers clean. Her grey-haired user patted her throbbing behind again, reached under her for the clit pendant and again pushed it into her anus, the thin chain once more cutting into her pussy. Only then was she allowed to drop back to her knees.

The King used an aerosol glue solvent in a spray-can to release her breasts from the desk, and ordered her around it, sitting her on the desk edge in front of his chair. A pool of glue under each reddened buttock fastened her in place again, her palms released from her hips only long enough to be given a new coat of glue, and firmly pushed onto the desk surface behind her. As before, skin bonded to varnished wood in seconds. Sitting on the edge of the desk, leaning back on her arms behind her, His Majesty's final touch was to lift each leg, and glue Susan's calves to her thighs, her exposed pussy right in front of him.

Clearly having had to exert himself a little on her last use, this time His Majesty ordered a glass of iced lemonade to sip while he again enjoyed watching Susan tormenting herself. Settling back into his chair to allow the slave under the desk to once more lick him, first clean, and then hard, he pressed the ice-dewed glass against Susan's sex. She gasped.

"Still bright eyed and bushy tailed, aren't you?" he sighed. "I bet with your sexual stamina, you're popular at orgies?"

"Yes Master," Susan agreed smugly, her pussy lips frozen.

Slaveworld orgies were great fun. Blind and deaf under a tight latex hood, mouth held open by a ring gag and hands cuffed behind her back, a slavegirl was just tossed into a pile of bodies. To be used by any unseen guest, as, how, where, and as often as they liked!

A lit candle pushed back into her mouth to hold, this time the King expected her to drip hot wax between her own legs. The longer drop, her collar not letting her look down, and her already tortured breasts getting in the way, hindered accuracy, but her master was in no hurry at all. Susan had all afternoon. His Majesty amused himself slapping new and existing dried wax off her breasts, clearly enjoying the swing and bounce of her slap-reddened flesh, even while he unfavourably compared, what he called her udders, to the firm, delicately pointed breasts of the twin blonde serving slaves now flanking his chair. The chained blondes, wearing only translucent harem pants and standing neatly to attention, waiting to be ordered into motion, watched Susan having her breasts slapped and dripping scalding candlewax onto her own pussy impassively.

"Now I want that cunt totally covered," he warned. "Completely closed, hood, clit ring, the lot!"

Arms pulled back behind her, palms glued to the desk and legs helplessly raised, Susan gasped in obedient lust as another slap stung a breast with a stinging crack, the firm heavy mound bouncing, and then swinging back for the next blow with a quiver. Even though she couldn't look down, she soon got her aim in; the way molten wax stung into her sex being quite unmistakable! It was incredibly difficult not to press her thighs protectively together, her ordeal made harder by disdainful looks the King's twins were now giving her. Like they could do better!

When Susan had again tortured herself to her user's

satisfaction, and he was hard again, the King pulled away the wax between her legs. Susan squealed as her remaining pubic hair was ripped out, His Majesty pushing aside the clit chain and again ramming his huge penis hard into her. Clearly he liked that first, soft, cry of pain when he first penetrated his chosen victim. Sitting on the edge of the desk she was glued to, Susan was in a very convenient position for the King to shaft, but he wasn't really able to spank her, having to content himself with occasionally twisting and squeezing her slave breasts to stimulate her to greater efforts to please. As she moaned and gasped in lust, pain and pleasure intermingled, looking over her user's shoulder, Susan was rewarded with a hastily hidden flash of envy on the face of one of the watching twins.

The lovely pair were in her cellblock she remembered now, which wasn't going to help her own status or treatment as ' teachers pet'. But to hell with that now!

"Thank you Master, thank you Master, thank you Master..." she groaned, as fingers twisted into her breasts.

Pussy stuffed to bursting point, she was expertly ridden to yet another orgasm. The tormenting clit chain, pushed aside by His Majesty's cock, tugged devilishly at her pierced clitoris with every deep, hard, thrust, pulling the pendant slightly back and forth inside her anus. She came and came again, wave after wave of pleasure washing over her firmly stuck-down body.

Lust-swollen breasts throbbing, panting, limp, trembling legs still invitingly raised, this time she had no idea how many times she'd been made to come when the King finally withdrew and splashed hot come over her sex. He stroked his semen onto her now baby-smooth belly, Susan surprised to be rewarded for her efforts with a light kiss on the lips. She responded eagerly, as his fingers slid easily across her semen-moist flesh. Many female slaves were clean shaven, but she'd been decorated with a neatly trimmed vertical tuft above her sex right from the beginning. She thought it looked attractive and had grown to like it, but had once again been reminded, her opinions counted for nothing! Only her compliance.

He was right not to trust her. Could she really condemn other Earth girls to this life of humiliation, pain and shame through inactivity if she was returned to Britain? Not turn herself in? The King then let her lick semen and her own juices off his fingers again, and the answer was obvious. Of course she could!

Mindlessly obedient now, totally compliant, after the King had recovered his breath, and the slave under his desk had licked him clean and hard again, Susan was secured in a new position. Sure the cheroot had been some sort of sexual stimulant to keep the King going now, she hoped his heart could take it. Her hands were glued to her own breasts, a winch-suspended pole pushed through her arms behind her back and raised, so that she could be bent forward, caned, and then taken from behind on her toes, hanging under her own arms. To avoid ripping the skin off her own breasts, Susan was forced to painfully squeeze and twist her own fingers deep into the heavy mounds as she hung under the pole from her elbows. His Majesty stood behind her thrusting hard and deep into her sex.

She didn't mind in the slightest. She was absolutely delighted to finally get her hands on her own ample flesh, the first time since being sold she'd been allowed to touch her own enlarged boobs. They were huge! And so heavy. She came again and again from that one.

Panting gently, a sheen of sweat on her skin, Susan swayed upright when the King pulled his cock out of her, head up and ankles together, still held in place under the winch chain with the pole threaded through her elbows behind her back. Her hands still superglued to her own breasts, she realised with faint disappointment that His Majesty had finally had his fill of her. The old man was exhausted.

The King flopped naked into his chair, his eyes closed, while his breathing gradually slowed. Susan watching, the grey-haired King's semen leaking out of her sex, surreptitiously squeezed her own breasts, trying not to moan aloud, palms and fingers still firmly bonded to the lust-swollen globes. The King finally sat up, studying her bound nudity thoughtfully as he enjoyed a light late lunch, sipping another cooling glass of iced lemonade. Finished, he stood and walked around her, first stroking her belly and then patting a buttock.

"Let's find out what you can really take," he decided.

Susan was bent over the desk facing him, her belly and palms stuck to the desk with the oh-so-useful superglue, breasts free this time so that the King in his chair in front of her could handle, squeeze or shock the firm, heavy mounds. From behind, taking turns when they tired, the twins, wearing strap-on dildos were set to whipping and screwing Susan, ordered to hold up her head by her hair so that the King could see her eyes. They were very enthusiastic, the brutal shafting going on and on and on, Susan wailing helplessly as she was made to come again and again, pain and pleasure a whirlwind fusion. After the initial rush, each orgasm was harder and left her further exhausted, her squeaks, yelps and cries becoming more plaintive, despairing!

When one of the twins finally made her cry out in ecstasy, the pair swapped over, both giving her a few whip strokes before the next strap-on dildo was pushed into her dripping sex. A half dozen paired whip strokes after each orgasm was the perfect pick-me-up, and again and again Susan found herself being forced to gasp and squeak in pleasure long after she thought she was spent. The King handling her breasts, her belly, forearms and palms still firmly stuck to the desk she was bent forward over, Susan found the twins' bellies brushing across her whipped scalded, throbbing, burning hindquarters as they ravaged her, very stimulating.

Inevitably, despite the viper kiss of twin lashes across her behind, Susan tired. The King started to use a small shock baton to deliver electric shocks to her breasts, which kept Susan obediently focused and hot for a good while longer. Uncounted bolts of agony engulfed the over-large melons, nipples seared, but as always she responded well to tit torture and dazed, barely able to think now, Susan found she didn't in any way resent being kept hot and wet in this way. It was especially satisfying for her when His Majesty decided the blondes shafting her would have to be punished for making such an unseemly fuss, the current passing through her body to theirs. They really were a soft and pampered pair of pets!

He screwed tight clamps down onto her nipples, which helped her to come again, and then he had his blonde pets thrust a full-size butt plug into her back passage, which kept her aroused a little longer. Sweat-gleaming, her pink ball gag was now buckled tightly back into her mouth, the King less tolerant of ecstatic squeals when he wasn't shafting her himself. And every time a shock to her breasts made Susan blink tears and sweat out of her eyes, she found him looking into her face with detached, attentive, interest.

In between ramming their strap-on dildos deep and hard into her helpless body, the pick-me-up whippings and the King's relentless tit torture continued. Legs spread wide, the soles of her shoes also glued to the floor, Susan realised she was slavering helplessly around her ball gag as she yelped and squeaked. Oh God! Utterly exhausted, she wailed around the mouth-filling restraint in sudden horrified understanding. He was going to have her fucked unconscious!

And the shafting and torture went on and on. The last thing Susan remembered was the King of England saying, "We really will have to see if there are more like you at home!"

She still wasn't sure if she'd passed her test, when she found herself the meat in a Royal slave sandwich that evening. He'd seemed to enjoy her once he'd got going, and the Queen seemed pleased. But then, nobody told slaves anything!

In a small African dictatorship, in a heavily guarded room in the cellars of the Presidential palace, a bright shimmering Gateway to another world hung suspended in a light copper framework. The exchange was going quickly and efficiently. Gold bullion, in exchange for five eighteen year olds — the deal was hopefully the first of many — the hooded, bound, naked girls, tied neck to neck with a single rope.

Pre-arranged, an RSP trooper with a portable receiver Gate had used the one-way Gate to jump into the middle of a national park the night before, making his way to the Presidential palace with a letter of introduction from the Ambassador. Now a stable two-way portal, out of reach of British detection, could be established in this cellar anytime the Slaveworld authorities wished. The Ambassador clasped hands with his old friend, as Captain Scott inspected the naked merchandise.

"You told me, but I didn't really believe it," the general said wonderingly, looking at the Gate.

"I know. Amazing isn't it?" the Ambassador agreed.

As they watched, two young women stepped through the shimmering portal and were led away, the second part of the deal. The blindfolded pair, carrying backpacks, were supposed to be dressed as ordinary tourists, so that they could blend in on the Realworld unnoticed. But the Slaveworld's security, used to dealing with either naked slaves or robed and veiled peasants, had got it just slightly wrong. In sprayed-on jeans, held in place with a far too tight broad belt, huge tits straining against snug t-shirts, the drop-dead gorgeous pair were going to turn heads wherever they went! Oh well, not his problem.

The shorter blonde's nipple rings were clearly visible under the strained material of her top, the pet-tag hanging from her earlobe labelling her a slave called Honey, listing her owner as Lady Abigail. The taller brunette's nametag said she answered to Precious, her owner, HRH Queen Victoria II.

The Ambassador suspected that anyone confronted with such voluptuous magnificence was going to be too distracted to look closely at what appeared to be single earrings. And even if they did, or body piercings set off airport metal detectors and a strip search revealed tattooed bar codes, serial numbers and Precious's brand, so what! The girls were obviously free to come and go, and carried large amounts of cash.

They might be mistaken for jet-setting call girls, but real slavery in this day and age? Preposterous! The President's men would have the two taken to the airport and put on a flight to Britain, where hopefully their expertly faked passports would get them back into the country. To do what there, the Ambassador wasn't quite sure, but he didn't see that they could do much harm. And the blindfolds ensured they couldn't identify either the Ambassador or his friend the President, which was all he really cared about.

He wondered how his unwitting alibi Marie was enjoying her first Slaveworld hunt. She'd been practicing with a tranquilliser-dart-firing automatic rifle when he'd last seen her. Had she chosen to drive and whip her one-time friend Ruth as a pony girl, stuffed with twin dildos, in harness and bridle and with her reins attached to nipple rings? Or drive another naked pony slave and hunt the former law student herself?

"Oh, almost forgot!" his friend said.

The President opened the wooden crate he'd been sitting on when the Ambassador stepped through the Gate. The young woman inside was hog-tied, her head encased in a tight leather hood, and white in contrast to the five black slaves Captain Scott was inspecting, but the Ambassador recognised the body immediately. He'd enjoyed it often enough. It was the Australian reporter!

"Someone, somehow, heard about her trial. Her embassy's been asking about her, so I had to tell them she escaped from jail. I thought you might like to have her?"

"Oh yes! Thank you very much!"

Captain Scott was quite amenable. While two RSP troopers held the hog-tied former reporter suspended facedown between them, he wrote across a buttock in marker pen PROPERTY OF THE BRITISH AMBASSADOR, and waved the trio on through the Gate.

Although she didn't know it yet, the lovely journalist had just stumbled onto a story any reporter would give her eyeteeth for. The story of the century! To allow her to make the most of the opportunity, the Ambassador decided he would have to ensure the blonde experienced every possible aspect of Slaveworld life. He chuckled to himself. She had simply no idea how interesting her life was going to become, or how much fun he was going to have with her!

Perhaps he would even let her keep a journal, and publish it in the Realworld as fiction. It might make interesting reading!

And now for the opening of next month's title:

TRAINED IN THE HAREM by MARK STEWART

CHAPTER 1.

Captain John Macklay stood on the poop deck and looked around with a stern expression on his face. The North-Westerly wind filled the sails sending the ship scudding smoothly over the sea, bound for Australia. He looked up at the sky where a weak autumn sun shone through the thin layer of clouds. He was in his element. The sea had been his life since he had first enlisted as a cabin boy at the age of fourteen. That had been some thirty years ago and, by hard work and diligence, he had worked his way up the promotion ladder until he had, at an early age, achieved his ambition and been rewarded with his Master's Certificate. He should have been very happy, instead of which he was disgruntled and angry.

He had only been in port for a fortnight, when the Owners had sent for him. There had been some difficulty in obtaining a cargo for his next voyage to India. Since his ship was due for a refit, they had pressed him into taking over from the present captain of this boat, who had suddenly gone down with a serious illness. On being told the destination and nature of the cargo, he had tried to decline the appointment, but they had used strong pressures to which he had finally succumbed. Fortunately he had found that the new crew under his command were sound and experienced sailors. Especially the bo'sun, Jack Noakes, who, whilst being strict with the crew, was a fair and likeable fellow.

The cargo, the cause of his displeasure, was convicts, eighty male and twenty five female. Silently he cursed the owners for forcing him to undertake the voyage, and the previous captain for falling ill just at the wrong time. The transportation of convicts was not the most favoured job for any captain, since it could be relied on that there would be trouble aboard during the long voyage. That the truth of this had been borne out so early into the voyage was the cause of the anger at present seething within him. He looked down onto the well of the ship where the convicts, heavily chained, had been gathered under the armed surveillance of those members of the crew who could be spared from duty.

John Macklay had been at sea long enough to know that discipline on board ship was essential. He prided himself on being a fair man but had never hesitated to implement this when necessary. He had seen, and ordered, men flogged during his time at sea and accepted this as part of the seaman's way of life. He had never felt squeamish until now. He was well aware that trouble with the convicts was likely at some time during the voyage and had to be stamped upon immediately, but had not expected it to raise its ugly head so soon into the voyage. His thoughts were interrupted as two of the crew emerged from the door beneath the deck where he stood. Between them, they were holding one of the female convicts, who was struggling to escape their grasp.

She was the cause of the captain's disquiet. He had been told that one of the women had started a fight below decks and he had, reluctantly, given the order for what was about to be done. With over a hundred convicts on board, it was essential to show them that bad conduct would not be tolerated. The bo'sun had advocated setting an example and he had agreed. He looked down on the trio standing below him. He was taken aback when he saw that the woman was, in fact, young and, beneath the grime, clearly very attractive. The shabby dress which she wore, did little to disguise the shapely body beneath. A pair of green eyes, set in a pretty face framed in a cascade of long blonde hair, stared back at him defiantly. He turned his glance to his left, where the bo'sun stood, stripped to the waist, and noticed the sack he was holding.

"I don't think the cat-o-nine tails should be used on a female," he whispered. "Use a rope's end instead, Mr Noakes, and on her backside, not her back. Over the cannon I think would be best"

"Aye, aye Sir," the bo'sun answered, unable to hide the

relief in his voice, and dropped the sack to the deck. He picked up a length of thick hemp rope and descended to the main deck.

Tanya Crawley, the younger daughter of a successful merchant, struggled in the hands of the two seamen. She was not used to being handled so roughly. All through her childhood and adolescence, she had been pampered, having been born to her parents late in their lives. At the tender age of eighteen, she was terrified at the predicament she had been deposited in during the last month and her terror had fuelled the repugnance which she felt, at that moment, for her fellow creatures. She looked at the rope in the bo'sun's hands and defiance seethed through her small frame. He was going to flog her. She, who had never had a hand raised against her before!

The captain cleared his throat. "Tanya Crawley. You are guilty of causing a serious disturbance. Such behaviour will not be tolerated on my ship. I trust that the punishment you are about to receive will be a lesson to you, and all the others, and that the rest of the voyage will proceed without further incident." He looked at the bo'sun. "Two dozen lashes, Mr Noakes. Proceed."

Under the bo'sun's orders, the two escorts dragged the struggling young woman to one of the ship's cannons. They forced her to bend over the breach and lashed her ankles and wrists to the cold metal and stood back. The bo'sun approached and lifted the woman's skirts high over her back and pulled down her drawers to her ankles. John Macklay, watching from the poop deck, saw a pair of long shapely legs and a delicious behind revealed. The woman turned her head and looked at the bo'sun, who had moved to her side, in time to see him raise his muscular arm high in the air. The look of defiance that unexpectedly burned in her eyes was not missed, either by the bo'sun or the captain.

An expectant hush fell over the ship, broken only by the rattle of the convicts' chains as they edged forward to get a better view of the woman's ordeal. If they had expected her to scream for mercy, they were to be disappointed. She had already made up her mind that, no matter what was done to her, she would not give them that satisfaction.

...to be continued

The cover photograph for this book and many others are available as limited edition prints.
Write to:-

Viewfinders Photography
PO Box 200,
Reepham
Norfolk
NR10 4SY

for details, or see,

www.viewfinders.org.uk

TITLES IN PRINT

Silver Moon

ISBN 1-897809-23-9 Slave to the System, *Rosetta Stone*
ISBN 1-897809-37-9 Bush Slave, *Lia Anderssen*
ISBN 1-897809-50-6 Naked Truth, *Nicole Dere*
ISBN 1-897809-51-4 I Confess!, *Dr Gerald Rochelle*
ISBN 1-897809-54-9 The Confessions of Amy Mansfield, *R. Hurst*
ISBN 1-897809-55-7 Gentleman's Club, *John Angus*
ISBN 1-897809-57-3 Sinfinder General *Johnathan Tate*
ISBN 1-897809-59-X Slaves for the Sheik *Allan Aldiss*
ISBN 1-897809-60-3 Church of Chains *Sean O'Kane*
ISBN 1-897809-62-X Slavegirl from Suburbia *Mark Slade*
ISBN 1-897809-64-6 Submission of a Clan Girl *Mark Stewart*
ISBN 1-897809-65-4 Taming the Brat *Sean O'Kane*
ISBN 1-897809-66-2 Slave for Sale *J.T. Pearce*
ISBN 1-897809-69-7 Caged! *Dr. Gerald Rochelle*
ISBN 1-897809-71-9 Rachel in servitude *J.L. Jones*
ISBN 1-897809-72-2 Beaucastel *Caroline Swift*
ISBN 1-897809-73-5 Slaveworld *Steven Douglas*
ISBN 1-897809-76-X Sisters in Slavery *Charles Graham*
ISBN 1-897809-78-6 Eve in Eden *Stephen Rawlings*
ISBN 1-897809-80-8 Inside the Fortress *John Sternes*
ISBN 1-903687-00-4 The Brotherhood *Falconer Bridges*
ISBN 1-903687-01-2 Both Master and Slave *Martin Sharpe*
ISBN 1-903687-03-9 Slaves of the Girlspell *William Avon*
ISBN 1-903687-04-7 Royal Slave; Slaveworld Story *Stephen Douglas*
ISBN 1-903687-05-5 Castle of Torment *Caroline Swift*
ISBN 1-903687-08-X The Art of Submission *Tessa Valmur*
ISBN 1-903687-09-8 Theatre of Slaves *Mark Stewart*
ISBN 1-903687-10-1 Painful Prize *Stephen Rawlings*
ISBN 1-903687-12-8 The Story of Emma *Sean O'Kane*
ISBN I-903687-14-4 Savage Journey *John Argus*
ISBN 1-903687-15-2 Slave School *Stephen Douglas*
ISBN 1-903687-16-0 Slaves of the Circle T *Charles Graham*
ISBN 1-903687-17-9 Amber in Chains *Francine Whittaker*
ISBN 1-903687-18-7 Linda's Trials *Nicole Dere*
ISBN 1-903687-19-5 Hannah's Trials *Stephen Rawlings*
ISBN 1-903687-20-9 The Pit of Pain *Falconer Bridges*
ISBN 1-903687-21-7 The Sufferers *Caroline Swift*
ISBN 1-903687-22-5 Bought and Sold *Tessa Valmur*

TITLES IN PRINT

Silver Mink
ISBN 1-897809-22-0 The Captive *Amber Jameson*
ISBN 1-897809-24-7 Dear Master *Terry Smith*
ISBN 1-897809-26-3 Sisters in Servitude *Nicole Dere*
ISBN 1-897809-28-X Cradle of Pain *Krys Antarakis*
ISBN 1-897809-32-8 The Contract *Sarah Fisher*
ISBN 1-897898-45-X Dominating Obsession *Terry Smith*
ISBN 1-897809-49-2 The Penitent *Charles Arnold*
ISBN 1-897809-56-5 Please Save Me! *Dr. Gerald Rochelle*
ISBN 1-897809-58-1 Private Tuition *Jay Merson*
ISBN 1-897809-61-1 Little One *Rachel Hurst*
ISBN 1-897809-63-8 Naked Truth II *Nicole Dere*
ISBN 1-897809-67-0 Tales from the Lodge *Bridges/O'Kane*
ISBN 1-897809-68-9 Your Obedient Servant Charlotte *Anna Grant*
ISBN 1-897809-70-0 Bush Slave II *Lia Anderssen*
ISBN 1-897809-74-3 Further Private Tuition *Jay Merson*
ISBN 1-897809-75-1 The Connoisseur *Francine Whittaker*
ISBN 1-897809-77-8 Slave to her Desires *Samantha Austen*
ISBN 1-897809-79-4 The Girlspell *William Avon*
ISBN 1-897809-81-6 The Stonehurst Letters *J.L. Jones*
ISBN 1-903687-07-1 Punishment Bound *Francine Whittaker*
ISBN 1-903687-11-X Naked Deliverance *Lia Anderssen*
ISBN 1-903687-13-6 Lani's Initiation *Danielle Richards*

Stiletto SM
ISBN 1-897809-88-3 Stern Manor *Denise leCroix*
ISBN 1-897809-93-X Military Discipline *Anna Grant*
ISBN 1-897809-94-8 Mistress Blackheart *Francine Whittaker*
ISBN 1-897809-97-2 Slaves of the Sisterhood *Anna Grant*
ISBN 1-897809-93-X The Rich Bitch *Becky Ball*
ISBN 1-897809-93-X Maria's Fulfilment *Jay Merson*
ISBN 1-903687-02-0 The Daughters of de Sade *Falconer Bridges*

Special Double Issues

ISBN 1-897809-06-9 Biker's Girl + Caravan of Slaves
ISBN 1-897809-06-9 Biker's Girl on the Run + A Toy for Jay